Teresa

May the Map
be an adventure in
your mind!

xo

The Map

A LOGAN NASH ADVENTURE

DAVE BURDETT

◆ FriesenPress

Suite 300 - 990 Fort St
Victoria, BC, V8V 3K2
Canada

www.friesenpress.com

Copyright © 2018 by Dave Burdett
Second Edition — 2018

map-thenovel.com

All rights reserved.

No part of this publication may be reproduced in any form, or by any means, electronic or mechanical, including photocopying, recording, or any information browsing, storage, or retrieval system, without permission in writing from FriesenPress.

ISBN
978-1-5255-0964-3 (Hardcover)
978-1-5255-0965-0 (Paperback)
978-1-5255-0966-7 (eBook)

1. FICTION, ACTION & ADVENTURE

Distributed to the trade by The Ingram Book Company

In memory of my father, taken by leukemia too soon.

You are missed.

The Map

"The world is a book and those who do not travel read only one page."

—St. Augustine

AUTHOR'S NOTE

I have always felt that I was born a hundred years too late. Ever since I was a child I have dreamed of little else than discovering a lost city in the Amazon or buried treasure on a deserted tropical island. I would read with envy about the adventurers of the last century and their amazing discoveries, yearning to experience all that they did. I didn't wish for fame or riches, but just the pure thrill and adventure of the quest. I came to realize that for me, it was more about the journey than the destination. I often embarked on my journeys alone, wishing there was someone who could truly appreciate the adventures I set out for myself. One day while on a jungle hike, I found myself standing on a bluff overlooking an amazing white-sand beach surrounded by lush jungle. A wave of inspiration washed over me.

"Hundreds of years ago, I bet great adventurers stood on this very spot," I said to myself. A plan began to swirl in my head. "What would be the dream of all true adventurers? To find a treasure map!" I vowed to set up the ultimate treasure quest. The only problem was that I would only have a token treasure to hide. The true treasure would not be the prize at the end, but rather the quest itself, and the amazing adventure it would take you on.

I decided that if I were to do this, I was not going to do it half-heartedly. The quest would eclipse any others from centuries past and would not be for the faint of heart. It would take you to every corner of the earth—from the tops of mountains, to the depths of the sea, and everywhere in between. The quest would challenge even the most hard-core adventurer.

This book is based on a quest to find actual treasure maps that I had hidden around the world, although for my own reasons, I have changed some of the locations in the story. The treasure quest that I had set up took me nearly two years to complete. I don't want to give away the details of how I set it up before you read the book, but I will tell you that was done in the same way.

Setting up the original quest was truly a labor of love, as was writing this novel. I hope my spirit for adventure shines through and transports you to exotic lands, and that you are now ready to join Logan Nash in his latest adventure.

PROLOGUE

Logan Nash slowly eased the frosty bottle across his dripping forehead, the cold sweat from the amber glass trickling down his face. He sighed contentedly as he stared out over the muddy, brown expanse of water that took on a saffron glow as the sun dipped toward the horizon. The small bar attached to the guesthouse where he was staying sat on stilts, perched on the edge of the mighty Amazon River on the outskirts of a small jungle city. It was a peaceful place where he could reflect. He replayed his recent adventures in his mind as he tipped back the bottle, eagerly emptying its contents. "Ah," he said with a smile, enjoying his first cold beverage in over three months.

The Amazon was one of the last adventurous frontiers, and despite the encroachment of progress from all angles, it was still largely untamed, a place where jungle tribes still existed with little or no contact with modern civilization. Logan had spent time down there before, and it was that yearning for adventure that had drawn him back. Rosa, a beautiful young Latina with raven-black hair, smoldering dark eyes, and a warm smile, flirtingly glanced at him as she wiped down the next table. Logan smiled at her and gave her a quick wink. She quickly turned away as her face turned crimson red.

Logan had always had an easy time with the ladies. He stood just over six feet tall and was deeply tanned. He had ruggedly handsome dark features, broad shoulders, and the muscular physique women liked. Beyond his physical features, he had gentle brown eyes that projected an aura of confidence, integrity, and sincerity, indicating to most people he met that he was someone who could be truly relied on. Logan held up his empty bottle to catch Rosa's attention as she worked at the small bamboo bar.

"Uno más cerveza, por favor, Señiorita." His Spanish was far from perfect, but over the years he had learned just enough to get himself into trouble.

Just then, a loud, energetic voice boomed out, "Make that dos cervezas, and put it on my tab."

"Sí, Señor," Rosa replied. She made eye contact with Logan again after acknowledging the newcomer's request.

"Hi, my name is Edward," the man said. "My friends call me Eddie. Mind if I join you?"

"No, not at all," Logan quickly replied as he sized up the stranger, whom he guessed to be in his early forties. Logan was naturally a bit skeptical of the stranger's motives and ran various scenarios in his mind. He figured there wasn't much of a timeshare market down here, and that if the stranger was looking to scam money from him, he was most definitely barking up the wrong tree. He thought he was fairly safe. There was also something familiar about the man, but he just could not put his finger on it.

Logan stood and gestured toward the chair across from him as he extended his hand. "Hi, my name is Logan Nash."

They exchanged firm handshakes.

"Thank you," Eddie replied. He pulled out the peeling white plastic lawn chair and sat down.

Rosa was prompt, and she set the beers down on the table while the men exchanged pleasantries. Eddie raised his beer toward Logan. "Salud."

Logan clanged the neck of his beer bottle against Eddie's. "Salud."

The men proceeded to down a good portion of their drinks.

"God, that goes down smooth," Eddie bellowed. "It's been weeks since I've seen one of these babies."

"Weeks!" Logan exclaimed. "Just imagine how good this sweet nectar would taste after three months of nothing but piss-warm, heavily chlorinated water."

"Three months!"

"Yeah, three months. Well, to make an extremely long story short, I started out in the Amazon region of southern Venezuela, hiring local guides along the way and going from one jungle tribe to the next until I reached the Amazon River. Then I took a small boat up the river here to Leticia, Colombia's main port on the Amazon."

Eddie was shocked to meet someone with such a passion for adventure, someone who ventured into the wilds of the Amazon on his own. He felt he was looking at a younger version of himself. "Wow, that sounds like an amazing adventure. I truly would love to hear more."

Logan felt a sense of appreciation for Eddie's genuine understanding of and respect for his accomplishment. "It really was amazing. And how about you? What brings you out here?"

"I'm a man after your own heart. I am trying to experience the last great frontier before it disappears. I spent a month in Peru, first in Cuzco, and then I hiked the Inca Trail to Machu Picchu, which was incredible by the way. I then made my way down to the city of Iquitos, where I began my journey down the Amazon River, stopping here at Leticia, but I eventually plan to end up in northern Brazil. In Belém."

The two men sat on the riverside patio in the sultry night air swapping tales of true adventures that only a kindred spirit could understand. Oil torches lined the railing of the patio bar, casting dancing shadows as the flames flickered. As the beer flowed, the laughter and decibel level of the conversation seemed to increase proportionately, all but drowning out the chorus of insects and beasts that made up the intense sounds of the jungle at night.

Rosa listened and watched the men intently, never really understanding a single word they spoke but desperately wishing she did. They spoke with such passion, and it excited her.

Eddie strained in the dim lighting of the bar to look at his watch, "Shit—1:30 in the morning already! I'm heading down river at 6:30 a.m.

An old man like me needs his beauty sleep." Laughter erupted from both men.

Logan grabbed Eddie's hand, firmly shook it, and said goodbye. "Eddie, this truly has been a pleasure. I hope our paths cross again."

"Me too, my friend," Eddie said. He began to stagger down the dimly lit hallway toward his room.

Logan walked over to the railing of the bar. The Amazonian water lapped against the pilings below the planking of the patio. In the still of the night, the jungle was deafening; it was a world like no other. He took a deep breath, drawing in the dense jungle air as he left the patio and returned to his sparsely furnished room illuminated by a single dim bulb. A rusty ceiling fan pulsed above his head. A small timeworn dresser with a few handles missing sat off to one side of the room, and on the other side was a saggy bed covered with a filthy sheet. Logan peeled off his damp black T-shirt and khaki shorts. The draft from the fan felt refreshing against his hot, sweaty skin. He sat on the edge of the threadbare bed thinking of Eddie's passion for travel and adventure, and Logan hoped that he, too, would still have that same incredible passion ten or twenty years later.

His thoughts were interrupted by a light knock at the door. He stood up, walked to the battered door, and turned the knob, cracking the door open a few inches. To his surprise, it was Rosa. Without hesitation, she gently pushed open the door, stepped inside, and closed the door behind her, never saying a word and never breaking the lustful gaze she had fixed on Logan.

CHAPTER 1

A mischievous smile crept across Colton's face as he emerged from the frothy black water. With the assistance of an incoming wave, he propelled himself onto the slippery edge of the cave entrance, the moonlight dancing across the grumbling sea behind him.

"Three years." Colton sighed, with only the cave-dwelling creatures of the night to hear him. "Finally finished. This will be my true legacy," he said.

Suddenly, as if struck by a rogue wave, he was overcome by crushing emotion and began to sob uncontrollably. It wasn't one feeling or thought that brought on the flood of emotions; it was an entire spectrum of satisfaction, pride, fear, pity, happiness, resentment, and anger. Although he was a deeply passionate person, he was not normally prone to such outbursts of emotion, but with tonight's sortie, his entire purpose for the last three years had culminated in the successful completion of his quest.

No, stop it, Colton," he said. "I will not sit here and have a pity party."

Colton was an extremely positive individual, almost sickeningly so. Three years ago to the day he had been diagnosed with late-stage leukemia and was given only one year to live. He was already an enigma to his doctors. However, he knew he was on borrowed time and refused to slip quietly into the night. He was a fighter with a lust for life that few in this world possessed.

Colton's thoughts quickly returned to the place where he was when he emerged from the sea a few minutes earlier. As if almost on cue, that same mischievous smile returned with a vengeance as he laughed out loud. "Yeah, this will really chap their collective asses."

Colton Edward Braxton III was born with a silver spoon in hand. To say he was the black sheep of his family was an understatement. His family was all convinced he had to be an illegitimate child born of some pot smoking bohemian hippy that somehow managed to infiltrate the ranks of the Braxton family. His family often said, "A true Braxton would never conduct himself in such a manner."

The entire Braxton family had shunned Colton because of the lifestyle he had chosen. He didn't fit in. He was a constant embarrassment to them. To them, life was limousines, country clubs, and fancy dinner parties, where they patted each other on the back, congratulating themselves on their incredible successes. Colton was born with an incurable case of wanderlust. He wanted to see and experience everything—not from the balcony of a five-star hotel that overlooked a pool surrounded by fat roasting turkeys in eight-hundred-dollar sunglasses, but to really see it and to see it down and dirty.

He would throw on a backpack and trek around the world, traveling on ferries, trains, and battered chicken buses—no first class for him! He had an insatiable thirst for adventure, which had taken him from swinging in a hammock in the Amazon jungle to the grueling trek to Everest Base Camp. He traveled wherever the wind took him in search of his next adventure, from the most amazing scuba diving sites to newly discovered ruins deep in some impenetrable jungle. Colton was a true traveler, not a tourist. He would always travel incognito, never letting anyone know who he really was. He would often go by his middle name, Edward, or Eddie as some friends called him. To look at Colton, unshaven and humping his backpack, you could almost hear the last coins jingling in his pockets. You would never guess he was a billionaire. His clean but casual unkempt appearance gave him the look of an eternal student working on his fourth degree, or someone recently divorced in the throes of an early midlife crisis having sold his worldly possessions, picked up a backpack, and revisited his youth.

It wasn't that he looked old. In fact, despite his age of forty-eight, he could easily pass for his late thirties or early forties. The only factors alluding to his true age were the smile lines on his well-tanned face and just a hint of gray that crept into the temples of his otherwise black hair. It would have given him a distinguished look, except for the four o'clock shadow he perpetually had on his face, giving him a more rugged outdoorsy look. He prided himself on staying fit and had the wiry toned body of a long-distance runner. His face had a friendly aura, and his warm hazel eyes were non-threatening in a way that made him appear approachable to everyone.

Occasionally someone would say to him, "Hey, you look like that billionaire guy. What's his name? Braxton. Yeah, Braxton."

Colton would laugh. "Yeah, I'm trying to save a few bucks staying in this roach-infested hostel with the likes of you guys."

Normally, everyone would have a good laugh, never realizing that they were sitting with a billionaire. Colton wanted it this way. It was imperative. He wanted to meet the locals and swap adventure stories with the other travelers, and he knew that would drastically change if his true identity were known.

He smiled as he recalled times he would show up at some pretentious black-tie affair just to see the mortified looks on the faces of the rich and famous as he strolled into the room in his faded jeans and casual khaki shirt. Sometimes this was better than a funny movie, and it amused him. His uncle, Elliot Braxton, had left his entire fortune of $2.4 billion to Colton at the tender age of twenty-three. He wanted to make sure that Colton received the majority of his estate, and he knew if he had left it to him in his will, his family would have spared no expense fighting its validity in the courts. When Elliot's health began to fail eight years before his death, he arranged for Colton to receive almost everything, leaving his biological children just enough to live comfortably. He could now live out his last few years vicariously through Colton, knowing he had made the best investment of his life. Elliot beamed with pride whenever he spoke or even thought of his nephew, who was a hundred times more of a son than either of Elliot's two biological sons would ever be.

In his youth, Elliot was considered the black sheep of the family, although compared to Colton he was a stuffed shirt. Elliot had found the family pressure to conform was too great, and he had eventually slotted himself into his proper place—one ordained by the Braxton name. The heart of an adventurer buried deep inside him had brought him to respect and admire Colton for being his own person. Elliot didn't envy Colton his nephew, but he despised his own cowardice for giving in to the immense pressure of his family to conform to the Braxton mold—a phony, pretentious existence, his behavior, his entire life all preordained by social status. Elliot looked at his family as you would an insect that you just wanted to squash.

The Braxton family fortune had been passed down through the generations. The Braxtons had originally immigrated to the Pacific Northwest from England in 1836. They began acquiring vast amounts of property, which diversified over the years into forestry, mining, and real estate.

Whenever Colton had attended a family function over the years, which was not very often, he was always surprised to walk out without a knife or two in his back, although if looks could kill, he would have been a worm entree long ago. Although no one in the Braxton family was hard done by, not by any stretch of the imagination, there was an incredible resentment toward Colton over Elliot having left his entire fortune to him. Colton's own father went so far as to try to have him declared legally insane in order to take controlling interest of his share of the Braxton conglomerate, Buccaneer Investments.

Colton knew that with little warning, he could be on his deathbed in agonizing pain, morphine dripping into his veins, but to look at him this day, he seemed to be the epitome of health and vitality. He had been given the option of having aggressive chemotherapy and medical treatments, which the doctors said could extend his life another year, perhaps even two. To Colton, living in a weakened state as a result of the chemotherapy and medication—virtually chained to a hospital like some rabid junkyard dog and living only for his next medical treatment—was not acceptable. *No thanks,* he thought. It would be a living hell that he didn't even consider an existence. Colton decided he was going to live like he never had, like it was his last day spinning around on this ball of dirt, as he often said. For all he knew, any day could be his last. He had no illusions of curing himself, going into remission, or even living a long life, but he did know that mind and body are capable of so much more than people usually think.

On the day Colton learned of his impending fate, it was as if someone had switched the light on. He knew what he needed to do. For reasons unknown to him, he felt a deep craving for everyone to know who Colton Edward Braxton III truly was. To most he was just some eccentric philanthropist who generously supported countless charities around the world and lived a wild carefree lifestyle to the point where he seemed to be a bit of a nut case. His family started much of the negative publicity, and, of course, it was blown out of proportion by the press. Colton was extremely proud that he didn't possess the Braxton greed gene, and it made him feel good to help people. Even though he had been extremely generous with his money over the years, his business interests flourished, a fact that further infuriated his family. He was glad to be known as a philanthropist, but there was so much more to him. There was his passion for true adventure and the incredible stories he had to tell. That was what really made Colton Braxton tick. He wanted—needed—people to know.

The idea materialized in Colton's mind: his legacy would be in the form of the ultimate scavenger hunt, an adventure worthy of himself. The details quickly formed in his mind, and on the very day he learned of his fate, he set the wheels in motion to prepare his legacy. He knew he needed to conduct the operation in utmost secrecy. He knew that was especially true since he was being watched like a hawk, not as much by the media, although he had always made an interesting headline for them, but by his family, who, like a flock of unconscionable vultures, were all waiting for his impending demise, anxious to rip off their piece of carrion.

His family was watching him closely, fearful that he would give away or squander what they thought was rightfully theirs. Colton couldn't help but laugh because they were totally right. He had no plans to leave anyone in his family one red cent. He had arranged to have his estate divided among various charities. Most of them were animal, environmental, and children's charities, and, of course, there was the prize for the ultimate treasure hunt.

Colton had designed a scavenger hunt worthy of a true explorer, someone with a lust for true adventure flowing through his or her veins. He hoped someone would seek out the treasure without a clue of what might be in store.

Colton was always a target for the media, but he usually managed to avoid the reporters like a cockroach in a light bulb factory. For him, cash was king, making it much harder to trace his comings and goings. In any year, he was lucky to be home for four or five weeks. It was not that he didn't like home, but there was a big world out there to be discovered and explored. He had gone as far as to have fake IDs made. They were great for hotels and booking agents, although unfortunately he did have to carry some official identification for airports, border crossings, and those pesky places that only accepted credit cards. He made sure that all his credit cards simply read C. Braxton. With his rugged appearance, staying at lower end lodgings, and using cheap transportation, people rarely made the connection.

He knew that when the first map was found, the media would try to retrace his travels. Colton snickered. "Have at it. I will give you a wild goose chase like you've never seen."

He had designed and manufactured a special map paper. The parchment was burnt almond with a watermark of a pirate's compass in the center of each page. In the top left-hand corner of each piece were Colton's handwritten initials, C. E. B. When completed, each page would then be waterproofed.

He had hidden four treasure maps in the four corners of the world. Each map fit together as part of the whole, with each containing part of the outline of the island where the treasure was buried. He realized that with two or perhaps even one of the maps and using today's technology, someone could easily extrapolate the location of the island. With this in mind, Colton ensured each map not only had riddles, clues, and directions to the next map, but also had part of the final instructions to find the destination. Without each piece of the puzzle, it would be utterly impossible to ever find the treasure. He went over and over each contingency, making sure that no one could complete the quest without all four maps, until finally he was satisfied. During the year that it had taken him to hide the four maps, he had traveled to sixty-three countries, never staying in the same town or hotel for more than two days. He had traveled to 204 different destinations including cities, towns, ruins, caves, and several dive sites. His original plans were that after the four maps were hidden, he would publicly release the fifth map that would start the quest to find the other four maps. This starter map was to be available to everyone. Colton had planned it this way, as he figured the grim reaper would soon be strolling down the path toward his front door.

The year came and went, and Colton still felt fine. In fact, to the doctors' amazement, the cancer, although not in remission, didn't seem to be spreading very fast. They had no answers for this, as they had first predicted that the spread would be aggressive.

Colton then decided he would not release the fifth starter map publicly, but rather he devised a plan where he would make seven copies of the starter map and hide them throughout the world. They would not be hidden as well as the other maps, so it would be possible to find one by luck or by a glance at the right time in the right place. The map did not say what the treasure was, or by whom or when the treasure map was made. In fact, the map was made to look quite antique. Colton figured a true adventurer would follow the map just for the hell of it, or even morbid curiosity.

He again took to the road, moving around incognito. Normally when he traveled, he completely made it up as he went. If he liked the place, he would stay a week, a month, or even three or four months until he felt like moving on wherever and whenever the wind took him. This was different, though. Colton had turned it into a game of cloak and dagger in his mind. He always felt as if he were being watched. Sometimes, but not often, he was right. One thing was certain: the quest had become an adventure unto itself.

Colton smiled. He thought he was quite clever with the placement of the seven starter maps. They had all been placed in locations that had special meaning to him, places with fond memories. The first map was placed in a sealed bottle and stuffed into the sand dunes of Lamu Island off the coast of Kenya. He smiled as he recalled running and leaping off the steep dunes, where he had spent a month in his younger days.

The second map found its home in the charming medieval walled town of Volterra in Tuscany. His quaint little hotel had a row of antique wine bottles displayed on a shelf. Colton lifted a bottle dating back to 1933, rolled up the map, and carefully placed the bottle back. The third map was sealed in a wine bottle and tossed into the East China Sea off the coast of the small Japanese fishing island of Yonaguni, where they had recently discovered underwater ruins that many speculated were the lost city of Mu, the Asian version of Atlantis. The fourth map was also sealed in a wine bottle and thrown into the Atlantic Ocean off the coast of the lush Portuguese island of Madeira.

The fifth map was placed in a fluorescent orange watertight case and placed in a small crevasse on the climbing trail that led to the top of Huayna Picchu, the jungle-clad peak that rose up behind the famous ruins of Machu Picchu. It was much less visited than the famous ruins, but when one thought of the site, Huayna Picchu was always right there in the mind's eye.

The sixth map was placed in a weighted waterproof case wedged in the rocks near a cave where a giant Pacific octopus spent his days before heading out at night to scour the waters off the coast of Vancouver Island, near Nanaimo.

The final of the seven maps was sealed in a lime green watertight case and placed on a small ledge below the water's entrance to Admiralty Caves, not far outside the quaint city of Hamilton in Bermuda. The cliffs above the caves had become a popular place for both young and young-at-heart daredevils to take the thirty-foot leap into the churning waters below. The way back up from the water required a climb out through the cave entrance. Colton figured the gaudy green case would be hard to miss and would be retrieved, if for no other reason than curiosity's sake. The British army had carved the caves from the limestone cliffs in the 1850s, creating a perfect fortress. They were used by the British forces until after World War II.

Admiralty Caves, now a tourist attraction, had also become a bit of a hangout for Bermuda's rowdier youth, but the park was silent when Colton went to hide the case. He'd partially covered his dive light, giving himself just enough illumination to unobtrusively slip out of the park undetected and return to the 50-CC scooter he'd left just down the road. After a frenzied few minutes of rummaging his backpack to find his keys, he soon was buzzing down the road like an angry bumblebee toward the quaint Victorian town of Saint Georges.

Bermuda had always been one of Colton's favorite places, and he had often found himself visiting. There was a feel about it, something intangible. Yes, it had gorgeous pink-sand beaches, quaint English charm, beautiful gardens, and great diving, but it wasn't any of those things that drew him back again and again. *Maybe it's all of them*, he'd thought as he sat in his porch swing outside his pastel lilac cottage in Bermuda and closed his eyes. The sounds had been magical. He'd heard the rumbling of the sea in the distance, which the song of Bermuda's tree frogs almost eclipsed. It was like a symphony to his ears. He'd finally felt at peace with his own mortality, knowing he would be remembered for who he truly was. A sense of relief and tranquility flooded over him as he'd fallen asleep.

CHAPTER 2

An icy chill ran down Logan's spine, and his heart pounded as adrenaline surged through his veins. Logan stood frozen in place like a statue, not wanting to even blink, fearing he might miss a word of what the news anchor was saying. As he watched the pictures on the screen, it all seemed surreal, like a dream you don't want to wake from but always do, despite lying there with your eyes closed. A million thoughts flooded his mind as he stood there soaking up every word. Suddenly, as if slapped in the face, Logan's trance was broken as the news anchor shifted to another story, although his heart still raced to the point where he almost felt dizzy. He rushed toward his office, solidly cracking his left knee on the coffee table as he hurried past. "Damn it," he yelled as he hobbled along undaunted by the pain.

Covering one wall in his office were three large mahogany bookcases, all perfectly arranged with a balance of books, along with various antiques and collectibles that he had found or procured in his travels. The overwhelming majority of the books were on shipwrecks, diving, and travel, with the remainder about archaeology and history. Others were adventure novels. There was a definite theme. The other walls in his office were similarly themed. One was covered with antique maps, while another was covered with tribal masks he had collected from every corner of the world.

A few years back, Logan had dreamed of nothing but treasure hunting and had become quite the accomplished tomb raider, but a nasty incident had given him a moment of pause, haunting him enough to make him step away entirely from that world. Museums, collectors, and even governments had used his services in the past, knowing he was a man who got the job done without the need for a long bureaucratic paper trail. Despite the nightmares of his past, it was still something that was close to his heart, a passion boiling under the surface. His office gave insight into the man he really was. From the top shelf of the center bookcase, he swiftly but gingerly removed a bottle. He slid a map from the emerald-green wine bottle and placed the bottle back in its rightful place on the shelf.

Logan felt his hands shaking as he unrolled the map, holding it open with his hands. He intently stared at it, seeming to re-enter the same trance he was in when he first watched the news broadcast. "Everything is here. Everything is here," he muttered. He held the parchment against the brass banker's lamp that adorned his oversized double-pedestal mahogany desk. "Yes!" The light revealed the watermark of a compass. His heart palpitated, and trepidation engulfed him. It seemed like it was just too good to be true. He slowly shook his head from side to side and whispered, "You know what they say. If it seems too good to be true, it probably is."

To Logan, finding a genuine treasure map was better than winning the lottery. He was waiting to either wake up or have someone come bursting through the door and scream, "Surprise, you're on Candid Camera!" He placed the map on his desk and examined it more closely, weighing it down on top with an antique Asian compass and an antique globe penholder on the bottom. He then settled into his black leather executive chair and swung it around to the matching mahogany computer desk that sat perpendicular to the main desk. Sliding out the keyboard tray, he wiggled the mouse, bringing the screen to life. He searched, "Colton Braxton + map." Almost instantly, the results page appeared.

Despite Logan's excitement, a sense of sadness tempered his mood. He didn't know Colton Braxton, or so he thought at the time, but he had a heartfelt respect for him. Braxton had done so much good with his money and helped so many causes that were close to Logan's own heart. From what he read about the man, it was clear he'd really enjoyed life. He was definitely not the typical billionaire, and he truly would be missed. Logan quickly scanned the first few entries of the search page and, finding one that looked reputable, and clicked on it.

At the top of the page was a photo of Colton Braxton. Logan paused. "No, it couldn't be, could it?" He said, as his mind flashed back to a drunken night at a riverside bar on the Amazon River years ago. *Damn, it looks like him, and it even fits with his lifestyle,* Logan thought, *no - it couldn't be.* He then began reading the text aloud as he scrolled down the page.

"Today after a six-year battle with leukemia, eccentric philanthropist Colton Edward Braxton III passed away at the age of fifty-one. Six years ago, he was given one year to live, but he defied all odds, living a full life for most of the last six years despite having chosen not to undergo any cancer treatments. Two months ago, he collapsed while hiking up Uluru in central Australia. Mr. Braxton was flown to his estate in rural Washington State, where he lived out his last two months under twenty-four-hour medical supervision until his passing today. As per Mr. Braxton's wishes, he was not given any life support.

"Colton Braxton III's stake in Buccaneer Investments is estimated to be worth in excess of $3.6 billion. He had several times been named America's most eligible bachelor. He was best known for his extremely generous nature and the many charities he supported, as well as for his often eccentric, if not outrageous behavior. Many were unsurprised at the bizarre contents of Mr. Braxton's last will and testament.

"It contained a list of the forty-two charities to receive an undisclosed amount to be administered by Mr. Braxton's law firm in strict confidence. The surprising revelation came in the form of a treasure map—actually seven identical treasure maps—that would give clues to find four other treasure maps, which would lead to a treasure of undetermined value. There was no further information on where the maps were located or when they were hidden, although in his will, Mr. Braxton indicated that he had hoped someone would have found the treasure while he was alive, implying the maps may have been out there for some time.

"In the contents of the will, there was a template of what the maps look like for use in authenticating them, when and if they were found, or if anyone is already in possession of one.

"On a related note, the Braxton family was apparently left out in the cold when the will was read. In fact, the only mention of his family was a brief statement saying, 'To my family I leave exactly what they deserve—absolutely nothing!' Adding a further twist to this story, the Braxton family has offered a one-million-dollar reward for an authenticated map providing the treasure has not yet been found. This has many speculating on how valuable the treasure might really be."

Logan's mind raced. A million dollars! *I could have a million dollars*, he thought. He also thought about what the treasure could really be worth—ten million? A hundred million? He thought about the pure rush of a real treasure hunt. He could be living one of those adventure novels he loved to read.

The script on the search page was followed by a picture and detailed description of the map. Logan carefully studied every detail. The paper was an exact match to his. It had the same granite-colored antique paper, the handwritten initials C. E. B. in the top left corner, and the identical watermark of a compass, which Colton Braxton had apparently designed for the production of his map parchment. According to the article he had read, after the maps were completed, any excess paper or templates made in designing the paper were destroyed. He thought that with technology today it would be easy to forge one, but until today no one knew the maps existed. Logan had had this map for over two years now.

Logan convinced himself he had to be skeptical and extremely meticulous, so he went over everything again and again. No matter how many times he tried to find fault in his map, he couldn't. It was definitely one of the seven maps. His mind flashed back to the day he had found it.

He had reached the climax of his weeklong, live-aboard diving trip and would finally be exploring the newly discovered ruins just off the coast of Yonaguni in Japan. He had read an article in one of the diving magazines about the area and had seen some of the amazing photos. The story and photos convinced Logan that he had to see the underwater marvel for himself. He was far removed from a regular hardcore diver—they were too warm and fuzzy for him. In fact, he took hardcore to a whole new level. When it came to diving he would push the envelope, as he did in many aspects of his life. He had taken his dive training as far as it could go, earning certification in a variety of disciplines: open water, advanced, rescue diver, dive master, dive instructor, cave diver, mixed gas blending technician, as well as being trained in Trimix and Helox technical diving. In all, he had amassed seventeen certifications, and he'd logged over two thousand dives in more than fifty countries.

Logan was an absolute wreck diving junkie, with more than eight hundred wreck dives under his belt. On several occasions, when there were no technical diving options available, he would find himself at 230 feet on regular air, pushing both limits of nitrogen narcosis and more dangerously, the limits of oxygen toxicity, where due to the effects of pressure, oxygen becomes poison. Logan had known divers who had died of oxygen toxicity, but they were all enriched oxygen nitrox dives that ended up deeper than they had planned. He had done several helium-based dives to over four hundred feet and felt comfortable at any depth.

On terra firma, ruins were one of Logan's passions. He had explored them all over the world: Angkor in Cambodia, Machu Picchu in Peru, Tikal in Guatemala, and Egyptian ruins in Giza, Luxor, Edfu, Alexandria, and Aswan, to name but a few. He figured he'd explored two hundred, three hundred, or maybe even more archaeological sites. To combine two of his favorite passions, ruins and diving, he knew the trip to Japan would be amazing.

They'd started their live-aboard trip in Okinawa and had gone down the chain of islands toward the island of Yonaguni. Logan had been more than pleasantly surprised at how great diving was during the entire trip, but today, this dive was why he had come. The dive group would be spending the next two days exploring the underwater ruins at Yonaguni. The ruins were situated in a channel, which was known for currents as swift as eight knots at maximum stages of the tide, making it advisable to time the dives at either low or high tide when the currents were slack. Logan knew that if they dove it outside those windows, it would be like flying down a raging underwater river.

On the second dive of the first day of exploring, the tides had started to shift, making the currents pick up. It's not as easy to take photos as on the first dive. No finning necessary, you just cruise along, and if you want to take a photo or a closer look, grab on and look for some leeward shelter in the ruins as you fly by.

When Logan's time below was up, after making a brief safety stop, he'd begun to slowly ascend toward the brightness of the surface above. As always, before breaking the surface, he'd taken a quick look to make sure there were not any boats cruising overhead. Just as he'd broken the surface of the water, something hard struck him on the forehead, right at the hairline. He'd felt a warm sensation as blood trickled down his face from the small cut that had opened when the bottle bobbing in the waves solidly contacted his head. Initially, he hadn't realized what he'd hit, or rather what had hit him, but he'd noticed the culprit out of the corner of his eye.

He had grabbed the bottle, noticing that it was sealed with a cork. He'd opened the front pocket of his buoyancy-compensating device, or BCD, and stuffed the bottle inside. The neck stuck out, but the closure on the BCD pocket was strong and the bottle was secure. Once everyone had collected together on the surface, the dive boat swung around to pick up the divers. Logan, as always, had been patient, waiting until everyone went up the ladder before ascending himself. Once he'd boarded, Logan removed his BCD and tank, and then strapped them down with the attached bungee cords. Another diver on the boat asked Logan about the cut on his head.

"Yeah, I got in a bar fight out there and got hit by a bottle," he'd jokingly replied.

Logan had slid the bottle out of his BCD pocket, almost immediately drawing the attention of the other divers, who were curious about what he had found. He could see that the bottle contained a piece of paper, and everyone had begun speculating, wondering if it was a love letter, a treasure map, or a laundry list. Everyone had an idea or had made a joke about Logan's new prize.

He'd reached down to his thigh, slid his dive knife out of its sheath, and picked away at the extremely stubborn wax that sealed the bottle. After a bit of cajoling, the cork had come free. He'd looked inside and saw a tightly rolled piece of paper, which was neatly tied with string at both ends. He'd tipped the bottle upside down, letting gravity deliver the paper into his awaiting hand, and then he'd tugged gently on each end of the string and begun to gingerly unroll the parchment.

"It's in English!" he said. This had been surprising considering they were in the East China Sea. "It seems to be some kind of treasure map with several riddles that lead to another map." No sooner had Logan spoken than he'd wished he had kept his mouth shut. He'd given everyone a quick look and began joking about the map being fake, saying it was some tourist's idea of a joke. Logan had known that the chance of the map being real was remote, but he'd decided to downplay it anyway and never let the map out of his hands.

He'd laughed, dabbing his forehead with a damp cloth. "Well, at least this will make an interesting souvenir, and all it cost me was a cut on the head," he'd said. Everyone had laughed.

Unbeknown to Logan, minutes before he and the other divers began their ascent, a 280-foot white and blue yacht with a helicopter strapped down on the aft deck had cruised through the channel. From the portside promenade deck, Colton Braxton reared back and flung an emerald-green bottle overboard. Not in his wildest dreams could he have imagined who drifted below the surface. He watched the bottle plummet into the choppy azure waves, disappearing in the frothy white wake astern.

This was the second time that destiny had brought Logan and Colton's paths together.

Over the years, Colton had often thought of that hot, humid night in Leticia, where he'd shared travel tales with the young kid so full of piss and vinegar. The recollection reminded him of a twinge of regret he had. He'd often wished he had a son or daughter, one with his adventurous spirit. Colton thought if he'd ever had a son he would've wanted him to turn out like that Logan kid, who had such a lust for life, just like his.

Adventure had become Colton's mistress, and despite many affairs, he'd never settled down. "Yeah, that kid would've made a great son," Colton had said to himself. He wondered what had become of Logan Nash.

CHAPTER 3

Insomnia gripped Logan for the third night in a row. He lifted his wrist and looked at the glowing hands of his dive watch, which seemed like spotlights to his tired, scratchy eyes. "Damn. 5:23 a.m." Logan sighed. "Bunch of crap," he mumbled, referring to the herbal sleep aid he had taken the previous two nights. Exhaustion engulfed his body, but still his mind spun like an out-of-control amusement park ride. He didn't comprehend the feeling of trepidation that hung over him because the map was a dream come true, and yet something still gave him a moment of pause.

The eastern sky took on a crimson hue as the sun ascended from the depths of night. Logan begrudgingly lifted himself from his bed, feeling robbed again of desperately needed rest. He slid open his bedroom patio door and stepped into the dawn's early light. The soothing Pacific breeze wafted over his naked body. He closed his eyes, inhaling the fresh ocean air as the powerful sound of the sea making its continuous advances and retreats on the shoreline filled his ears.

To someone looking in from the outside, it seemed like Logan had it all. He had made the move from the Pacific Northwest to the Big Island of Hawaii. On many trips to the islands, he had fallen in love with the place because of its perfect climate and friendly people. For the most part, Logan loved living in such a tourist-oriented locale, and except for the occasional arse who always seemed to be miserable no matter where they were, people generally were much more fun and relaxed when traveling on vacation. That was the side of people he loved to see.

He had bought a place with an ocean view just south of Hilo. It was his piece of paradise. Of all the Hawaiian Islands, he loved the variety that the Big Island offered—the beautiful beaches on the west side, the jungles and waterfalls to the north, and of course, the famous Volcanoes National Park to the south. It was a photographer's paradise and lent itself perfectly to his long-term plan, or so he thought.

He had opened a small photography studio in town. He did fashion photography, family portraits, and weddings, although much of his work was outside assignments consisting of underwater photography, aerial photography, and tourist photo safaris. The main use of his studio was a showcase for his underwater, nature, and travel photography.

He had not yet breathed a word of the map to anyone, not even to family or friends. Logan knew every one of them, if they believed him, would tell him that he would be out of his mind not to take the Braxton family's million-dollar offer. He had followed his heart his entire life. His heart told him that this was an adventure beyond anything he could have hoped for, that it was a real quest with the possibility of untold riches at the end. Logan's mind screamed. *One million dollars!*

He didn't want money for just for the sake of having it, but it could give him the freedom to travel, explore, and enjoy life, and, if wisely invested, it could set up his future. Taking the Braxton's one million dollars was the prudent thing to do. Logan thought; *What happens if I spend tens of thousands of dollars traipsing around the world only to find it's all a hoax, that the treasure is only a few trinkets in a box. Or what if someone beats me to it? Could I live with myself knowing I threw away one million dollars? But what if I sold the map to the Braxtons and later found out the treasure was one hundred million dollars?*

Logan didn't want to live with regrets. He asked himself if he could accept the fact that he was too much of a coward to go after what he considered a dream come true. His head throbbed. Between his mind racing with decisions and his inability to drift into sleep, he had become a poster child for tension headaches. He popped a couple of pain tablets and stepped into a hot shower. He leaned his hands against the still cold tiles of the shower wall and closed his eyes as hot water pulsed against his muscular broad shoulders.

Then he was struck with a moment of clarity like a bolt of lightning. The map was his destiny. It would be what defined him as a man. Logan had always said he wished he had been born a hundred years earlier when true explorers were still making great discoveries. The map may not have been a new discovery, but it was a once in a lifetime, priceless adventure. However, he still struggled with whom he should entrust with his plans. Logan's family would think he was completely out of his mind, so he figured he'd tell them after the fact, if he found the treasure. The person whom he trusted the most was his best friend, Zackary Cook, who still called Seattle home. They had shared many adventures together. No matter how crazy it was, Zack was gung-ho, which was quite a contrast to his career as a web designer.

Zack was quite an interesting character. Normally, when you think of a computer geek, you think of a scrawny pencil neck with pasty skin and thick glasses, but he was quite different from that. He was quite athletic, with the body of a runner. He loved almost every sport—running, tennis, hiking, and especially skiing. He also loved traveling, but he never got to do as much of it as he liked due to his work schedule and his wife, Pam, who thought Logan was a bad influence on him, probably because whenever they went off on one of their adventures they often came back with interesting and bizarre stories.

Zack claimed that he had a famous heritage, that he was a descendant of the famous British explorer Captain James Cook. He said a child of Captain Cook had accompanied George Vancouver, who had served under Captain James Cook, when Captain George Vancouver set out with his own ship and discovered the Pacific Northwest. Not only did he not have proof of this, but also after Logan did some checking, it appeared the story was completely fabricated. Zack said it was a great pickup line to use on women because they seemed to be fascinated whenever he told the story. Logan knew Zack could really spin a yarn.

Logan looked at his watch and saw that it was 6:42 a.m. He knew it was just a bit early to call Zack, who was self-employed and rarely crawled out of bed before 10:00 a.m. He would give his friend a chance to wake up and have his morning coffee before Logan told him about throwing away a guaranteed million dollars.

Still wearing only a towel around his waist, Logan walked into his office and flipped open his day timer. For him, it was all or nothing, so if he was going to search for the treasure, he was going to devote all his time to the search. He didn't have any photo shoots that he couldn't cancel, except one later on this morning, a single mother who had arranged to have photos taken of her two kids. Logan had been busy the day they had come in and couldn't do the shoot, but the kids stood out to him because they were so well behaved, something you certainly don't see every day. He sat down and made a list of everything he needed to do to temporarily shut down his business. Even as he made his list, opposing feelings of excitement and regret ebbed and flowed through him. He prayed he had made the right choice, but he knew in his heart that searching for the treasure was just something he had to do.

He got dressed and headed into the kitchen to make some breakfast. As adventurous as he was, he was extremely predictable when it came to his breakfast. He ate the same thing every morning—scrambled eggs, cereal, yogurt, acai berry juice, and of course, he washed it all down with a large cup of coffee. If he was in one of his favorite countries, such as Thailand, then he'd have banana pancakes. Normally, Logan always went for a run in the morning, but due to his lack of sleep during the last few nights, he just couldn't find the energy. Besides, this morning he had a lot to do. With his list in his hand, he headed out the door and hopped into his Jeep. It was another typical day in paradise. It wasn't even 9:00 a.m. and the sun already felt hot, though it was kept in check by the cool breeze as he sped down the road.

Logan slid the key into the lock on the door of his studio and with a loud click, the deadbolt slid open. He stepped inside, swiping the light switch on as he entered. He paused for a moment, slowly rotating, as he looked at all his photos that adorned the walls of his studio—so many memories of so many adventures. Logan thought he was about to embark on what might be his greatest adventure yet.

He pulled out his day timer, and again began making all the necessary calls needed to close the studio temporarily. He looked at his watch, noting that it was 10:20 a.m. His one remaining appointment was scheduled for 10:30 a.m. Logan had planned to call his friend Zack, but he would have to wait until after his photo shoot. As if on cue, the single lady who had made the appointment walked in the door. It couldn't help but warm his heart to see the smiling faces of her two children. *What are their names again?* he wondered.

He extended his hand. "Hi, Gloria. Nice to see you again. I'm so sorry, but I forgot your children's names."

"Finney and Amelia," Gloria replied. "Finney is three years old, and Amelia is seven."

"A pleasure to see you both again," Logan said, nodding at the kids.

As he carried on with the shoot, he thought what amazing and cute children Finney and Amelia were, with their beautiful smiles. They were so well behaved, too. It was a perfect farewell shoot before he embarked on his adventure. Logan wasn't superstitious, but he thought this had to be a sign. In fact, when the photo shoot was done, he refused to take any money. Gloria thanked him while Finney and Amelia waved goodbye with big smiles.

After Gloria and the kids had gone, Logan immediately went into the back and began to print off the photos. He packed them up and put them into his outbox with a stack of other envelopes that needed to be sent out as part of the shutdown. His fingers were ready to set the alarms as he paused in the doorway and took a long look into the now dark studio, again a gamut of emotions running through him, a mix of excitement tempered with uncertainty. *Well, this is it.* He had no idea of how long or where the treasure quest would take him, but it was that uncertainty that was part of the treasure quest's romantic appeal.

Logan needed to clear his head, so as he often did when he wanted to think, he drove north to Akaka Falls State Park. He loved the natural beauty of the area. Parking the Jeep, he got out and was soon walking down a jungle-clad path to a clearing with a beautiful view of the falls. He stepped off the path to the edge of an embankment and sat down. The sun inched toward the horizon, giving a photogenic orange hue to the falls. Logan sat alone with his thoughts as the falls thundered in his ears.

After a period of reflection, he extracted his cell phone from his pocket and scrolled through his phone book until he reached Zack Cook's number. After two rings, Zack picked up.

"Hey Logan, I haven't heard from you in ages! What the hell you been up to?"

"Ah, the wonder of call display." Logan laughed, surprised that Zack had even answered. Normally he would let the answering machine take the call and eventually, usually two or three days later, return the call.

"Zack, I was just wondering what you're up to for, oh, say the next month or two? Or maybe five?"

"Depends," Zack said tentatively.

"Oh, come on, Zack! You aren't going to do nothing except bang away on that silly keyboard." Logan laughed.

"Hey," Zack replied, trying to sound indignant. "Believe it or not that silly keyboard is how I make my living."

"Well, my friend, how do you feel about getting away from that computer for a while?"

"Go on, I'm listening."

With a big sigh, Logan said, "Are you sitting down?"

Zack chuckled. "Of course. I'm practically glued to this chair."

"Good, because I'm about to tell you a bizarre tale. I guess that would be the best way to describe it." Logan told Zack the entire story, starting with finding the bottle while diving in Japan and ending with hearing the news broadcast about Colton Braxton's death, and about his will that included the map. Everything seemed to be going well until he told Zack that he could sell the map to the Braxton family for one million dollars but had decided instead to hunt for the treasure himself.

Logan pulled the phone away from his ear as Zack screamed. "A million dollars! A million frickin' dollars! What the hell are you thinking, Logan?"

"Of all people, I thought you'd understand. You know I live for this shit," Logan replied.

"I know you live for extreme travel, and no matter how bizarre of an adventure you go on, I'm normally not the least bit surprised, but we're talking about a million dollars," Zack said. There was a pause as Logan not only gathered his thoughts, but also started wondering if Zack was right.

"I'm sorry, Logan," Zack said, now pacing around his office, no longer glued to his chair. "I know you live for this shit and this really must be like a dream come true for you, but I just can't stop thinking about what a million dollars could do for you."

"I know. I've thought long and hard about this, and it's just something I have to do. I know if I don't, I'll regret it for the rest of my life."

"Okay. You know I'm there for you. What do you need?"

"First and foremost, you have to promise to tell no one about this. No one. Not even your wife. Promise?"

"Okay, my friend. Tell me what I can do."

As much as Logan trusted Zack, he knew how hard it was for couples living together to keep secrets from each other. He had to tell his friend anyway.

"I'm pretty sure I've figured out the location of the first map, but I'll scan it and e-mail it to you with my findings. If you could confirm them before I run halfway around the world, it would be great. It would be even better if you could come along. You know it will be a real adventure."

"God, Logan, I wish I could, but I really can't get away in the next few weeks," Zack said. Even as the words left his mouth, he was already thinking of a way he could escape work and join Logan on his adventure. For now, though, he would put his computer skills to work and help that way.

Logan had not discussed any remuneration with Zack, but the bonds of friendship were so strong between them that it was not necessary.

Zack knew that if Logan found a valuable treasure, he would be more than generous to him. He knew he would have a hard time accepting any reward from Logan. Not only was his business booming, but it would be out of friendship he was helping, not for any potential financial gain.

Logan sent off his findings and a scan of the map that he had saved to an e-mail draft earlier, as he and Zack talked a bit more. Immediately upon hanging up the phone Zack headed to his computer and opened the scan of the map and began to confirm Logan's findings.

CHAPTER 4

A large puff of smoke from the thick Cohiba cigar slowly drifted into the expansive and dimly lit study of Dr. Victor Kane. He intently watched the world news on his large screen TV mounted in an opening of a wall of books that would humble most libraries. As he watched, a slight grin spread across his pockmarked face, while the wheels turned in his head, already beginning to formulate a plan to find the Braxton treasure. It was what he did—finding treasure, no matter what it took.

Despite being only in his mid-forties, Victor looked much older. His once dirty-blond hair was now mostly gray. He also sported a goatee mainly to cover up a large scar on his chin that he had received courtesy of a knife. The goatee also gave him a sinister appearance. Victor stood only five feet nine inches tall, but he was a stocky, powerful man who not only knew his way around a weight room but had also earned his black belt in karate.

He was born of an Irish mother and a Dutch father. He had received his doctorate in archaeology but found that acquiring antiquities by slightly less than legal means was immensely more profitable. Over the last two decades, he had amassed one of the most extensive private collections of antiquities in the world. His collection included everything from ancient Egyptian artifacts to shipwreck coins, and everything in between. Victor Kane was one of the world's most notorious black-market antiquity dealers. On several occasions, he had found himself in trouble with the law, but with his wealth and connections he'd never even received as much as a fine, let alone jail time.

He had gained quite a reputation for getting what he wanted. The problem was with how he got it. What Victor was truly notorious for was letting other people discover, dig up, or find an artifact, only to have it end up in his hands. Ruthless didn't begin to describe him. More than one treasure hunter had disappeared over the years after an encounter with him. He leaned back in his chair, drawing in a mouthful of cigar smoke and closing his eyes in contemplation. "Yes!" he said. "I will have that treasure." Ways to get it began to run through his mind.

Over the years, Victor had developed a vast network of contacts throughout the world that he knew he could trust, or rather he knew would not dare to betray him. He settled into his desk chair, and from the top drawer of his desk he removed a black book. He flipped through it, pondering whom he should entrust with this task. He grabbed the phone and began to set his plan in motion.

He thought about the seven starter maps. He wondered how many of them had been discovered and if the person who had discovered them had any clue of what they possessed. Victor had found that one of the greatest resources for information was the Internet—blogs in particular. In general, people loved to brag about anything of interest they may have found, and there were thousands of sites that he had used in the past to lead him to an artifact, often duping a novice would-be treasure hunter out of his find.

As soon as he had contacted his most resourceful cronies, he began searching blogs and websites in earnest to see if anyone had obtained one of the starter maps. "Unbelievable," Victor muttered to himself. He couldn't believe the number of people that had either claimed to have some sort of treasure map or know of someone who did. Some were quickly weeded through, since many had attached pictures that were obviously not the Braxton map. He shook his head. He couldn't believe some of the ridiculous claims he found. However, Victor also found several leads worth pursuing.

"Oh, I'm sorry, Mr. Kane. I didn't mean to disturb you," his maid said.

"No problem, Margaret. What time is it?"

"It's 9:15, sir."

"A.M.?" Victor yelled.

"Yes, sir. It's 9:15 a.m.," Margaret answered. She slowly backed out of the room.

He had been sitting at his computer desk for nearly eleven hours without so much as a snack or even a bathroom break. Suddenly, Victor felt an urgent need for both.

In a few minutes, he returned to his desk, coffee in one hand and a couple of pastries in the other. He set down his makeshift breakfast and picked up his list. He had eighteen names, six of which looked promising. Victor had already contacted all of them by either e-mail, blog post, or phone call. He had also dispatched his henchmen to the locations of the possible maps where he was lucky enough to obtain any of the particulars. Meanwhile, he had his computer experts tracking down the identities and whereabouts of potential leads through e-mail accounts, usernames, and IP addresses. The thought of sleep didn't even cross his mind. He was obsessed with finding the map.

Another day passed. Victor had been burning the candle at both ends. He rubbed his eyes. He had a hard time focusing on the computer screen. His eyes felt as scratchy as sandpaper, his back ached, and his head throbbed. He finally realized that he needed to sleep before he collapsed.

In the past day and a half, he had followed over fifty leads, and between himself and the people working on his behalf, he had eliminated all but five of them. He thought, *who knows? With seven maps out there, one—or perhaps all five—could be real.* He slowly dragged himself up the wide wooden staircase to his massive bedroom, and in the same clothes that he had worn for the past two days, he collapsed onto the bed. As soon as he closed his eyes, the room began to spin, but only for few seconds before he fell into a deep sleep.

In a few hours, Victor awoke feeling confused, not knowing how long he'd been asleep. He quickly looked at his watch. "Oh, thank God," he said, his voice groggy from sleep. "I only slept four hours." He knew he could have used more rest, but he had much more pressing things on his mind. He quickly jumped into the shower to refresh himself, threw on some clean clothes, and made his way back down to his office. He became irritated with himself for needing sleep when he saw that he had three messages and eight e-mails that he had missed regarding the map. He picked up his cell phone and called his voicemail inbox, listening to his messages as he simultaneously started reading his e-mails.

He was on his second e-mail when suddenly he felt his heart skip a beat. It was a reply regarding more information on a treasure map that the diver had found in the East China Sea. The diver had described the map that another diver on his boat had found in a bottle. The description perfectly matched the map described in the will of Colton Braxton III. If it had only been the map's description, Victor would not have been so excited, but along with it was a scanned photograph someone else aboard the dive boat had taken of the diver. By pure chance, the photograph had caught a corner of the map. Unfortunately for Victor, most of the map was hidden, but in the corner he could clearly see the initials C. E. B. This information, combined with the description provided by the diver, led him to believe that the map was genuine. He had asked the diver if he remembered who it was that had found the map, but he could not remember the man's name. The diver did tell Victor when the dive trip had taken place and told him the name of the company that owned the boat.

Victor was on the phone with the dive shop within ten minutes, but despite all the silver-tongued charm that he tried to muster up, the person on the other end of the line would not reveal the identity of the man who had found the map in the bottle. As soon as Victor ended the call, he yelled, and with a violent swipe of his hand the phone was torn from the wall and flew across the room into the mantle of the large stone fireplace. He was in a rage. He was used to getting what he wanted. He knew he would eventually get the information, but he was severely irritated that he would be slowed in his quest to acquire the map. He was so certain that this was a genuine lead that he planned to take it upon himself to retrieve the information from the dive shop. Within two hours, Victor was on route from Amsterdam to the Schiphol Airport, where his private jet was being fueled and readied for the flight to Okinawa.

At the airport, Victor boarded the plane flanked by two of his henchmen, whose looks alone were enough to intimidate even the toughest of customers. On the flight, he sat quiet and stone faced, his anger boiling within and ready to be unleashed upon the unsuspecting dive shop owner.

Before leaving Amsterdam, he had contacted a source in Okinawa that would pick up the trio at the airport and take them to the dive shop. Victor, despite his short temper and anger, thought it best if he tried to reason with the owner or offer to buy the information before resorting to violence. He lacked an ounce of compassion for anyone or anything, but he didn't want any legal hassles slowing him down now. He was pretty sure he could buy the information. After all, everyone had his or her price.

Victor embraced the warm breeze that stroked his face as the door of the plane opened. It felt good on his stiff muscles after the long flight. The immigration formalities went smoothly and before long he was en route to the dive shop. The timing was perfect. It was about to close, and from the reports he had received the owner was the only one there. Victor and his two henchmen parked the car about a half a block away, and from there they began to make their way toward the shop while the driver lagged behind to serve as a lookout. With a clang of a bell, Victor opened the door of the dive shop, followed closely by his men.

"Sorry, gentlemen, we're closed," bellowed a voice with a distinctive Southern accent from the backroom.

"If I could have but a moment of your time, sir," Victor replied, trying his best to sound cordial.

"Okay. Just a minute."

Before long, a blond-haired man in his forties wearing nothing but a pair of surfer shorts emerged from the backroom. At a glance, it was apparent that he spent a lot of time in the sun as well as drank more than his fair share of beer. He sported quite a substantial beer gut.

"Hi, my name is Dick," he said. He tried to size up the three men in his shop, as they certainly did not appear to be divers. "What can I do for you gentlemen?"

"Good day," Victor replied in his politest voice. "My name is Dr. Victor Kane, and these are my associates, Rolf and Maarten."

Dick immediately recognized the name. "Oh, yes, Dr. Kane, we spoke on the phone. I'm very, very sorry you made a trip all the way out here, but I'm afraid that I can't give out my clients' names. I'm sure you can understand that."

Victor could feel his blood pressure rising. "Yes, I understand that, but it's not like you are divulging confidential medical records," he replied. "Besides, I will pay you quite handsomely for two minutes of your time. Please, just give me a name." He reached into his jacket pocket and pulled out an envelope. He slapped it on the counter, his irritation now apparent.

Dick's eyes were fixed on the envelope, and he began to feel that Victor Kane and his no-neck goons meant business. His sense of self-preservation kicked in. He ran through in his mind what he could use for a weapon if it came to that.

"Look, mister, I've been more than polite with you so far, but I don't want your money. Now please leave my shop."

Victor just laughed and shook his head. "Oh, Dick, Dick, Dick. You do drive a hard bargain." He reached into his pocket and withdrew another thick envelope and banged it on the counter. "There. Twenty thousand dollars for doing nothing but being a typical rude American," Victor snarled, his voice ripe with distain.

In a show of bravado, Dick said, "I don't know who you think you are, but get the hell out of my shop immediately or I'll call the police." He reached for the phone.

Victor snapped. With a violent backhand swing, he knocked Dick to the floor. He yelled to his henchmen. "Lock the door and then drag this piece of shit into the backroom." Immediately, Rolf headed toward the door to lock it and close the blinds, while Maarten opened the counter door and reached down to grab Dick.

Just in time, Dick regained enough of his senses to throw a wild kick that landed squarely on Maarten's nose, breaking it, sending blood spraying and Maarten stumbling backward, clutching his face in pain.

Dick scrambled on all fours into the backroom and headed for a spear gun he had hanging on the wall. He lifted himself off the floor and grabbed the spear gun from the wall, grabbed an arrow, and as quickly as he could, fumbled to load the gun. Suddenly, Victor's powerful hand ripped the arrow away from Dick. Victor then grabbed Dick's throat, pressing in on it like a rapidly closing vise.

"So, you want to kill me?" Victor frothed. He then reached into his jacket pocket, pulled out a switchblade, and clicked it open. "Rot in hell." He drove the knife deep into Dick's belly and then jerked it upward, slicing him open. He released his grip on his neck as Dick grabbed his abdomen, which was gushing blood. Dick stared wide-eyed at Victor as he silently crumpled into a heap on the floor, and after a few convulsions, his body went limp. The pool of blood spread like ripples on a pond. Both Rolf and Maarten were standing in the doorway, Maarten still holding his nose.

"Forget him. Just look for any evidence of my contacting him, and for files of his dive charters," Victor barked. "Bastard! No wonder he didn't want to give me the name." Right there on the back desk were notes and research relating to the map, and notes about the person who had found the bottle, along with the contact information. He picked up the paper, and his eyes widened as he reached up and stroked the scar under his goatee. Then he gave a sinister laugh that would make the hairs on the back of your neck stand up.

CHAPTER 5

Logan popped the cork from a chilled bottle of Gewurztraminer at the exact moment the phone rang, startling him just enough to spill wine on the kitchen floor. "Hey, Zack! It had to be you. No one else could have such impeccable timing. What's up?" Logan said.

"What do you mean?" Zack asked. "What timing?"

"Doesn't matter. Great to hear your voice, my friend. So, what do you think about the map scan?"

"You were definitely right. The clues are extremely cryptic but working backward from the answers you came up with, it fits perfectly. I think you're spot on. I can't believe you figured that out! Just for fun, before I looked at your conclusions, I spent a few days trying to work out something, but eventually came to a dead end."

"I'm glad you agree. The clues weren't much to work with, but when you have the answers, it seems easy," Logan replied, as Zack began to read the clues on the map for the millionth time.

"You're good." Zack said, as he began to read the clues out loud. "Half a millennium before this date in Gotham's history and half a millennium after the death ended this twelve-month reign of this familiar name."

"Through nature's silky fingers you must go, to where they have, but as the old saying goes, don't…"

"Yeah, I think you're right, Zack." Logan said, interrupting him. "I also think that good ol' Colton Braxton wanted to make this a bit of a challenge. Are you sure you can't join me?"

"Not right now, but trust me, I am working as fast as I can to free up my calendar. You know I've always wanted to go to Asia."

"I know. You better be free to join me on my next leg of this treasure hunt. Besides, this one should be easy. I feel like I'm going home since I've spent so much time over there."

"Remember, anything you need, call me and I will try to either get this work done or see if I can postpone it for a while. After all, why should you have all the fun? Oh, and make sure you have fun!" Zack laughed.

Logan hung up the phone and double- and triple-checked his list, which was a habit he had acquired over the years. A quick glance at his watch showed that it was almost that time. He had made a few copies of the map. He locked one of them up in his safety deposit box, another in his safe, and he left the third copy with Zack. He would never let it out of his sight, just like his passport. He sincerely hoped Zack and he had deciphered the clues correctly, because if they hadn't, it was back to square one. In all the time spent researching, neither Logan nor Zack had come up with any other scenario that fit everything anywhere near as perfectly as their answers to the clues.

The unmistakable honking of a taxi horn broke the silence. Logan took one last look around, threw his backpack onto one shoulder, turned out the lights, and with a loud click the deadbolt was set. The taxi driver jabbered on as they drove, but Logan was lost in his thoughts and didn't hear or respond. The one-way conversation rambled on anyway, despite Logan completely ignoring the man. At the airport, he paid the taxi driver, leaving him with a generous tip, as was his habit, and then made his way to the check-in counter. He had spent so much time in airports he could almost go through the motions on autopilot. After he checked in, he went through security and bought a snack.

As Logan impatiently waited for his flight to board, he thought about the cryptic clues and how the pieces of the puzzle fit together. One of the pieces, Gotham, was easy—often, New York was referred to as

Gotham, but to find an important date in the history of New York was more than daunting. Equally difficult was to find a twelve-month reign of someone, not knowing what century, what country, or even what kind of reign. It could be referencing the reign of a king, a queen, a mayor, even a top bowler.

It had taken Logan hundreds of hours of cross-referencing. Thousands of possibilities had to be weeded through, but after what seemed like a project without an end, he had concluded that the New York date was the year it was chartered as a city in 1686. From there, Logan had a starting date from which to search. On the other end, AD 686, was the year that Pope John Paul V died, ending his twelve-month reign as pope. The year in the middle was AD 1186.

In AD 1186, on what was once the mighty city of Angkor, monarch Jayavarman VII built an amazing temple named Rajavihara, or royal monastery, which was since renamed Ta Prohm. Ironically, Ta Prohm was also one of Logan's favorite ruins at the Angkor site in Cambodia. Over the years, he had made three trips to the Angkor site. He found it incredible, and the vastness of the site would take years to explore fully. Unfortunately, each time he went, he only had about a week. He had always made the most of his time, getting there first thing in the morning and staying until late in the afternoon. He never slowed down. Exploring ruins energized Logan.

The next piece of the puzzle seemed to just fall into place, especially after so much exploring of the Ta Prohm ruins. Nature's silky fingers were obviously the massive roots of the silk cotton trees that intertwined themselves among the crumbling ruins. The last piece jumped out at Logan as he scanned through the thousands of photographs he had taken over the years. The photo showed a headless group of Buddha statues at Ta Prohm. The clue had read: "They had lost their heads; don't lose your head!"

Logan had checked all the possible flights available and found the quickest way for him to get to Angkor was to fly into Bangkok, and from there catch a flight to Siem Reap, Cambodia, which was the town just outside the Angkor archaeological site. Logan was much happier flying into Bangkok instead of Phnom Penh. He had spent some time in the Cambodian capital, but he was not only more comfortable and familiar with Bangkok, he also thoroughly enjoyed the city and would have one evening there before his morning flight to Siem Reap.

Logan wasn't sure how he was going to react when he actually got to Angkor. He was already so keyed up and antsy to get searching for the map that he could hardly imagine the excitement once he was there. Flying to Siem Reap would definitely be a treat for him, since on all his previous trips he had taken the brutal sixteen-hour overland trip. Logan just smiled when he thought of some of the amazing stories he had from his overland adventures into Cambodia, which included everything from collapsed bridges to broken down vans.

Of all the extensive travel Logan had done, he had spent the most time in Thailand; it was like his second home. He loved everything about it: the smells, the food, the amazing beaches, the rock climbing, the awesome diving, and the incredible temples. The people were some of the friendliest in the world. His heart beat faster just thinking about it and all the amazing memories he had from past adventures. The flight seemed to take forever. Logan tried to sleep, but he couldn't, at least not right away. Fatigue finally got the best of him and he drifted off. Unfortunately, he didn't go to that happy place that dreams are made of, but rather to a dark place where the demons of his past had haunted him for many years. His body convulsed back and forth in the seat of the aircraft as he suddenly found himself underwater. A deafening shockwave drove his face into the sand. He felt his lungs starting to burn, and the warmth of his own blood swirled around him as imminent death stared him in the face.

As the rocks crumbled down one by one, the light in the distance dimmed. *I don't want to die like this!* Logan silently screamed, but no one could hear him. His body desperately wanted to inhale, but his extensive diving experience told him to fight the reflex action, that inhaling meant certain death. With every second that passed, his lungs burned more, craving life-sustaining oxygen. *Stay calm! Stay calm! Stay calm!* Logan chanted to himself. He knew that panic was his worst enemy and it would deplete the precious oxygen left in his body. Gaining leverage with one leg, he tore his other leg free from the pile of coral rocks that had pinned it to the cave floor. He could feel the flesh ripping from his leg through his neoprene wetsuit as he wrenched it from the death grip of the jagged rocks.

Through his own black blood that swirled in a hedonistic dance with the fine silt of the cave he could see a faint blue light. It seemed a mile away.

Logan's desire to live was almost superhuman. Most men would have perished by now. He feverishly swam toward the light, oblivious to the pain of the deep gash in his head or the skin that hung like ribbons in the wind from his shredded leg. He knew he had to concentrate on staying calm and keeping his heart rate low. He let his mind drift back to the games he used to play in the pool, where he would sit on the bottom to see how long he could hold his breath. In the comfort of the lotus position as he rested on the pool bottom, he had held his breath for over five minutes many times, but this was far from a sunny pool. Here time seemed to stand still, and no matter how far he swam, the majestic blue light still seemed so far away.

After what seemed like an eternity, Logan finally reached the opening. No, no, no! Too small! He felt on the edge of blacking out. He felt his vision narrowing, and his lungs were ablaze. He hastily removed his BCD and tank, which were useless to him anyway. *Damn it! The opening is still too small!* He frantically began to dig in the sand just enough to wedge his body through the narrow opening. With his last ounce of strength, he pushed up from the sandy bottom toward the surface sixty feet above him as everything suddenly went black.

Logan jolted awake, bathed in a cold sweat. He looked around, feeling as though everyone was staring at him, but no one was. It was all so vivid, like it had just happened. His heart was pounding. He could feel the pain, and it sent shivers down his spine. Logan starred out the window of the plane and saw the lights of Bangkok below, but he was still lost in a trance. He remembered waking up on the deck of a dive boat that had rescued him from the choppy waters of the Caribbean

Sea. He had blacked out on his ascent to the surface, only being saved from drowning by the buoyancy of his wetsuit. Except for a few scars on his leg and a scar under his hair, the physical injuries had healed, but it was a nightmare that took him a long time to recover from, one that visited him from time to time. After all, it's not every day that someone tries to kill you.

Despite all that had happened, Logan could feel that same adrenaline rush that had once surged through his veins. He had often wondered what happened to the man who attacked him and had stolen the greatest shipwreck treasure Logan had ever found. A slight grin came to his face. "At least I got one good slash in," he said softly. He was still bitter at not only almost losing his life, but a once in a lifetime treasure. He finally snapped to, and the sense of excitement returned as he began to focus on the task at hand. He continued to stare down at the lights of Bangkok. They were a welcome sight, but even once on the ground, the plane seemed to take forever to taxi to the terminal.

Logan could feel the humidity seeping into the jet way as he deplaned. He relished the sultry night air. He loved the heat. You would never hear him say it's too hot. He collected his luggage, went through immigration, and was soon out the front door of the airport.

"Khao San Road, please," Logan told the taxi driver. Every taxi driver knew where Khao San Road was. It was the center of the backpacking universe. Logan thought it was one of the most incredible places on the planet. No matter what time day or night, it was happening on Khao San. The vibe on the street was something that you had to experience to understand. Over the past few years, there had been a shift from the domain of the backpacker to a combination of backpackers and flashpackers, but still it was the ultimate travel melting pot.

The taxi pulled up at the end of Khao San Road, which was a pedestrian street during the evening. It was packed with thousands of people. Logan smiled as he stepped out onto the street, feeling like he was home. He threw on his backpack and started to make his way down to one of the old haunts he had stayed at several times in the past. As he entered the hotel and walked toward the counter, a friendly Thai girl greeted him with a huge smile. "Sawatdee," Logan replied and proceeded to check in.

Despite being short on sleep, he just could not resist hitting the street for a few hours. Besides, he knew he was way too keyed up to sleep. Logan had never had a problem with anything going missing from his hotels in Thailand before, but in this case the map, along with his passport, were securely strapped to a travel pouch under his clothes. It had been two years since he had been to Bangkok, but the second he had stepped into the street, he felt like he'd never left. He slowly strolled up and down Khao San Road, taking in the sights and sounds that brought back so many memories—memories of friends he had met, travel stories swapped, and of course, memories of women that he had spent time with in Thailand. He thought he would engage in one of his favorite Khao San Road activities: people watching while enjoying an ice-cold beer. He stopped at one of his favorite outdoor restaurants and pulled up a chair. A friendly waitress greeted him, and he ordered a beer. Though it was late, he couldn't resist ordering his favorite dish, Thai green curry.

Time passed quickly as Logan watched and listened with intrigue as every possible kind of person walked by. By the time the waitress returned with his green curry, he was ready for another beer. "God, that smells good!" Logan said quietly, salivating, as the aroma of the sweet spices filled his nasal passageways. He raised his beer in a toast. "Well, Logan," he said softly, "here's to the adventure of a lifetime."

A playful chuckle filled his ears. "What are your imaginary friends drinking?" asked a sexy woman with a Southern accent whom Logan hadn't noticed before.

"Oh, God. Now I'm embarrassed," Logan said, taking in the woman's looks with pleasure. She had long, tanned legs covered only by an extremely distracting mini skirt, and she was wearing a cut-off top that revealed a firm midriff and curves in all the right places. Although Logan had not meant to stare, he felt like he had taken an inordinate time making his way to what only could be described as a stunning face. The first thing that jumped out at him was her incredible smile. He was a pushover for a beautiful smile. The woman had long blond hair and ice-blue eyes that seemed to look straight into his soul.

"Do you mind if I join you and your imaginary friends?" She asked playfully.

Still flush with embarrassment, Logan replied, "No. I don't mind. Please do. Uh, they, my imaginary friends, have to leave anyway."

She giggled and sat down. "Hi, my name is Savannah Devereux."

"Hi, Savannah. I'm Logan Nash. I love your accent."

"Why thank you, Logan."

"You have to be from Louisiana."

"Yes! Oh, my God, you are good! I'm from New Orleans! And you are from … California?"

"You got the right side of the continent. I used to live in Seattle, but there's too much rain there, so I now make Hawaii my home."

"I love Hawaii! Oahu? Maui?"

"No, actually the Big Island, in Hilo, to be specific. It's one of the rainiest spots in Hawaii, but much better than Seattle. I love the incredible variety that the Big Island offers. So, Savannah, is this your first trip to Thailand?"

"Yes, but I'm a little leery about traveling on my own. My friend was supposed to come with me, but she broke her leg. I don't normally come up and talk to strange men in strange countries, but you and your invisible friends seemed so cute."

"Thanks, I guess. I'm glad I didn't scare you off. I'm not completely insane, you know. In fact, I hardly ever talk to make believe friends."

"How about you? Have you been here before?" Savannah asked.

"I'm proud to say I have. I have made several trips here. It truly is one of my favorite countries in the world."

"Well, Mr. Logan Nash, it looks like I picked the right crazy guy to talk to. Maybe you can show me around."

Just the thought of that sent Logan's pulse racing, not to mention his hormones. He couldn't believe he had forgotten why he was here for a few minutes, and beyond that, he was shocked at the intense attraction he felt for Savannah. *Thanks, fate,* Logan thought, realizing that the timing could not have been worse. He knew he had to concentrate his efforts on finding the next map, and time was of the essence. He couldn't believe that the thought of postponing the trip to Cambodia actually crossed his mind, but it did because he didn't want to lose the opportunity to get to know such an amazing woman.

Logan and Savannah became so engrossed in conversation that the competing pounding music of a dozen bars and nightclubs, the loud boisterous conversations of a thousand people streaming by, and the hundreds of street vendors hawking their wares all blended into muffled background noise. He found the conversation intoxicating. It was like they were two soul mates that had gone their own way, and then years later picked up exactly where they had left off. He found they shared so much in common that it seemed too good to be true. Not only was she strikingly beautiful, but she was also intelligent and interesting.

Could this be what they call love at first sight? he wondered. *God, Logan, get a grip on yourself. What are you thinking? Start thinking with the big head, not the little one!*

Before he could stop himself, Logan asked, "How do you feel about taking a trip to Cambodia?"

CHAPTER 6

While Logan was preparing for his adventure to Asia, and while Zack slaved away in front of a computer screen to confirm Logan's findings, Dr. Victor Kane was back at his Amsterdam estate formulating a plan of his own.

A pleased grin spread across Victor's face as he studied the papers that he had retrieved from Okinawa. "Thank you very much, Dick," he said. It was obvious to him that the late Dick Fletcher had planned to go after the treasure himself. He had been good enough to do most of Victor's legwork for him, and his payment was being left to bleed to death on a dirty dive shop floor. Being as cold blooded as he was, Victor did not feel an ounce of remorse. In fact, he felt justified having offered Mr. Fletcher what he thought was more than a fair deal.

Victor picked up one of the papers. "Logan Nash. Well, well, well, it looks like we'll meet again," he whispered. He again rubbed his hand on the scar beneath his goatee. At the dive shop, he had been pleasantly surprised to see Logan's name.

It has to be the same Logan Nash. It has to be!

Victor's mind wandered back five years to St. Thomas in the US Virgin Islands and his encounter with Logan Nash. Although he was surprised that Nash was still alive, even he had to admire his determination and resourcefulness to escape the predicament that Victor had left him in. "I think you will make a worthy adversary, young Mr. Nash," Victor said.

Victor walked over to one of the towering bookshelves in his office and tipped back the third book in on the second shelf. Smooth and silent, like a high-tech elevator door, the bookshelf slid open to reveal a hidden room. It was full of rare and valuable treasures and antiquities valued in the hundreds of millions of dollars. They were displayed in a way that would have you believe that you were walking into one of the world's finest museums, and it was, except it existed for the pleasure of only one man.

Victor walked over to a gold cross adorned with alternating rubies and diamonds, each gem well over two carats. It was arguably the greatest Spanish artifact ever found. He knew on the open market it could fetch upward of twenty million dollars. Victor punched in his electronic code, lifted the glass lid, and gently removed the gleaming cross from its indigo velvet home. He cradled it as one would a child. It was a true thing of beauty, something he would never part with, something he had killed to acquire. As he caressed it, admiring its beauty, he thought about Logan Nash, the young treasure hunter who had been good enough to find what Victor considered the jewel in his vast collection of artifacts and antiquities.

By pure chance, Victor had been on vacation in St. Thomas for some time in the sun and a bit of scuba diving. Although not what one would consider a hardcore diver, he'd found that in the world of treasure hunting, it was good to be able to go wherever the treasure might be without having to rely on hired help, or at least to be there to oversee what was happening. When it came to treasure, he had found greed often overruled common sense in most people, and when it came to him, that could be a deadly mistake.

He had become extremely efficient at greasing peoples' palms in advance, thus creating a vast information network loyal to him—as long as the money flowed. This was especially true when it came to anything to do with diving or ruins—two of the richest sources of treasure. This had been the case in St. Thomas. He and his associates had chartered a dive boat to scout out easy pickings, always making sure the owner, the boat captain, and the dive master were compensated in a way that surpassed anything they could ever have hoped for. One night as Victor sat down to eat dinner, he'd received an intriguing phone call.

"Hello, Mr. Victor, dis is Dudley, da captain of da dive boat you were on 'tree days ago," he'd said in a thick island accent.

"Yes, Dudley, I remember you. What can I do for you?" Victor had asked.

"I remember you say dat you pay good for information."

"That depends on what you have for me." Victor had been extremely intrigued.

"Last two days a young man hire da boat, go far out on da outer reef. Between dives, I see him making notes about shipwreck, and he bring up a couple of coins, too. But da last dive he very excited. He say we go out early tomorrow morning."

"Have you told anyone else?" Victor had asked.

"No, mon. No one. Me tell you first."

"Okay, Dudley, don't tell anyone. If I find something valuable, I will make it well worth your while – very well."

"Yes, sir. Tank you, sir. We will leave at 7:00 a.m. in da morning. Da young mon's name is Nash. Logan Nash."

"Thank you very much, Dudley. Be relaxed in the morning, like nothing has happened, and just go out as planned. We will follow you from a distance and rendezvous with you after Mr. Nash is under the water."

The next morning at the break of dawn, Victor and his men had waited behind a shed, boat at the ready. It had been another typical day in paradise: hot and sunny, with just enough of a breeze to hold the stifling humidity at bay.

Logan had pulled up to the dive shop in his rented Jeep Wrangler. At the water's edge, he'd seen Dudley waiting by the boat. As Logan cheerfully walked toward him, Dudley had looked away.

"Good morning, Dudley. It looks like a perfect day to go diving," Logan had said. Dudley nodded, giving Logan a quick glance and then looking away.

Dudley had untied the boat from the dock and they headed off across the azure sea, a slight chop causing the boat to skip across the water like a flat stone flung into a pond. Victor had been watching as the boat shrank against the horizon.

"Okay, let's go," Victor had said, causing his men to jump into action with military precision. In seconds, they were skipping over the waves, keeping enough distance between them and Logan's boat not to draw attention.

After several miles, Dudley had slowed the dive boat. Victor had immediately slowed his boat and pulled out a pair of high-powered binoculars, watching as Logan checked his GPS and gestured to Dudley to adjust their position as he suited up. Victor had watched as Dudley tossed the anchor overboard, and then sat down with a sullen look on his face, which worried Victor as he wondered if Dudley would tell Logan of his plan. He had seen the guilt on Dudley's face from 300 yards away.

Dudley had informed Victor that the site was a coral outcropping that ranged from a few feet below the surface to sixty feet deep, which would explain how a ship could easily run aground, since they would not expect such a shallow reef so far out to sea. Still, he'd intently watched as Logan donned a set of double tanks, leading him to believe that Logan planned to spend a fair bit of time down there. At that depth, decompression really wouldn't have been an issue, unless he was down for a long time.

Within a few minutes, Logan had rolled back and plunged into the Caribbean Sea, disappearing below the waves.

Victor and his men had sprung into action, throttling up the boat and hastily making their way to Logan's location. He'd known that in the shallow water Logan would easily see a boat overhead, so he'd waited a way off for about fifteen minutes. He had hoped that by then Logan would be too busy digging in the sand to notice the boat overhead. Victor's boat had slowly eased its way alongside the other boat.

"Good morning, Dudley," Victor had said.

"Morning, sir, I, I just want to say please don't hurt da kid. He's a good guy."

Victor's demeanor had immediately changed, and his slight smile turned into a scowl. He had known he couldn't trust Dudley, but he had wanted to see what trinkets young Logan found before he decided what to do about it. Victor had ordered one of his men to watch Dudley, and he and one of his men had put on their dive gear to check out what Logan had found.

After Victor had found out where the dive site was the previous night, he had done some checking and discovered that there had been a shipwreck found there about forty years ago. Over the years, the site had been extensively excavated. To his knowledge, it had been picked clean, although he knew hurricanes could stir up wreck sites that were even three hundred fifty years old. Still, he had been skeptical about anything other than maybe a few coins being found, but he'd felt obliged to check it out. Victor and his bulky henchman had been ready to enter the water, and they'd both been armed with knives, spear guns, and a small explosive device that Victor had brought along just in case he needed to get rid of one of the dive boats. They'd seen where Logan's bubbles had broken the surface, and after penetrating the water, they'd headed toward his position. They'd spotted Logan digging under a coral head a few feet from what appeared to be a small cave, and they'd slipped behind another coral head before Logan noticed them.

Victor had intently watched Logan violently gouging away at the coral, which had piqued his curiosity, but he hadn't needed to wait long until his eyes suddenly widened as Logan extracted a coral-encrusted gold cross. Victor couldn't believe his eyes. The cross Logan had found was huge, and even though it had still been half covered with coral, he'd seen jewels sparkling in the light of the shallow water.

Out of the corner of his eye, Logan had caught a glimpse of the two men. He'd immediately stuffed the cross into his BCD pocket, hoping that they had not seen it and wondering what the hell other divers were doing way out there. He had taken a quick glance at his dive computer and had noted that he was well within the safe zone, so, with no fear of decompression sickness and no time for a safety stop, he headed quickly for the surface.

Victor and his henchman had followed. Logan, being much younger and experienced in the water, had easily won the race to the surface, but the moment he had looked up, he was staring down the barrel of a 9mm semi-automatic pistol.

Within seconds, the two men had flanked Logan, their spear guns at the ready. "Mr. Nash, I presume?" Victor had gloated.

"Please, please, Mr. Kane," Dudley had begged, only to have his groveling cut short by Victor, who had raised his spear gun, firing the razor-sharp spear through the center of Dudley's neck. Dudley had clutched at his neck and stumbled across the boat, plunging over the other side. Logan heard him thrashing for only a few seconds, and then all was silent.

Victor had ripped open Logan's BCD pocket and wrenched out the cross, while Logan remained stunned over what he had just seen. His heart felt like it was beating out of his chest, and his mind had raced a mile a minute with possible scenarios about the outcome of the confrontation—most of which would end badly. Logan had seen Victor reach for his dive knife, knowing that the stranger was going to kill him, especially after he had witnessed him murdering Dudley. There would be no bargaining now, he knew, as he had his only bargaining chip taken from him.

Time had seemed to stand still as Logan was hit with a moment of clarity, knowing that he had to act quickly and decisively. He figured there was no way he could reach the dive knife on his thigh quickly enough, but being a well-prepared wreck diver, he always carried a spare knife on his BCD strap. In one lightning quick move, he brought his right elbow back, striking Victor's henchman in the throat, while with his left hand he slid out his secondary knife, slashing it toward Victor's neck. Victor had quickly lunged back, saving his life, but the knife had torn into his chin, sending blood spraying across Logan's facemask.

Logan had quickly dived beneath the boat to avoid the gunfire from Victor's man that had been stationed to watch Dudley. He finned downward for the safety of the cave. Victor's man in the water had been gasping for breath and was unable to give chase. Blood gushed from the deep wound on Victor's chin, but he had known he couldn't leave Logan alive. Even miles out to sea, he could have been rescued, and that would be game over. Victor grabbed the spear gun from his injured man and gave chase, a steam of blood flowing from his chin as he swam. Logan had already reached a depth of thirty feet and was descending fast, and Victor had seen that he was heading for the cave entrance. Without a dive light, Victor had known that there was no way he could have followed Logan into the cave. The distance between them had increased, and Victor raised the spear gun and fired. The spear had spiraled through the water toward Logan, striking the manifold that connected the two tanks.

The impact caused the manifold to crack open, deflecting the spear away from Logan, leaving him unharmed. The shot had been a one in a million event, hitting the manifold in the one place where Logan could not isolate one tank. The air violently erupted from the tanks, emptying them in seconds with a thunderous roar. Logan had sucked in his last precious lungful of air and darted into the cave opening.

Seeing the devastating result of his spear, Victor had known that Logan couldn't hold his breath for long, but just to be sure, he pulled out the explosive device he had planned to use to blow up the dive boat. He'd set the timer for fifteen seconds, placed it at the cave entrance, and began swimming away as quickly as he could. It had not been a powerful device, but it was more than sufficient to collapse the cave entrance. The blast had been enough to send a small shockwave Victor's way. "Goodbye and thank you, Mr. Nash," Victor said to himself as he ascended toward the surface, feeling dizzy from the loss of blood, which had only been enhanced by his exertion in the water.

He climbed up the boat's ladder, and while stripping off his diving gear, he had chastised his men with a tone of utter disgust. "Thanks a lot for your help down there. I don't even know why I pay you morons. Now sink that other boat and let's get the hell out of here."

Victor held a towel on his chin, and despite his pain and the ineptness of his men, he felt like a kid who just gotten a new toy for Christmas. The cross would be the crowning jewel of his collection.

Coming out of his reverie, Victor admired the cross for a minute more in the lavish confines of his secret museum room. The cross was so much more beautiful now than when he had first acquired it from Logan Nash. He thought of all the painstaking time he had spent to clean and restore it to its original pristine condition. He carefully placed it back in its blue velvet home, almost as if he were placing it back in the azure waters from which it had come just five years earlier after resting in the depths of the Caribbean for centuries.

Victor read Dick Fletcher's notes for what had to be the tenth time. "Yes, good old Dick did his homework," he muttered. Dick even had two private investigators watching Logan's every move. It appeared to Victor that if he had arrived in Okinawa any later, Fletcher would have already gone after Logan himself. Suddenly, as if the actual letters had come to life, the answer leaped off the page right into Victor's mind. "Yes, that's it! That's brilliant! Victor, you are truly a genius," he said aloud. "Yes, you have truly outdone yourself this time."

He closed the bookshelf, went to his desk, and picked up the phone. "Good morning," he said. "I want to—"

CHAPTER 7

A moment of silence filled the air. Logan chastised himself. "Shit, nice going Logan, now you scared her off." To his surprise, it turned out to be a good silence.

"Cambodia? You're kidding me, right? Oh, my God! I so wanted to go to Cambodia! Well, uh, I really wanted to go to Angkor. I've done so much reading about it. It is so amazing! So awesome! Please tell me that's where you are planning to go."

Logan grinned. "Believe it or not, yes, Angkor is where I am heading, and you'll be happy to know I have made several trips there as well. I'll be more than happy to play tour guide with you."

Savannah flashed Logan a playful look, as if to say, "Behave!" She then leaned over the table, cupped her chin in her hands, and looked deeply into Logan's eyes. "Well, Mr. Nash, this is all very sudden. Can I trust you? After all, you do sit and talk to imaginary people, and now you want to whisk me off to the middle of nowhere."

"Yes, and yes," Logan replied.

"I've always followed my instincts and they haven't let me down yet. Besides, where else could I find such a cheap guide?" Savannah chuckled.

"Cheap? Who says I'm cheap? You haven't got my bill yet." Logan did his best to sound serious, but Savannah wasn't buying it. She gave him a seductive wink and smiled.

Logan glanced at his watch, noting that it was 3:15 a.m.

"Past your bedtime?" Savannah smiled.

"No, my mommy usually lets me stay up until 3:30." He laughed. "Actually, I was thinking more practically." Logan couldn't believe he'd said that. "I was due to fly out to Siem Reap tomorrow morning, but we will have to wait for the next morning. I know a place here on Khao San Road where if we take your passport at 8:00 a.m., we can get you a Cambodian visa by 5:00 p.m."

"Sounds like a good plan," Savannah agreed, pushing back her chair and standing up. Logan followed suit.

"So, do you need an escort home?" Logan asked.

She smiled and moved in close to Logan, pressing her breasts against his muscular body. She leaned in and kissed him on the cheek. "Good night, Mr. Nash. How about we meet here at 7:00 a.m. for breakfast? Well, actually in a couple of hours," she chuckled, bidding Logan good night again in her sexy Southern accent.

"That sounds great! They make great banana pancakes here," Logan replied. His heart pounded from having Savannah's body pressed up against his and from what he thought was the most sensual peck on the cheek in history. He smiled and thought, *Yeah, she wants me. She's just playing hard to get.* Logan couldn't take his eyes off her as she drifted into the sea of late night revelers that still crowded Khao San Road. Logan sighed deeply and headed back to his hotel, suddenly tired from the long flight, the excitement of the quest to come, and his chance encounter with Savannah. He wondered about the meeting for a moment, his natural wariness percolating to the surface despite his fatigue, but he dismissed it. Or at least he tried to.

Yet, even as he walked among the throngs on the street, a battle raged inside his head. On one side, he felt as giddy as a schoolboy experiencing love for the first time, and on the other side he had the opportunity of a lifetime to find a treasure that could allow him the ultimate in financial freedom. The adventure of the treasure hunt itself was a real bonus too.

Shaking his head, Logan thought, *Idiot! Why couldn't I just take her number and call her in a week or two? Because, you don't think a woman like that would wander the streets of Bangkok long before someone else swept her off her feet?*

The boxing match raged on in his head, and no matter what the practical side said, he wanted to see Savannah again. Their next rendezvous at breakfast couldn't come fast enough.

Soon, his alarm clock jolted him awake. He rolled over, turned it off. He squinted through the morning haze at the bright red numbers on the clock - 6:00 a.m. "Nice," he said sarcastically. Even though he'd been exhausted, he'd had a hard time falling asleep. He figured he'd only slept for an hour, though he hoped it was more than that. He got up and rummaged around in his backpack for a few minutes before pulling out a bottle of pain relievers. He reached for a bottle of water and popped down a couple of the pills. "Yeah, I should have had a bit more water last night. Or less beer." That caused him to laugh, which only served to make his head hurt more. Still feeling half asleep, he stumbled into the shower. The water felt refreshing. His head started to clear, and despite the lack of sleep, the anticipation of the day was more than enough to get his engine running.

When Logan backpacked, he never really concerned himself with dressier clothes, and he had not this time either, but he found himself digging through his rucksack, trying to find something that looked presentable for his breakfast with Savannah. "This is the best I have with me," he mumbled. He dressed in a golf shirt and khaki shorts.

He arrived at the restaurant a few minutes early and ordered a coffee. Right on cue, he saw Savannah. The morning sun behind her gave her an angelic appearance. She seemed to float down the street in her little white sundress. Logan stood as she approached and greeted her with a peck on the cheek and a hug. "Wow, you look stunning, Savannah."

"Why thank you, kind sir, and good morning to you as well."

They sat down, ordered breakfast, and seemed to pick up the conversation exactly where they had left off the night before. When they had finished their breakfast, Logan paid the waitress, and as always, left a very nice tip. Although the wait staff wasn't accustomed to being tipped as much as they were back home, he thought they deserved it, as they not only worked hard, but the service was fantastic.

Across the street and a few feet down from the restaurant was a small travel agency that Logan had used many times. He had always found the service reliable. The older Thai woman that ran the place never seemed to age or change in any way. He greeted her upon entering, introduced Savannah, and arranged for her visa. Logan had previously arranged his own visa back home, as he had thought that he would be in a rush. *Strange how some things work out*, he thought.

"Well, Ms. Savannah, it's 8:10 a.m., and we have a whole day to enjoy Bangkok before we're off to Cambodia."

"Well, Mr. Logan, I'm all yours for the day, to do with as you please." She had most definitely mastered the art of seductive insinuation.

Though Logan preferred many of the beautiful islands that dotted the waters in Southern Thailand to Bangkok itself, it was still such an amazing and interesting place that he enjoyed immensely. He also knew it well. Logan and Savannah started their day with a short walk from Khao San Road down to the Grand Palace. They had a good laugh at the not so flattering pants and skirts they had to borrow there to cover up their bare extremities. As with many temples, the dress code was strictly enforced. Savannah was taken aback in awe at the incredibly stunning and lavish temples that adorned the grounds of the Grand Palace, which had first been built in 1782 but sparkled as if it had been built last year. She listened intently as Logan gave a running commentary that would have rivaled any umbrella-toting tour guide.

After a quick stop at Wat Pho to see the world's largest reclining Buddha, they grabbed a tuk tuk. With a loud whine, the three-wheeled motorized rickshaw was off, spewing exhaust into the air. They weaved in and out of Bangkok's insane traffic in what was not the safest or even the cheapest mode of transit around. Yet, if traffic got really snarled, it was faster than taking a taxi. Savannah was certain her white dress would not be quite as white after a day of Bangkok's pollution wafting around her in the open tuk tuk, but still she enjoyed it like a kid on a thrill ride. Logan had seen all the sights many times, but he felt like it was the first time for him too, as he experienced it all through Savannah's eyes. Her excitement was contagious.

They strolled around, taking in the plethora of sights, sounds, and smells of the street markets with everything bought and sold in an animated show of bartering. Logan had become an expert at the bartering. In Thailand, it was all part of the fascinating game of shopping. He thought that a visit to Bangkok would not be complete without a stroll through Patpong, the famous, or rather infamous, red light district, which in the late afternoon was just beginning to stir, ready to take on the night like no other place in the city. It was one of Thailand's many enigmas that all stirred together to make the city such an amazing place.

Logan hailed a taxi to take them down to the Chao Phraya River. Like a large anaconda, the river weaved its way through the sprawling metropolis. It was just before sunset when they jumped aboard one of the river buses that plied the waters. Logan had always been amazed at the precision the drivers had, pulling up full speed to a perfect stop almost every time, unloading and loading dozens, sometimes hundreds of people in seconds. There was no dilly-dallying. If you did, they would just take off without you. Logan was impressed by the speed and efficiency of their operation. As he and Savannah made their way down the river toward Khao San Road, the sun had begun to set. The one upside of the heavy pollution was the incredible cascade of colors that painted the horizon with a romantic backdrop.

As they neared Wat Arun, one of Bangkok's most picturesque temples, Savannah squeezed herself between Logan and the railing of the boat. Logan's heart jumped as he confidently slid his powerful arms around her firm waist, interlocking his hands and pulling her tightly against his body. The wind blew her golden hair against his face. He could smell her perfume and feel her squirm ever so slightly against his body. His heart pounded, and his emotions raced.

I want to take her now!

The boat that once seemed to be racing down the river seemed to slow, like a snail going up an icy hill. Savannah closed her eyes, reached her left arm back, and slowly ran her fingernails up Logan's thigh. He breathed heavily, and it required all his willpower to restrain himself from taking her at that very moment. He pulled back her hair, revealing her soft sensual neck, and gently leaned forward to give her a soft kiss. Savannah sighed, and he could tell she wanted more. Logan had always said that life was a series of snapshots defined by moments of such intensity as to be seared permanently into memory, making it part of who a person was. This is one of those moments.

After what felt like an eternity, the boat slid up to their stop. Logan grabbed Savannah by the hand and hurried her off the boat. They weaved in and out of the throng of people sauntering down the alleys and streets as they hastily made their way back to Khao San Road.

Savannah's hotel was the closest, so without debate or even a word spoken, the choice was made. They hurried up the two flights of stairs to her third-floor hotel room. She fumbled with the key, but finally opened the door. Logan immediately kicked the door shut and pinned her against the wall just inside the door, passionately kissing her as his hands began to explore her luscious body. She began to disrobe Logan as they became a lustful entanglement of urges and desires. They danced their way across the room to her bed, where they passionately made love with an intensity neither had ever felt before. They came twice in moments of intense ecstasy, and neither of them broke the silence that had begun the second Savannah slid her sleek sexy body in front of Logan's hours earlier on the river boat.

"Oh, shit!" Logan yelled in a state of panic, looking at his watch.

"What's wrong?" Savannah asked. She ran her fingers down Logan's muscular chest, her fingers heading south.

"It's 9:45 and the travel office closes at 10:00."

"I guess you better just get those cute little buns of yours dressed and hurry down there and pick up my passport while I take a nice, hot, soapy shower," Savannah said. She was lying naked on the bed.

Logan frantically got dressed, putting his shirt on backward and causing Savannah to erupt with laughter. "Easy, tiger, I'll still be here when you get back. If you hurry," she said, giving him a sexy wink.

Logan blew her a kiss and ran out of the room, down the stairs, out of the hotel, and down the street, jostling a passerby. "Excuse me," he said, as he made his way down the packed Khao San Road.

Logan knew that Thailand had two seasons: hot and hotter, both with extreme humidity. By the time he arrived at the travel shop, he was dripping in sweat.

"Made it!" Logan said to the old Thai woman, who, from what Logan could see, worked fourteen hours a day, seven days a week.

"Just barely," she replied in broken English.

Logan finally started to catch his breath as she handed him Savannah's passport and plane tickets.

"Usually people must pick up their own passport, but I know you long time, Mr. Logan. A shuttle bus will take you to the airport at 6:00 a.m. You and your lady friend have a good time." Logan just nodded and rushed out.

He hurried back to Savannah, who was freshly showered and in the process of putting on another stunning dress. "Girl, you just look better every time I see you," Logan said.

She smiled. "I'm starving. I guess I worked up quite an appetite."

Admiring how beautiful she looked, Logan pointed to her oversized suitcase on wheels. "I hope you do have some clothes and a good pair of boots for hiking and exploring the ruins in there."

"You bet I do," she said. She nestled against him, giving him a long passionate kiss. "Now, let's go have some nice, spicy Thai food, a few drinks, and, if you're a good boy, we can come back here for dessert."

After a very late dinner, they returned to Savannah's hotel and made passionate love deep into the night. Logan could feel his emotions spiraling out of control. *Am I falling in love with Savannah Devereux?*

CHAPTER 8

Savannah rested her arm on Logan's leg and kissed his cheek as they sat in the minivan headed for the airport. Logan smiled, but he was lost in thought. He knew he was falling for Savannah. *Can I tell her the real reason I'm going to Cambodia? And then what? When I figure out the next map, what do I tell her then? How am I even going to search for this map with Savannah all over me?* He knew whatever he decided, it would have to be soon. As hard as he had fallen for her, he still cursed the timing of it.

Even moving towards Angkor was enough to re-ignite the lust for adventure in Logan. He had planned to put his whole heart and soul into this treasure hunt. It was something that would change his life, define him as a man. *Would it be a solo journey, or would it be one shared with his new unexpected love interest?*

They checked in and boarded the plane. Within minutes, Savannah had fallen asleep. Logan spent the entire flight staring at her, as if trying to peer into her soul. *Was this real? It felt real. Could he trust her with his extraordinary secret? Did he want to lose her over this?* These questions and a hundred others spun around in Logan's head. The reality was that he barely knew her, but he felt he had known her for years. No one had ever gotten past his defenses so quickly or easily. Logan had found with many of his past relationships that at least until he knew someone well, he was very guarded, but for a reason that he could not explain, he had granted her an instant backstage pass to his life.

Life was all about taking chances. "What the hell," Logan muttered softly. "I took a big gamble and gave up a million dollars only to spend tens of thousands of dollars on a treasure that may or may not exist, with no guarantee that I'll find it first. Why not go all in?" Logan decided that he would tell Savannah about the maps and the treasure as soon as they checked into the hotel. Having finally made the decision, a feeling of calm settled over him. He felt that if there was a chance of their relationship going anywhere, he had to be honest. Logan laughed. "Yeah, that's a first for me. Planning my future after a few days."

Savannah was jostled awake by the impact of the aircraft touching down on the tarmac. "Good morning, Sleeping Beauty," Logan said.

She stretched and yawned. "I think I must have really needed that sleep."

"It's still early. How do you feel about checking in and then scooting off to the ruins for a while?"

"As soon as you feed me, okay?"

"It's a deal. I know a great little restaurant just a block from the hotel."

After the overly air-conditioned plane, the heat and humidity hit Savannah like a slap in the face. "God, it seems much hotter here than in Bangkok."

"Don't worry, you'll adjust fast. They just had that plane way too cold," Logan replied, relishing the sultry air. They hopped in a taxi and before long, they were unlocking the door of their hotel room. Savannah scampered over to the balcony overlooking the pool area, which was adorned with beautiful trees and a prism of tropical flowers. "Oh my God, Logan, this is amazing." She screeched, running back toward him, jumping up, throwing herself into his arms, and wrapping her legs around his waist. "Are you sure you want to go to the ruins right now? Because I can think of something much better for us to do."

Savannah jumped out of Logan's arms, and before he had a chance to answer, she began to strip off her clothes. Logan couldn't resist her as she stood naked in the middle of the room, the sun from the still open balcony glistening on her perfect taut body. Logan tore off his own clothes and ravaged her with pure animal lust.

"Logan Nash, you truly are the most amazing lover I have ever had," Savannah said softly, her voice showing her satisfaction and fatigue.

"And you, girl. You are so bad. We are supposed to be tromping around ruins right now. You know how easily I'm distracted by you?"

"I hadn't noticed," she said, knowing full well she had Logan wrapped around her little finger. "What's the hurry, baby? I bet you the ruins are going to be there for a long, long time, and I would like to think I'm more important than some old stones."

Logan thought this was going to be as good a time as any to reveal the true reason for his trip to Angkor and the circumstances of his arriving at this point. "Savannah, I have something very important to talk to you about." He started to get dressed. "Get dressed and we'll talk. Otherwise, I'm going to be far too distracted by that hot bod of yours." He winked.

Savannah began to get dressed, a worried look on her face, like a child who was about to be punished for being bad. She obviously didn't know what to expect. Logan could see the worry in her eyes.

"What's wrong, Logan? Did I do something wrong? Do you want me to go back to Thailand? Are you married? Tell me!"

Logan took Savannah in his strong arms and held her tight. "Relax, baby. It's nothing like that at all. I just want to tell you the real reason I'm here. It's a long and complicated story. All I ask is that you just let me finish, and then you can ask any questions you want. Okay?"

With a stressed look on her face, Savannah nodded.

Logan began to reveal his life to her. It was a story more amazing, one filled with more drama, excitement, and danger than any book. She sat in silent awe on the edge of every word. He started from his early treasure hunting days and how he gained possession of the map. Savannah sat open-jawed in horror as he relived the tale of his encounter with an evil man named Kane who had robbed him of his greatest find, killed his friend, and left him for dead. For nearly two hours, Logan regaled her with his tales of adventure. When he finished, he asked, "Do you have any questions about anything? I think you are an amazing woman, Savannah

Devereux, and I don't want any secrets to jeopardize what we've started. If you want to, I would love to make you part of this adventure."

Savannah seemed to be stunned. She didn't know if she should laugh, cry, or jump for joy. She felt like she had just been taken on an emotional roller coaster, especially since Logan told the story with such deep passion. She had a much deeper respect for him.

"I… I don't know what to say, Logan."

He could see the tears welling up in her eyes.

"I am honored that you would want to make me part of this," she said, "but it's just all so overwhelming. I am so sorry to hear about that evil man who tried to kill you. It broke my heart hearing that you had to go through that horrible ordeal."

"That's okay. It was a long time ago. Are you going to be okay?" For reasons unknown to Logan, she began to cry. He took her in his arms and held her tight, questioning if he had done the right thing in telling her.

After a good cry, she silently lay against Logan's chest and listened to the beating of his heart. He was so strong, yet so tender. It hadn't even been three days yet and she felt closer to him than she had ever felt to anyone. She was at a crossroads and didn't know which way to turn.

After a while, Savannah composed herself and began asking questions. Many men could easily put their life into two hours, but certainly not Logan Nash. She had a thousand questions for him, and once she started, the floodgates opened, and a barrage of questions ensued. Logan answered every one the best he could in the hope that she would better understand him and where he was at now.

He was perplexed at the situation. He had thought his excitement about the treasure hunt would be infectious. *Maybe I just threw too much out there too fast.* After all, they only had known each other for a few days. Logan asked himself if he had said something wrong, something that may have upset her. He replayed the last few hours over in his mind and prayed he hadn't blown a relationship that appeared to have such incredible potential.

"Logan, do you mind going for a walk or having a drink? I just need a little time to myself."

"What's wrong? Is there anything you want to talk about?"

"No, I just need a bit of time. Please, Logan."

"Of course. I'll be back in about two hours. Is that enough time or do you need more?"

"No, that's perfect. Thank you for being so understanding."

There was a sadness in her eyes that hadn't been there before. Logan couldn't help but feel there was something wrong that she wasn't telling him, something that went beyond being affected emotionally by his life story. Logan felt she was hiding something from him, something she was too embarrassed or scared to tell.

What could possibly be so bad that she thinks I would not understand?

Logan returned after three hours, bringing with him a few snacks, since they hadn't made it to the restaurant. Savannah had fallen asleep. She looked as peaceful as an angel, but a glance at the tear stains on the pillow told him that she had cried herself to sleep. Logan hoped all would be back to normal in the morning, that a good night's sleep would cure all, but he was afraid that the demons that haunted her would return in the morning. Logan felt he was back in that spiral of emotions, and he felt anxious this time that he wouldn't like where the ride would stop.

CHAPTER 9

Logan awoke early to run down to the restaurant, so he could surprise Savannah with breakfast in bed. Before leaving the room, he took the time to leave a note for her just in case she woke up. After all, she had already been asleep for ten hours at least. He returned in less than twenty minutes, entering the room carrying a large serving tray of fresh fruit, waffles, steaming fresh papaya muffins, and of course, two cups of coffee. The mouth-watering smells wafting from the serving tray began to stir Savannah's senses.

"Mmmm. Whatever you have smells positively delicious." She spoke in a muffled voice, her eyes still closed with her face buried deep in the thick, fluffy pillow.

Logan sat down beside her, leaned over, and kissed her shoulder. A purr of approval emanated from under the pillow. *A good sign*, he thought, sensing at least some improvement in her mood. "Yes, my dear. All kinds of goodies await you. You must be starving."

Savannah rolled over, sat up, and gave Logan a tender kiss. "Thank you."

"Oh, it's no big deal. I was hungry too, so my motives weren't purely unselfish."

"No, Logan. Thank you."

Logan realized that she was not speaking of breakfast, but rather was thanking him for giving her the time and space she had needed the previous evening.

"You're welcome," he said softly. He wanted to ask more about why she had acted the way she did, but he thought he would give her the time she needed to come to him and not push the issue, which seemed to be a sure way to drive her away.

They had moved from the bed to a small wooden table that sat just inside the balcony door. It was adorned with fresh tropical flowers, no doubt cut from the many flowers that graced the courtyard and surrounding gardens. Savannah closed her eyes. "God, I wish I could bottle this smell. I would call it Scent of Paradise."

Logan drew in a deep breath, savoring the powerful fragrance of the flowers and the inviting odor of the food. He delighted in the sounds of the tropical birds cheerfully welcoming the morning, and as he gazed outside, he relished the rising sun that bathed everything in a soft light. A warm breeze blew into the room, carrying the rich fragrance from the nearby gardens and caressing Logan and Savannah's skin like the touch of a gentle lover.

As they finished their breakfast, they planned for the day, with Logan going into more detail about exactly where he believed the map would be found. Between Logan and Zack, they had gone over and over their findings. "The moment of truth is almost here. We'll soon see how good of a treasure hunter I really am," he said. There was a twinge of doubt in his voice.

Normally, Logan would hire a rickshaw for the entire day, but this was one time he didn't want anyone hanging around wondering why they'd been at the same set of ruins for six hours. A short walk from the hotel was a shop that rented motorbikes. Within a few minutes, they were on their way. Safety was obviously not a major concern, as helmets weren't even offered as an option.

At the gates to the Angkor Archaeological Park, they purchased a four-day pass. Logan had figured even if they found the map right away, Zack and he would need time to figure out the location of the next one.

If it were anywhere near as difficult as this one, they'd need lots of time. As soon as he found the next map, he had planned to scan it and send it to Zack, while he worked from this end for now anyway. After all, the Internet is the same anywhere.

Savannah gasped with awe as they sped past one impressive set of ruins after another. "Oh, Logan, can we just stop here for a few minutes?"

He laughed and shook his head. "Don't worry, girl. We'll have lots of time to explore all the ruins, but it's down to business first."

They continued along until coming to a set of ruins that looked like they had not been restored. In fact, they looked like they had just been found. The ruins were left that way to show people how Angkor looked when it was first rediscovered, almost becoming one with the jungle, the giant roots of the banyan and silk cotton trees so intertwined as to form a symbiotic relationship.

"Logan, this is so amazing. I feel like I'm the one discovering this site," Savannah gasped.

"Ta Prohm," Logan said proudly, as if the ruins were like his own child.

Ta Prohm had always been one of Logan's favorite sets of Angkor ruins, maybe apart from the Bayon. He had spent many hours on his previous three trips exploring every nook and cranny of the site. With child-like exuberance, he grabbed Savannah by the hand. "C'mon, let's go."

An evil twisted hand of wood reached down, its long tentacles flowing over and through the stone structure, digging its fingernails deep into the ancient soil. Savannah craned her neck as they drew closer to the tree that towered above them, her mouth dropping open, the roots alone dwarfing the ruins. Logan knew exactly where he wanted to go, which he desperately hoped was also the place he needed to go. After a few minutes, they stood at the entrance to a room and were staring at a posse of headless Buddha statues.

The clue had not been specific about exactly where the map would be. Would it be under a Buddha? Maybe buried under the rubble strewn among them? Under or wedged in the wall next to them? Now the hard part truly started. He just wanted to start digging, poking, and tipping, but two huge obstacles stood in his way. The first was the endless parade of tourists that sauntered through, never seeming to give them more than a minute or two alone. The second and more serious of the problems was that if they were caught damaging or defacing the ruins in any way... well, he didn't even want to think of what would happen to them.

Logan stood in the room of headless Buddhas silently waiting for a sign from them, for them to speak to him. He chuckled and thought how silly it was hoping that a headless statue might speak to him.

"What's so funny?" Savannah asked.

"Sorry, I think I'm losing my mind," he replied, shaking his head in frustration.

Logan was studying every inch of the room, trying to think like Colton Braxton III. *Where would I hide a map if I were you, Colton?* He knew it would have to be somewhere that couldn't be found accidentally. *How did you do it, Colton? Did you sneak in here at night? Did you come here during the rainy season when there are many less tourists? Maybe you were just quick as a cat and only took a minute to hide the map?* Logan turned these and other questions over in his mind as he meticulously walked among the headless Buddhas. He also questioned how the weather and the years would have altered the hiding place. Any obvious signs would have disappeared with time.

Logan instructed Savannah to inspect the entire room for anything that seemed out of place. He knew that she wasn't experienced in the field of archaeology or treasure hunting, but he wanted to make her feel part of it all, and who knew? She might just stumble across the map. For the next two hours, they inspected the room, though with a constant stream of interruptions. All the while, they tried to appear inconspicuous.

Suddenly, Savannah screamed. Logan felt his heart jump out of his chest.

A voice from nowhere asked in broken English, "Are you looking for something?" A split second later, a grim-faced security guard stepped out from behind a stone doorway. Logan stood temporarily frozen while he tried to think up a believable story.

"You scared the hell out of me," Savannah said. "As a matter of fact, I am looking for something. I rubbed my eye and one of my contacts popped out."

The security guard looked puzzled. He didn't understand most of what Savannah had said between her Southern accent and rapid speech.

Logan quickly interjected, pointing to his eye and slowly explaining it to the security guard, who apologized for startling them and proceeded to help them look for the phantom contact lens. As Logan pretended to search, he smiled. He was proud of Savannah's quick thinking. After fifteen minutes, the guard gave up and informed them he had to continue his rounds. Logan asked the guard a myriad of the most ridiculous questions he could come up with. His plan worked perfectly. Despite the guard's attempt to be polite, the cringe on his face told the story, begging Logan to let him go and stop the barrage of stupidity.

At the first break in the conversation, the guard scurried away like he had been freed from prison. Logan thought he had annoyed him enough so that he wouldn't come back for some time, but he knew if they stayed too long, he would become suspicious. Logan also knew they had to get much more aggressive in their search. He directed Savannah to keep watch both for security guards and tourists while he started moving rocks and cautiously tipping the Buddhas to see if the map was hidden under them. He had a deep respect for the site and didn't want to damage anything and was careful to return everything that was moved to its original position.

Another hour passed, but they found nothing. They had checked every moveable object. The frustration began to show on Logan's face. Had he deciphered the clues wrong? Did they need to expand the search? All he knew was that the day had been spent without yielding any results. It was time to leave Ta Prohm.

"We need to get out of here for the rest of the day, Savannah. Do you want to go look at some other sites or call it a day?"

"Let's go walk around that one with all the Buddha faces," she said, pressing up against him and stroking his chest.

"The Bayon you mean?" Logan laughed, thinking how cute her description was, prompting her to slap his backside.

Logan seized Savannah, pinning her against the ancient wall and kissing her passionately. "Thank you for your patience and quick thinking today. You really saved our asses with that guard." He rested his hands on the wall beside her head. He placed one of his fingers in a crack between the stones, causing a loose piece of stone to shift. Logan's pulse quickened. He didn't want to get his hopes up, but it didn't sound like stone on stone. He surveyed the room, pleased that no one was there, and asked Savannah to go stand guard. She swiftly went to her post, as she could hear the urgency in his voice.

Logan dug his finger into the small crevasse, desperately trying to free it, but to no avail. He flung his daypack off his back and retrieved a pen, instantly proceeding with his task. After a few seconds, he felt the object move. He clawed it forward until he could grab it with his fingers. Logan slid out a thin wedge-shaped piece of plastic made to match the rocks of which the walls of Ta Prohm were constructed. His heart raced out of control as he saw a small latch on the inner edge of the pseudo rock wedge. Like a treasure chest of gold, the map appeared as he opened the plastic case. He gingerly removed the map from the case, stuffing it into his backpack as Savannah yelled for Logan to hurry up. Voices approached.

Logan grabbed Savannah by the inside of her arm and began to escort her out, his heart still pounding on his ribcage.

"Did you get the map, baby?"

"Yes. Yes I did. I didn't get a chance to study it, but the paper is the same. It has to be the first map," Logan replied, his voice overflowing with excitement. Almost as important as the map itself, finding first the bottle and now the cleverly disguised rock wedge gave Logan clues as to how Colton Braxton's mind worked.

They rode away from the site, Logan's head spinning. It was brutally hard for him to keep the speed of the motorbike down, as all he wanted to do was get back to the hotel and start studying the map. *Relax, relax, relax!* Logan thought. Savannah held him tight, wrapping herself around him on the back of the bike. In their rush to the hotel room, Logan left the keys to the bike in the ignition, practically dragging Savannah up the stairs. Once inside the room, he pulled out the map, carefully examining every inch of it and nodding.

"It's the map! We've found it," Logan sighed, relief in his voice. "I've got to scan this and e-mail it to Zack, so he can start working on the next clue."

"I've got a plan, baby. You do what you have to do here, and I'll go get us a bottle of the best wine I can find. We'll celebrate!"

"Yeah, that sounds great. You sure you don't mind?"

"Not at all. I think a party for two is a must."

While Savannah left the hotel in search of a bottle of wine, Logan pulled out his laptop and scanned the map. He then wrote an explanation to Zack, attached the scan, and fired the e-mail off into cyberspace.

A couple blocks down from the hotel, Savannah stopped at a small bench beside the Siem Reap River and sat down. Digging in her bag, she pulled out a cell phone and began to hesitantly enter the number. After three rings, her call was answered, and she spoke, her voice quivering. "Victor? It's Savannah."

CHAPTER 10

"What in the hell is going on there?" Victor roared. He was incensed at the fact that he had not heard from Savannah for days. "I explicitly told you to contact me every day."

"I'm sorry, but it couldn't be helped. I think you will forgive me once you realize how much progress I've made."

"Go on," Victor replied.

Savannah told him about how their not so chance meeting in Bangkok went and how she had easily gained Logan's trust. At this point, as far as Victor knew, she was still in Bangkok with Logan. He knew that Logan had arranged a flight to Bangkok, and he had Savannah arrive in Thailand on a flight before him, so she could follow him and make contact.

"I've got a little surprise for you, Victor. I gained Logan's trust, so he asked me to join him on his treasure hunt."

"Where are you now?"

"Siem Reap, in Cambodia."

"I know where Siem Reap is," Victor barked. "Is that where the first map is hidden? When are you planning to hunt for it? Have you had a chance to make a copy of the map?"

"I will try to copy the map, but Logan never lets that thing out of his sight. He has already found the first map."

"When? What did it say?" He despised the fact that he wasn't there to be in complete control of everything. He knew he needed to rely on others, and his network of contacts were both varied and widespread, but despite knowing he had limitations he still felt that no one could do the job as good as he could—no matter what that job was.

Victor began to feel his boiling blood bubble down to a simmer. "You've done great, Savannah. Try to send me a copy of that map. In the meantime, I think I will have young Mr. Logan Nash working for me without even knowing it." His devious plan developed further in his mind. "Yes, gain his full trust and don't let him out of your sight. He seems to be quite clever when it comes to deciphering these clues, so I'll just let Mr. Nash help me find that treasure." He was happy with how things had unfolded. "I still need a copy of that map as soon as possible, because if I could find the next map before Logan, it would be so, so sweet watching him search in vain for a map that wasn't there." He began to laugh at the thought of it. "Call me whenever you can. I would prefer you call me every day, but don't do anything that will make him suspicious of you."

"I won't, but I thought I was just to copy or steal the map and then go back home."

"You've done your job so beautifully that the plans have changed. Like I said, we will let Logan work for us, with you being the perfect incentive to make sure he gets the job done. If it's money you are talking about, I will triple what I'm paying you if you can lead me to the treasure. Plus, of course, all expenses and a very nice bonus once I have possession of it."

"Thank you, Victor. I'll be in touch soon." Savannah ended the call. No sooner had she pressed the end button on her cell phone, then tears began to run down her cheeks. She was struck with a wave of guilt that smothered her to where she felt she couldn't breathe. She knew she needed to compose herself, get a bottle of wine, and return to the hotel with a smile beaming across her face, even though she felt her soul ripping apart inside.

"This is just another job," she said to herself. She tried to shake the demons that were battling within her. She knew she would be paid extremely well. *It's not exactly a chore to travel around the world treasure hunting and making love to a hunk like Logan Nash*, she thought. Beyond the monetary gains she knew she would receive, she knew what happened to people who betrayed Victor Kane. A shiver ran down her spine at the thought of what he was capable of and willing to do if anyone crossed him.

Savannah hurried to the store, grabbed a bottle of the best wine she could find—grimacing at the outrageously poor selection—and hastily made her way back to the hotel. In the lobby, she stopped at a large mirror that adorned the wall to make sure she was presentable when she returned to the room. She paused in horror at what she saw. It wasn't that her eyes were red or puffy anymore, but at that moment she didn't feel beautiful. It was as if she were looking into her own soul. All she saw was a prostitute that would do anything for money, even if it meant deceiving such an incredible man, who didn't deserve such a fate. She could feel the tears once again begin to well up in her eyes. Savannah blinked rapidly, doing everything she could to fight back the torrent of tears that strained to break through the dam of emotions just beneath the surface. She pulled herself together and went up to their room.

"I'm back, baby! Let's celebrate!" She entered the room with a smile so plastic she was sure Logan would see right through it, but he failed to see the pain and guilt that were so apparent on her face. He had found the first map, he was falling in love, and he felt that his life was coming together. Raw emotion had trumped all caution and common sense, leaving him vulnerable.

Savannah did her best to shove her emotions to a dark corner in her mind. Otherwise, she knew she couldn't carry on. After a short time, she felt herself feeling better, convinced in her own mind that Logan would be okay, that she would be okay. She ignored the gnawing in her soul.

The candles flickered as the pair lay spent on the floor, exhausted from the raw, passionate lovemaking. Savannah's body trembled with a sense of fulfillment that she had only dreamed of experiencing. Logan rolled over on his side, still panting from the marathon love making session. He looked deeply into her mesmerizing blue eyes. He opened his mouth to speak, but nothing came out. He felt so close to her that he honestly thought he had found his soul mate. He wanted to tell her that he loved her, but the words refused to leave his lips.

"What is it, Logan?" Savannah asked, wiping the sweat from his forehead.

"You are so beautiful," he replied. He didn't know why part of him held back, even though it felt so right.

"Tell me everything about yourself, Mr. Logan Nash."

"Everything?"

"Yeah, I want to know everything about you. Tell me about some of the most amazing places you've traveled."

Logan had revealed part of himself to Savannah a few days earlier, but he gladly opened up to her about his travel and adventures. He began to entertain her with incredible stories of travel adventures that completely captivated her. He spoke with such passion it was impossible for her not to be caught up in it. He made her feel like she was right there with him. He really was the most interesting man she had ever met.

"Logan Nash, you truly are larger than life," she said. It caused him to blush just a little, but he still carried on with his tales of danger and high adventure.

The next few days passed like a blur to Logan. He tried to spend a few hours a day working on the cryptic clues in the map, but most of the day was spent hand in hand with Savannah, running around the ruins of Angkor like two lovesick teenagers. Watching her experience the magnificent ruins with such wonder, Logan felt like he was experiencing it for the first time himself. After a few days of nonstop exploring, they decided to take a day and relax by the pool. It was such an incredible setting, and they hadn't taken the time really savor it. The hot sun seared their skin at the apex of the day. Logan kicked his feet, splashing water as he sat on the edge of the pool, his legs dangling in the water.

"Savannah, I know you had planned to travel around Thailand, and I hope this trip here was worth taking some of your time away from there," Logan began. "But I have to head back to Hawaii for a while. I would love for you to come with me, but I will totally understand if you want to travel around Thailand. It's an amazing country."

Savannah knew this was the perfect opportunity to create even more desire in Logan by making him feel that he might lose her. "Oh, Logan, I have had the most incredible time with you, but Southeast Asia is somewhere I've always wanted to travel. Can you give me a couple of hours to think about it?" She batted her big blue eyes.

"Of course," he replied. He kissed her on the forehead as she hopped off the side of the pool into the refreshing water. Logan wondered if he had done the right thing. *Should I put the treasure quest on hold and travel around Thailand? Should I have insisted harder? Should I tell her how I really feel about her?* Logan tortured himself with these questions, wishing that she had instantly said yes.

Savannah slowly backstroked across the pool in her tiny bikini, the sun glistening off her firm, tanned, wet body. Logan was completely enamored with her, and even after such a short time, he couldn't imagine her just stepping out of his life. *Damn*, he thought. *Is this really love or just a case of severe infatuation?* Either way he couldn't take his eyes off her as she glided across the water like a sleek scull on a flat pond.

Savannah glanced Logan's way. She could see the desire in his face, and she knew her plan was working. A small grin appeared on her face. She was proud of her powers of seduction. *Yeah, I'll just let him stew just a bit more.*

Logan swam over to her, letting her know he was going to pop up to the room, take a shower, and work on the clues for a while. He gave her a gentle kiss. He could not only taste her luscious lips, but also that of chlorine mixed with suntan lotion. "You taste like summertime." He smiled.

"Summertime?" she replied, not exactly knowing what he meant, but taking it as a compliment. *Yeah, just a little bit longer*, she thought.

Logan returned to the hotel room still dripping from the pool and decided that the wisest thing would be to take a shower first and then get to work on the clues. He had talked to Zack a couple of days earlier, but his friend hadn't made any headway yet. *Damn, why did Colton have* to make the clues so difficult? Whatever happened to clues like walk ten paces south, and then fourteen paces east?*

Despite the heat and humidity, Logan liked a nice hot shower; it made him feel clean. Minutes after he stepped into the shower and began to lather up, the door opened. Savannah slid into the shower and pressed herself against Logan.

"Okay, I'll come with you to Hawaii," she said casually.

"Really? I'm thrilled! What changed your mind?"

"I guess Hawaii isn't such a hardship. It's not like you're taking me to North Dakota in January," she replied. She used a monotone voice to imply she was doing Logan a favor. "Besides, I might miss those cute buns of yours." She snarled, now sounding like a temptress, who, true to form, firmly slapped him on the backside.

"No, ma'am, I think you'll have a very good time there," he said as he began to kiss her just below her ear.

"Start that and you know where it leads," she said. *Yes, I definitely have this man wrapped around my little finger.* She thought only of her own desires, not of her task demanded by Dr. Victor Kane.

CHAPTER 11

Victor reclined in the plush leather chair situated next to the massive fireplace in the center of his expansive office. He took pleasure in the wise decision he had made to use Savannah to seduce Logan. He was happy to have Logan do all the work in finding the maps and working out the meaning of the clues. It would make it easy for Victor to then just step in and take the treasure from him. For him, it wasn't as much the hunt as it was the possessing. He often took more pleasure in stealing someone else's work than when he acquired it on his own. As the fire crackled, he was taken back to when he first met a young Savannah Devereux down in New Orleans. She was only a child then, just nineteen. "Six years ago," Victor muttered. "Time really does fly."

He had just returned from procuring a nice set of Spanish shipwreck coins from an unnamed wreck outside the port city of Vera Cruz, Mexico, an area of the Caribbean that was littered with shipwrecks over the centuries. Since he was already in the Americas, Victor thought he'd spend a few days in the colorful city of New Orleans.

In a strange twist of fate, at the very moment that Victor had begun to reminisce about his first encounter with Savannah, halfway around the world her mind flashed back to the same event, although with a very different perspective.

Victor thought about how he'd been sitting in a lively bar just off Bourbon Street when a vivacious young thing in an extremely low-cut dress had come over and begun flirting with him. She'd taken his breath away. She'd acted quite drunk, so Victor had thought he had his entertainment lined up for the night. As it turned out, she'd not only taken his breath away, but she'd also taken his wallet. She'd slipped out the back under the guise of a trip to the ladies' room. Naturally, Victor had been furious, but he'd also been embarrassed that he was so easily taken by a beautiful woman. After all, he was far from your typical mark on Bourbon Street. He was probably more paranoid and street smart than any ten people combined.

Savannah had had no idea from whom she had stolen. Victor Kane was someone you just did not steal from and live to tell about it.

With the help of a few of his connections, it had taken only a couple of hours before he'd found out where Savannah had been last seen. One of his connections had known who she was, and a connection of his had spotted her at a bar on St. Charles that was frequented by tourists. Victor had initially planned to wait until he could get her alone, and then she would find out what happened to someone who stole from Victor Kane. He'd watched her, biding his time and waiting for his opportunity. He had been amazed at the ease with which she took down her marks. He'd felt almost as if he were watching a prodigy. There didn't seem to be a single man that could resist her wiles. She'd taken down mark after mark with the efficiency of a surgeon. He had followed her to a half a dozen bars, becoming more intrigued by the minute. His rage had diminished, but not disappeared. After all, she'd stolen from him. However, as he'd watched her in action, he had developed a respect for her talent.

After taking down another fat drunk, Savannah had headed for the rear exit of the bar. Victor had been waiting for her. He'd grabbed her arm in a viselike grip the second the door had closed behind her. He dragged her to a dark corner of the alley.

"Let me go, you creep, or I'll scream!" Savannah had cried in terror.

"Yeah, maybe we can get the police here and you can explain the dozen or so wallets in your purse," Victor replied without a hint of worry in his voice.

She recognized him from the bar on Bourbon Street. "I'm sorry, mister. I'm so sorry. I just needed some money. I, I have nothing, nowhere to stay, nothing to eat—"

"Really?" Victor replied, cutting Savannah's ramblings off in mid-sentence. "It looks to me like you took in over a grand tonight, and I'm not stupid." He felt insulted. "You are obviously very good at what you do."

"Please, please don't hurt me." She'd begun to cry, fearing for her life.

"Do you have any idea who I am?"

"No, no, I'm sorry. I'm sorry. You can have all the money, just don't kill me."

Suddenly, from down the alley a male voice had shouted, "Hey, let that girl go or I'll come over there and kick your ass." The gruff voice had come from one of the many people that make the back alleys of New Orleans their home.

"Get lost and mind your own business," Victor shouted back.

The homeless man began to run toward Victor armed with a rusty piece of rebar. Victor hadn't flinched. He'd just stood there, still gripping Savannah's arm as the man approached.

Just feet away, the man had raised the bar to strike him. In one swift move, Victor pushed her to the ground and wrenched the bar from the hands of the homeless man, and he'd then savagely beaten him to death right in front of Savannah. Throwing the blood-stained bar into a dumpster in the alley, Victor reached down and picked up Savannah by the arm like a rag doll. "You know, little girl, I was going to kill you, but you have an incredible talent. You have a choice now. We can leave here and talk about your coming to work for me, or you can join your friend."

Stunned at what she had just witnessed, Savannah could not speak. All she'd been able to do was nod as she trembled in fear. He looked like a madman, and she'd been shocked at the ease at which he'd killed. He was pure evil. *Oh, Savannah, what did you get yourself into?* she wondered.

"One other thing. Don't even think of going to the police with what you saw. I will find you. There is nowhere you can hide. Anyone who betrays me wishes they are as lucky as that stiff in the alley."

She'd tried to walk, but Victor had dragged her out of the alley. She'd felt like all her strength had left her. Never a religious person, she'd found herself silently praying as she stumbled in the clutches of a murderer. *Oh, God, please let me make it through the night!*

"Do you understand what I said?" he'd asked her.

"Y… yes," she'd stammered.

"I'm not going to kill you. We are going to go have a talk, okay?" He softened his voice, seeing the terror in her eyes. "I'm going to let go of your arm now, but don't run away."

She'd known that to run would have meant certain death. She believed him when he said he would find her anywhere. Her arm had gone numb from his powerful hands, causing a tingling sensation from her shoulder to her fingertips.

He'd opened the passenger door to his rental car and motioned for her to get in. She didn't know if she were being driven to her death. *Is he going to rape me and then kill me? Or does he really just want to talk?*

She'd always considered herself a fighter, a strong person who could stand on her own, but she'd felt small, weak, and insignificant next to this powerful, evil man. Still trembling, she'd slowly slipped into the front seat. Victor had slammed the door and walked around the front of the car watching her every move, and he'd gotten into the driver's seat.

"My name is Dr. Victor Kane."

Doctor? What the hell kind of doctor would do such things? she'd thought, not knowing if she should tell him her real name, use a false name, or say nothing. Hell, did it really matter? *I'll probably be in the swamp getting eaten by gators an hour from now anyway.*

"What's your name?"

She had known she couldn't lie to him. "Savannah Devereux."

"Savannah, that's a beautiful name. I'm sorry for what you had to see back there in the alley, but it was either him or me," Victor said.

To Savannah's surprise, they'd driven into the city when she'd been sure that he would have been headed for the bayou. They'd pulled up to what looked like a very nice hotel. Victor had looked down at himself. "Shit," he growled, taking off his bloody suit jacket. "At least the black pants conceal most of the blood." He laughed. She had been shocked at his cavalier attitude about what he had done, treating the situation as if it was something commonplace. He'd rolled up his jacket, jammed it under his arm, and escorted Savannah into the busy hotel lobby. Something inside her had just wanted to scream out for help, but she had lost all courage.

With the array of colorful characters that New Orleans attracts, they had slipped through the lobby and up to Victor's room without a second glance from anyone. They'd entered a large suite with a separate living room and bedroom. Savannah had felt very nervous, afraid that Victor would attack her and kill her if she fought back. The terror that had surged through her veins had begun to return.

Victor had seen the skittish way she was acting. "Please relax. I told you I was not going to hurt you." He'd said that in a deep authoritative voice as he'd motioned to the table in the living room. "Sit down."

They'd both sat down. "Savannah, I don't know if you realize how good you are at what you do."

"You mean stealing wallets from horny guys?"

"No, well, that's part of it, but it's so much more. You can seduce them in minutes. You make them feel special. You are a great con woman." He'd complimented her with a twinge of respect. "You are risking a lot for a few bucks. One of these days, one of those guys will catch you, and you'll either end up in jail or in a back alley. And for what, a few lousy bucks?"

Savannah had always thought she'd done fairly well. She didn't always get a lot of cash, but she'd been getting better at picking her marks. "What are you trying to say, Mr. Kane?"

"I'm saying you work for me. There were many times I could have used someone like you to romance an item or information from someone."

"I'm not a hooker."

"God, listen! I'm not talking about hooking. I'm talking about using your seductive skills to get information, to distract someone, or to retrieve something." Victor had become visibly irritated. "You have a natural ability to make people trust you."

"Thank you. All I ever had were my looks."

"Yes, you are a stunning young lady. I can help you develop that talent, and I guarantee you'll make more money than you ever thought possible. Plus, with me you'll have protection. No one will mess with you. No one."

To Savannah, it had sounded like a skewed version of a pimp/hooker relationship, but she hadn't seen any other way out of the situation. "When you say money, what are we talking about?"

"What kind of money are you pulling in now? And don't lie to me."

"Tonight, would have been my best night ever. I had about twelve hundred dollars. I usually do okay. I don't know. I guess I pull down about a hundred fifty, sometimes two hundred per mark, unless someone takes it from me." She remembered on several occasions the money she'd worked hard to steal was stolen from her by other scumbags on the street. She'd normally just give it up because they threatened to hurt her if she didn't, and she knew if she didn't look pretty she wouldn't make anything.

"How would you like to make ten times that and live in a nice house, not in a shithole on skid row with all those other crackheads?"

Savannah had always dreamed of a better, normal life. "Okay, Mr. Kane, what do you want me to do?"

He'd smiled. "Good. Tell me about yourself. How did you get into this line of work?" Victor had been curious because it was odd for such an incredibly beautiful young woman to be doing what she did.

Savannah told Victor her sad story. *It's odd,* she'd thought. *Just a couple hours ago I was terrified to death of this man, and now here I am about to tell him my life story.*

Tears had begun to run down her cheeks as she'd told about how her mother had died in a car accident and her alcoholic father had raised her, though he hadn't given a shit about her until she was about twelve or thirteen and becoming a woman. She'd wept uncontrollably as she relived the nightmare of being raped by the fat drunken bastard, reeking of stale booze and cigarettes. For about three years, the rapes became a nightly occurrence, until she hadn't been able take it anymore and had poured anti-freeze into her father's drink. At the tender age of sixteen, she'd walked out her front door, leaving her father convulsing and vomiting on the filthy kitchen floor, never knowing if he had lived or died, and never caring.

She had lived on the streets ever since. What she did had become her way of punishing those same drunk slobs that she associated with her father. She would flirt with them, steal their wallets, take the cash, and then throw the credit cards into the street, only to be snatched up by other much more unscrupulous people than herself before they even hit the ground. She'd usually find a half decent place to sleep, food to eat, and she had had enough money to buy some nice clothes, which was important for her to carry on with her seductive game. She'd completely broken down as she told Victor of her dreams of what she had hoped life would someday be for her, the family she hoped to raise, the places she wanted to see. It had hit her hard in the moment that she realized the brutal murderer sitting across the table from her was probably going to be the only friend she would ever have.

CHAPTER 12

Savannah was fast asleep long before the aircraft left the ground in Bangkok. Logan gently stroked her hair as she wrapped herself tighter in a cocoon of blankets. Logan could hardly believe he had only met her just over a week ago. He felt he had shared years of memories in the past nine days, not to mention the spectrum of emotions that was thrust upon him. He could completely understand why she had drifted off so quickly, as he too felt the weight of emotional exhaustion pressing down on him. He knew he was crazy about her, but he tried his best to maintain a remnant of the protective wall that guarded his heart. For some unknown reason, she didn't like to talk about her past. Logan hadn't pushed the issue, again deciding to give her the benefit of the doubt, hoping she would eventually confide in him.

Logan could feel his eyelids getting heavy and his head bobbing as he fought to stay awake. He furrowed his brow and wondered why he was fighting the urge to get some desperately needed rest. He gave himself one last pat down, making sure the two maps were securely attached beneath his clothes, and took a couple of blankets and made a cocoon of his own. Within minutes, he was out like a light.

As was often the case, the flight back to Hilo would require a change of planes in Honolulu. Logan awoke to a friendly voice on the intercom informing them that they would be landing in twenty minutes. He couldn't believe he had slept the entire flight, as he always had trouble getting any quality sleep on planes.

"Good morning, cutie pie," Savannah said in her soft southern accent.

"Morning," Logan replied in a low growl. He stretched like a lion that had just awakened from a long nap. "How long have you been awake?"

"Not long, but at least long enough to find out you don't snore," she teased. "You don't, do you?" She realized that this was the first time she had seen him sleep, having always fallen asleep before him, and waking up after him.

"No, well, not unless you get me really drunk."

"Oh, Logan, look! It's so beautiful from the air," Savannah exclaimed as the plane dropped down toward the lush tropical island.

"If you think it looks good from a plane, I'll have to take you on a helicopter ride. You'll be amazed."

"I'm going to hold you to that, Mr. Logan Nash."

With a quick screech of the tires, the plane was on the ground. Since they had to deplane and clear customs and immigration, Logan thought why not start their time in Hawaii with a bang. It would be a nice surprise for Savannah.

While she waited to retrieve the luggage, Logan slipped away for a minute to place a call. In his photography business, Logan often used the services of the helicopter companies and knew of several that would be more than happy to help him out if they weren't booked up. In a few minutes, he returned as if he had only scooted off to the washroom for a minute. "Man, I hope I remembered to throw away that pizza I had sitting on the coffee table," he joked.

"Are you a messy little boy?" He shrugged and rolled his eyes.

Truth be known, Logan was an extremely neat person, who, except for what he was presently working on, always kept his house looking more like a show home than a bachelor pad. Logan strolled right by the connection gate and continued. "Isn't this where we need to catch the next flight?" Savannah asked.

"No, there's a problem with that flight. Way too many people on it."

"Okay."

They seemed to be leaving the departure area, and the next thing Savannah knew she was walking out onto the tarmac heading toward a bright yellow and black helicopter that resembled a giant bumblebee. "No way! Is this for us?"

"I want to make a good impression on my girl. Besides, I feel I have to make up for that first impression on Khao San Road." Logan laughed, remembering how they met.

"Thank you. You are so sweet," she replied, dropping her luggage to give him a big kiss.

"Good afternoon, Logan." A large Hawaiian man called out to them from the helicopter as he ran and relieved Savannah of her bags. "You must be Ms. Devereux. A pleasure to meet you." He said politely, giving her a slight bow.

"Please call me Savannah," she said with a big smile. She was already impressed with Hawaiian hospitality.

"Kabos! Good to see you again. I see you had to rush over and meet the beautiful lady," Logan joked.

"Hey, can you blame me? She's gorgeous!" he replied, causing Savannah to blush.

"That she is," Logan agreed.

"You two just stop it or you'll give me a big head, and I won't be able to get on the helicopter. Kabos. I don't think I've ever heard that name in my life. It's very nice."

Logan laughed, and Savannah looked a bit puzzled. "What's so funny? I do think it's a nice name."

"Ask him what it means," Logan replied, still laughing.

Before Savannah could ask, Kabos chimed in. "I don't think my parents liked me very much, although Logan always tells me that they must have known how I would turn out."

"What do you mean?" she asked.

"Kabos means swindler," he replied. He had a great sense of humor about his name.

"Well, I for one think Kabos is a great name," she said.

Logan helped strap Savannah into the co-pilot's seat on the left side of the aircraft, so she could get a better view.

"Are you sure you don't want me to sit in the back seat with you?" she asked.

"No, there is some incredible scenery and I want you to get a good look at my newly adopted home," he replied. "Plus, we're not heading straight to Hilo. It's going to be a bit longer out of the way trip, so we can cover most of the islands. Are you up for a scenic tour?"

"Oh my God, yes!" she said, unable to control her excitement.

"Hey, Kabos, you have enough fuel to do this trip?" Logan asked, knowing they would not be flying in a straight line.

"I don't think it should be a problem. We had a slight tail wind and I can push this bird almost four hundred miles before refueling, so at the very most you'll have to walk the last thirty or forty miles to your place," Kabos replied, trying to sound serious, but obviously joking.

"Now do you see, Savannah? The name fits him very well!" Logan jabbed back.

"Oh, you boys behave," she said, feeling comfortable already.

Logan couldn't stop smiling for the next couple of hours as they toured along the string of islands. He could see the exhilaration on Savannah's face, the sparkle in her eyes. He was completely taken with the incredible scenery of the islands himself, but on this trip, he found his sights were fixed on the beautiful blond sitting just a few feet away from him. Kabos made sure that Savannah got a true taste of everything. They flew over lush jungle mountains and valleys, towering waterfalls, and breathtaking coastlines where the various depths of the water and reefs covered every shade of blue she had ever imagined.

They had planned the flight perfectly, swinging around the south end of the Big Island just as the sun began to plunge into the deep indigo abyss. Savannah was pinned against the glass in awe as they flew past one of nature's most spectacular shows: the Kilauea Volcano. They followed it from the erupting cone as the lava flow made its way down to the sea, culminating in a spectacular crimson waterfall that erupted into towers of steam as it shook hands with the cool cobalt waters of the Pacific.

"Oh my God, I've never imagined anything so spectacular," Savannah whimpered, tears running down her cheeks. Within a few seconds, the whimpering turned into uncontrollable sobbing.

Logan and Kabos were at a loss. They sat silently, not knowing what to say. The transformation from jubilation to sadness hit them unexpectedly. There was obviously something going on in her head that even Logan knew nothing about.

The sheer beauty and splendor of the sights she had just experienced made Savannah think how far she had come from a scared and abused teenager on the mean streets of New Orleans. She was taken back to how her life was and how she dreamed she would one day be enjoying exotic locations with a man she loved. This was her dream, but it wasn't her own. Oh, how she wanted her life to be her own again. She wished what she had with Logan was real. She was falling in love with him, despite how she tried to emotionally distance herself. She knew her life was not her own, and that she would cause of the demise of the best person she had ever met. She knew what Victor Kane had planned for Logan. Savannah collapsed against the glass at the front of the helicopter, now weeping hysterically.

Logan gestured for Kabos to fly to Hilo as fast as he could. He could see the panic in his eyes and the pain on Savannah's face. His heart pounded as he struggled in his mind to find an answer as to why she was crying. Logan grappled with the question in his mind. *What horrific demons can be haunting this beautiful woman?*

CHAPTER 13

Logan helped Savannah from the helicopter. She had finally stopped the flood of tears, but the pain on her face was still there. She was extremely embarrassed to have broken down in front of Kabos and Logan that way, on what started out as such an incredible day. She couldn't bring herself to look either man in the eye, walking with her head hung low.

Kabos tagged behind with Savannah's luggage, giving them the space they needed to talk, but it was apparent that she didn't have anything to say.

Logan helped Savannah into a taxi while Kabos helped the cab driver load the luggage in the trunk.

After helping her into the taxi, Logan pulled Kabos aside. "I am so sorry. You didn't need to see all that." He apologized for the awkward situation and tried to stuff a couple extra hundred-dollar bills in his shirt pocket.

"No, man! You're my friend, I don't want your money. I feel for you. I wish I knew what I could do."

"Me too, Kabos. Me too," Logan said, giving the big Hawaiian a heartfelt hug. *Kabos has always been a friend I can rely on*, he thought.

When Logan got in the taxi, Savannah was scrunched into one corner, her head in her hands. He wasn't at all upset with her, but he was troubled about what would cause such an outburst. Again! Despite all the misgivings he felt, he knew it was too late. Though their time together was short, he cared deeply for her and just couldn't kick her to the curb. He desperately wanted her to open up to him and trust him.

The taxi driver could sense this wasn't one of those fares where you chitchat with the passengers, so the trip from the airport to Logan's house was wordless, except for a location stated by Logan as they pulled away from the airport. From the taxi, Logan toted both sets of luggage while Savannah slowly shuffled behind, her head still hung low. He unlocked the door of his home, set the luggage inside, and went to retrieve her. She had only made it halfway up the walk.

"It's okay, baby. I know just what you need." He comforted her as he took her into his living room, sitting her down on a soft camel leather sofa. He then hurried to his linen closet and returned with a nice plush comforter. Even though it was hot outside, he could see her shivering. Logan gave her the comforter and headed into the kitchen, where he filled a kettle with water and put it on the stove. On his return trip to the living room, he stopped to raise the temperature on the thermostat for the air conditioning to make it warmer inside. Then he loaded cedar logs into the fireplace and lit a fire. He couldn't even put into words how smelling burning cedar logs made him feel. It was almost a sensory overload, a smell that reminded him of the best times of his childhood at Christmas or sitting by a romantic campfire. Logan hoped it would make Savannah feel better.

He stood in front of the fireplace and watched the flames lick around the logs, the subdued light imparting a warm glow to the darkened room. Logan closed his eyes and drew in a slow deep breath, filling his lungs with the calming scent. The crackle and popping of the fire filled the otherwise silent room. Logan thought about how perfect the scene almost was, the roaring fire, the powerful scent of burning cedar, and the woman he was falling in love with. Only she was a million miles away.

He returned to the sofa where Savannah had curled up and handed her a steaming cup of hot chocolate. As she accepted the sweet-smelling hot chocolate, she began to cry again. Tears streaked down her face.

"Logan, why are you so good to me? I don't deserve it. Believe me, I really don't."

"Please, Savannah. Talk to me."

"I truly wish I could, but I can't." She whimpered, grappling with whether she should tell Logan the whole story. She knew what the consequences might be if she ever betrayed Victor. He said she was an employee of his, but the truth was he owned her. Over the last six years, she had witnessed his brutality several times, and the thought of that rage being unleashed on Logan was more than she could bear. She couldn't imagine how Logan would react if he found out that she worked for the very man that had left him for dead, a man who had stolen from him.

Logan curled up beside her on the sofa and cradled her tightly against his body. They both fell asleep as the fire dwindled to a pile of glowing embers that filled the air with the aroma of burnt cedar. Logan awoke to the loud annoying ring of his home phone. Savannah stirred, but she did not wake up, so Logan rushed to grab the phone before it rang again. As he grabbed the phone, he looked outside and saw the reds and pinks of the first hints of dawn. He glanced at his watch and saw it was 5:42 a.m. "Shit," he mumbled. He picked up the receiver, his voice still groggy from sleep.

"Logan? Where the hell have you been? I've been trying to reach you for two days." It was Zack, and a sense of urgency came through loud and clear.

Logan realized in all the drama of yesterday, he hadn't bothered to turn on his cell phone or to check his e-mail and phone messages. He looked down at the answering machine and noted that the display indicated twelve messages had come in. "Sorry, Zack. I've had a serious situation I had to deal with."

"Everything okay? Anything I can do?"

"No, but thanks. What's up?"

"I've got a nice surprise for you."

"You haven't figured out the map already, have you?"

"I think I have, but I would like to see if you agree with my conclusions. I hate these damn cryptic clues," Zack grumbled.

"Believe me, I know what you mean. Give me a few hours and I'll call you back."

"One other thing. I think I can join you on the next leg of your treasure hunt. Just helping you with these maps has really got me stoked."

"That is fantastic. Okay, I'm going to get to this and I'll talk to you soon."

Even as he hung up the phone, he realized that he needed to tell Zack about Savannah. "God, he's going to think I've lost my frickin' mind," Logan muttered to himself. First, he gave up the chance of a million dollars, and then he fell for a girl almost instantly.

Logan took a quick peek into the living room. Savannah was still sound asleep, all curled up on the sofa. He reached under his shirt, retrieving the map that was still attached to his body. He wore the same clothes he left Thailand in two days ago. "At least I'm not one of those people who sweat a lot." Logan laughed, thinking he really could use a shower, but he was too excited and anxious to check out Zack's findings.

Walking over to the desk, he sat down and read the clue.

"On the year its neighbor was born, this not yet grown child was torn. To the young place you must go, to the den of water like a sandbar in a storm, changing with the seasons and years. Go where you are forbidden to go. Read the signs."

Logan was utterly amazed that Zack had figured it out so quickly. He wondered if he could have solved the clue had he not been so caught up with Savannah. "It looks like I might have to give Zack a bigger piece of whatever pie I find." Logan chuckled.

The phone rang again. "Zack? Calling twice in ten minutes? To what do I owe the honor?"

"Very funny, Logan. In all my excitement to tell you about my findings, I remember I left something out of the e-mail."

"What do you mean?"

"I designed a program that uses a huge map data base, and then I entered the partial outline in the corner of the map."

"And?"

"Boy, impatient in the morning, aren't we?"

"You do realize that it's only about dawn here."

"Anyway," Zack said, "the program came up with nine possibilities. Four in Indonesia, two in the Arctic, one in Thailand, one in the Philippines, and one in the South Pacific."

"Wow, that's quite a list," Logan replied.

"I know. Once we get the next map, we can probably pinpoint the exact island."

"Then I guess I better get to it and check your findings. By the way, kudos to you for figuring it out so quickly. You're not half as slow as I thought you were." Logan facetiously said.

"Yeah, thanks. You're a real friend!" Zack joked back.

"Okay, talk to you soon Zack."

Logan hung up the phone and went into his office. He sat down at his computer and opened his e-mail account. As he read, it all made sense. Canada became a country in 1867, the same year the United States acquired Alaska from Russia. It occurred to him that Juneau meant young, and so Juneau, Alaska, must be important. And yes, den of water: the Mendenhall Ice Caves at Mendenhall Glacier. Like the glacier, the ice caves were continually changing like a sandbar in a storm. Apparently, there were warning signs not to enter the caves, as they had become very unstable. Zack went on to say he couldn't find a reference to follow the signs, but everything else fit perfectly.

Logan shook his head. "Working backward is a lot easier than blindly struggling through a million possibilities." He quickly searched the findings on the Internet and couldn't find any fault with Zack's conclusions. "I'll be damned. I guess I'd better dig up some warm clothes. It's off to Alaska." He felt exuberant that everything seemed to be progressing so well.

It was late May and the temperatures could still be cold in Alaska, especially at night, not to mention that after Southeast Asia and Hawaii, it would feel chilly even in mid-summer.

Savannah entered his office. "Logan?"

"Good morning, beautiful. How's my girl this morning?" He tried his best to sound positive.

"Better. I don't know how I can thank you for being so patient with me. You really don't deserve this. I've got a few things I need to work through. I just need some time."

"You don't have to go through it alone. I want to help you. I'm here for you. Please let me into your life."

"I can't. Not right now anyway." She wrapped her arms around him, squeezing him tight.

"Whenever you're ready, baby. Whenever you're ready."

They walked into the kitchen, the sun beaming through the windows. Together they made breakfast. It seemed to cheer Savannah up, and she flashed him a little smile. It warmed his heart to see even a little happiness in her face.

"So, I guess you'll want to go shopping for some new clothes today," Logan said.

"I should be okay. Don't you remember how large a wardrobe I have with me?" Savannah asked. She looked puzzled.

"Yeah, but I don't think you'll want to wear any of those clothes in Alaska."

It dawned on her that Zack must have figured out the map. "You guys didn't figure out the—"

"I can't take the credit for this one, but yes, Zack figured out the next clue."

"I thought we would be here weeks, maybe months." Savannah's voice was filled with excitement as well as disappointment, as she had hoped to spend some time in Hawaii getting to know Logan better.

"Me too, but it looks like we're off to Juneau. Are you up to going? If you wanted to just hang out here in the sunshine, you are more than welcome." He gave Savannah the option knowing she was a bit tender now, but at the same time he was not comfortable leaving her alone in her state of mind.

"No way! I've never been to Alaska. I really want to go, if you don't mind me tagging along." She batted her eyes innocently.

"Mind? I would miss that cute little smile of yours if I couldn't see it every day," he said, giving her a kiss on the forehead.

The news seemed to perk her up. She quizzed Logan on Alaska as they ate their breakfast on the back patio of his seaside home, the morning sun still low in the sky glistening off the water.

In the back of her mind, she knew she needed to call Victor, but she tried her best to push the thought away, at least for the time being. She wondered if Victor or one of his minions were in Hawaii watching their every move. Not knowing if or when she was being watched made it almost impossible to lie to Victor, because one thing was certain: she absolutely did not want to be caught in a lie to him. Her mind was consumed with how to get out of the predicament, not just the immediate one, but how to permanently escape from Victor's clutches.

Logan's stress was eased somewhat as Savannah was in a good mood again. He didn't want to waste any time, and so they hit the shopping mall preparing themselves for all weather conditions. He knew that he could pick up any ice climbing equipment he might need in Juneau, and most anything else on the off chance he forgot something. As he made the travel arrangements, all he could think was that he wished he at least had a day or two to relax, but he realized that time was of the essence. He called Zack and coordinated meeting times and places in Juneau, remembering he needed to talk to him about something.

"One more thing, Zack," Logan began.

"What's that? I think we've covered everything."

"I forgot to mention something I picked up in Thailand."

CHAPTER 14

Savannah pressed tightly against Logan, sheltering herself from the biting wind that buffeted them as they walked down the quaint streets of Juneau's downtown area. May could be such an unpredictable month in Alaska, warm and sunny one day and revisited by the chill of winter the next.

"Couldn't just meet him at the hotel, could you?" Savannah complained as they hiked through town toward the Mount Roberts Tramway to meet Zack.

"Sorry, baby. I said you could wait in the hotel."

"You know I hate to miss out on the fun," she said, her teeth chattering.

"Yeah, I can tell you're having a blast." Logan laughed. "I bet you're happy now we got that nice warm jacket for you. I had a feeling those sun dresses might not cut it."

"Brat!"

"You know I love to tease you," Logan said, giving her a quick kiss. "We're almost there. It's normally such a nice walk."

Before long, they had made their way through the downtown area, down Egan Drive to the base of the tramway. Dressed only in a sweatshirt, Zack stood in front of the entrance to the tramway. He was obviously freezing.

"Zack, great to see you," Logan said. The two men gave each other a brotherly hug.

"And you must be Savannah," Zack said, smiling and offering her his hand.

"Yes, and you must be Zack. A pleasure to meet you." She smiled back, giving him a dainty handshake.

"Likewise, and may I say you are even more beautiful than Logan described."

"Thank you Zack. Logan, you never told me he was such a charmer."

"You won't be saying that for long. Just wait until you get to know him," Logan joked.

"Jeez, Logan! Why couldn't we just meet at the hotel? It's frickin' freezing out here."

"See? I'm not the only one," Savannah said.

"Yeah, yeah, yeah. When I made the plan, I hoped we would be enjoying a much warmer day. The weather seems to be deteriorating by the hour, so I think a trip up the mountain may not be a lot of fun. How do you two feel about a few cold ones?"

"Lead the way," Zack replied, his arms wrapped around his chest for warmth.

"Hey, Arctic Man, are you okay to walk back downtown or would you like to catch a taxi?" Logan asked.

"Thought you'd never ask," Zack replied, instantly at the side of the road hailing a cab, causing both Logan and Savannah to laugh.

Within a few minutes, they sat on wooden stools in a bar. The smell of stale beer wafted through the air, along with the laughter of early season tourists making the most of the blustery day. As the two men entertained Savannah with story after story, each more outrageous than the last, Logan realized how much he had missed Zack's friendship and company. Savannah laughed harder than she ever had in her life. All the feelings and emotions that tortured her had slipped away for the time being, completely engulfed in the genuine fun that she had been caught up in. There was nothing phony, nothing pretentious, no games. *This is what true friendship is all about*, she thought. It was something she had never experienced in her life, but something she had desperately yearned for.

Logan knew that he wasn't the only one searching for the treasure, and that the potentially large amount of money involved could make people act unpredictably. At least he was the only one to have the Cambodian map. He hadn't seen anyone following him, but he was always on the lookout. He wanted to find the next map as quickly as possible. However, they needed supplies, and a day to catch up with Zack was exactly what the doctor ordered.

The next morning, the trio was off to procure their ice climbing gear. Later in the summer, it was possible to reach the ice caves on solid ground, but it had been a particularly hard winter and late spring, so they would be heading up the ice. Logan had talked to a few of the guides that gave the ice caves tours, pretending to be interested in taking a cave tour. Naturally, the caves being their passion and their business, most were happy to go on and on about them. Logan found out about the main caves and what dangers they held. He also wanted to know about which offshoots and crevasses that the guides would go into or cross over, and which ones they would avoid.

After leaving the third tour agency of the morning, Logan was beaming from ear to ear as he went to meet Savannah and Zack, who were busing shopping up a storm.

"You look like the cat that just swallowed the canary, Logan," Zack noted as Logan swaggered toward them.

"Well, when you're good, you're good, and I'm good!"

"Don't leave me in suspense." Zack threw his arms up in mock disgust.

"As I mentioned, I went to get some information on the caves. Colton obviously didn't hide the next map where some tourist fumbling along would find it, so I asked about other caves or offshoots, and I found out a lot of interesting information that will definitely help us."

"If they know where these caves are, then wouldn't they find the map?"

"That's the beauty of it. There are a lot of caves so unstable even these hardcore ice cavers won't go in them."

"And we are?" Zack asked, his voice filled with uncertainty.

"I guess we'll find out."

"Logan, you know I'll try almost anything, but I don't know if I'm up for this, and I'm virtually positive that Savannah isn't."

"You're right. I can't ask either of you to endanger your lives. I'm going to get radios so we can keep in contact. Savannah will stand guard outside the caves, and you go only as far as you feel comfortable. I'll go the rest of the way alone. As long as we don't fall into a crevasse the hike over the glacier should be safe wearing crampons."

"God, Logan. I know you've done a lot of caving, but that was either dry caves or underwater caves. This is something totally different. I don't know if I like you going into places that even professional ice cavers won't go." Zack was genuinely worried about his safety.

"Thanks, mom, but it's that adrenaline rush that makes us feel alive." Logan gave Zack a confident wink.

"Hi, guys! What's going on?" Savannah chimed in as she came over carrying an arm full of clothes.

"Oh, nothing. Logan just decided he wanted to be cryogenically frozen."

"What?"

"It's nothing. Zack is just being a worrywart. We were just doing a bit of preplanning for our ice cave adventure."

"What did Zack mean then? Is it dangerous?"

"Nothing I can't handle, girl." Logan gave her a big kiss.

"Oh, rent a room you two."

"We have." Logan and Savannah laughed.

Despite the outward confidence that Logan showed, he wondered what he was getting himself into. For hardcore ice cavers not to enter certain caves, they would have to be considered almost suicidal, or at the very least, extremely dangerous. He knew that ice caves changed drastically over the months, let alone over the years.

He bounced questions around in his head. When had Colton hidden the map? May, June, July? Would it even be possible to find the map? Could it now be buried under ten feet of ice, or has the ice melted and the map has blown away? No, Colton would have planned for those events of nature, but how? He nodded as he thought to himself. *Yeah, if Colton Braxton could hide it, I can find it.*

The next couple hours were filled with gathering up everything that they could possibly need on their sortie into the ice caves, including every possible contingency that could occur. One thing that Logan had learned well in his cave diving experiences was that triple redundancies were an absolute must. A saying often heard in cave diving circles popped into his head: "People who dive in caves, die in caves."

The more that Logan thought about it, the more he thought it best that he goes alone when they reached a junction of any danger whatsoever. He knew he was not only much better prepared, but more importantly, he had learned about his ability to remain calm in the direst situations. He had made a life of living on the edge and flirted with death on more than one occasion.

"Okay, guys. I think we got everything." He was studiously going over his list.

"You're going to need to find the treasure to pay for all this stuff," Zack joked.

"Yeah, thank goodness for credit cards." Logan said, only half joking. He was a bit shocked at what the treasure hunt had already cost him.

"I think we should have a quick lunch meeting, somewhere quiet so we can go over our plan," Logan said. "I've got some rough maps of the caves, but I think we have to be prepared to improvise."

For the next hour and a half, they sat in the corner of a quiet rustic diner. The smell of pine, stale beer, and greasy burgers blended in a way that made the aroma perfectly fit the setting. Ten-year-old country music echoed throughout the diner, which was made completely of wood. The dusty wooden walls were held up by thick wooden beams. There were bare wooden rafters covered in a thousand cobwebs, and, of course, a worn and splintered wood floor was complemented perfectly by the slightly grubby overall appearance of the diner, giving it an authentic gold rush town feel, although purely by accident.

Logan checked his watch. "It's 1:25 p.m. Let's head out to the glacier just to see what kind of crowds are out there. We are going to have to go into the caves without anyone seeing us. If the weather is favorable, I think we should leave under the darkness of the night, so we are well into the caves before anyone else is even having their toast and coffee."

There was a much more serious tone in Logan's voice, cold sober like a general preparing his troops for battle. It was a side of Logan that Zack had seen before, but only when he knew he was heading into a situation of potentially deadly consequences. He couldn't help but recall a time years ago when Logan was planning a free hand climb, a climb that no one in their right mind would attempt. Logan was a good climber, but often he would climb well beyond his abilities and training, pushing himself to new extreme limits.

Zack laughed and shook his head. He could see in his mind exactly what would happen if Logan completed his task tomorrow. Without fail, every time he succeeded in cheating death he would offer up his famous quote with a huge grin: "You're never more alive than when you're on the verge of dying."

CHAPTER 15

A bone-chilling dampness filled the air as the night temperature dropped below freezing. On the off chance anyone was out in the middle of the night, all three were dressed in dark clothing. Despite them all having several lights, only Logan carried a small infrared flashlight to lead the way. Savannah and Zack trekked single file behind Logan, who seemed to cross the rocks without making a sound. They marched into the blackness at a steady pace, blindly following in Logan's footsteps, trusting him to warn them of any impending danger. The eerie silence gave Savannah a foreboding feeling. She knew they couldn't yell and scream as they went along, but from the time they arrived at the glacier, not a word had been spoken.

They strapped on their crampons, which were a necessity for the glacier, and as a precaution, carried ice axes. The eastern sky began to cast a ghoulish glow over the ice, bringing to life menacing ice creatures and their devilish shadows that occupied the vast ancient monster's back.

In the deathly silence of the night, you could hear the monster groan as it clawed its way down the valley, ripping apart ancient rock formations that had clung steadfastly throughout history.

Logan stopped and stood silently, in awe of the mighty monster into which he was about to enter. As the sun crept higher into the sky, the dark monster now took on a hue of opalescent blue.

"Oh my God, Logan! It's indescribable!" Savannah whispered, breaking the silence. "It's incredibly beautiful."

"It's also dangerous," Logan said.

Zack nodded in stunned agreement as he peered into the azure cavern that appeared to be lit from inside its cold walls, glowing like a blue cathedral. Logan went over the plan one last time. As if they were soldiers heading into battle, Savannah and Zack never once questioned him, trusting in their leader to keep them safe. There had been signs outside warning of the dangers of entering the ice caves. *Are those the signs that Colton meant?* Logan thought. *No, there had to be another sign, but where?*

The initial passageway looked stable and safe, but erring on the side of caution, they slowly and meticulously made their way through the cave, not knowing exactly what they were looking for. Logan was certain that he would know it when he saw it. Water droplets pelted them as they walked gingerly down the frozen tunnel that almost appeared fluorescent blue as the sun pierced the thick ice. The ice caves were truly a thing of beauty, filled with open spaces and narrow ice tubes, all with the glow of the ancient blue ice that had witnessed passing centuries. "This is where they take the tourists. We have to look for a place few would go," Logan said.

The cave's beauty was deceptive as it was fraught with danger. At any moment, the entire cave could collapse, crushing them. The sun overhead melting the ice also caused pieces of rock and ice to fall from above that could injure or even kill an unsuspecting caver. A crack in the ice below could plummet the person to a violent and quick death. Being buried alive in an icy grave was also a possibility. After a while, the trio came to the end of the tourist trail, where there was a small opening with a warning sign saying not to enter because of unstable conditions.

"This has to be it," Logan said, the excitement apparent in his voice.

"Logan, I'm scared. I don't think I can go in there," Savannah whimpered.

"You don't have to. Zack, you and Savannah stay here. We'll keep in touch by radio. Hand me my harness." Logan asked, as he pulled the long climbing rope from off his shoulder.

Zack pulled off his backpack and dug around his bag feverishly. "Shit, shit, shit. Logan, I can't believe what I did. I set the harnesses down to repack my bag, and I must have left them on the ground by the truck. Should we go back?"

By the long pause, and the look on his face, Zack could see that Logan was agitated, but he quickly regained his composure. "No, we have no time to go back. I'll just tie the rope around my waist as a precaution, and you do the same. Feed me rope as I make my way down the passageway. It looks fairly level, so hopefully I won't need it," Logan said. He loudly exhaled a sigh of frustration. "It's early in the season, so the ice should still be fairly stable."

"Logan, don't push it too far," Zack said.

"Ah, you know me." He winked. "It's early in the season, so hopefully we'll have the cave to ourselves, but let me know if company comes."

"What should we tell them?" Zack asked.

"Just throw the rope in and try to cover the entrance. Pretend you're admiring the cave until they leave. I know you can bullshit as well as anyone." Logan laughed as he blew Savannah a kiss and headed into the narrow passageway.

Logan cautiously made his way down the jagged corridor. He reached up and clicked the headlamp he wore as the fluorescent blue turned indigo, dimming to black as he entered deeper into the bowels of the icy world.

"Shit," Logan muttered. He had come to an impasse where a section of the cave had collapsed. "What the hell am I doing?" He knew the changing ice could make finding the map impossible. "No, I must believe Colton would have thought of that. Think, Logan, think. How could he assure it could still be found years later?"

Logan radioed back to Zack and Savannah. "It looks like I'll be doing a bit of digging, if you're wondering why my progress has stopped."

"Okay, but be careful," Zack said into the radio.

Logan pulled out his ax and began to clear away the frozen obstruction, trying not to create another cave-in. He unzipped his coat, as he could feel the sweat pouring down his back from the exertion of making an opening. With a hefty tug on one large pyramid of ice, he had created an opening just large enough for him to squeeze through. He couldn't risk making the opening any larger, as the remaining ice chunks were already balancing precariously like a house of cards.

"Here goes nothing." Logan sighed as he lay on his belly and slithered through the runty opening.

"Well, I'll be damned," he said. His headlamp illuminated a small sign partially melted into the ice. At first, it appeared benign, warning of the dangers of going any farther, but suddenly he noticed in the corner of the sign the initials C. E. B.

"Follow the signs," Logan grinned as he recited part of the clue.

A bit farther along, the ice cave widened to the point where he wasn't shuffling sideways, until he reached a fork in the cave. He smiled again, as only one passageway had a warning sign. As he carried on, sporadic rock began to appear under his feet, and the height of the cave shrank until he was crawling along ground.

"No, no, no!" Logan said in frustration as he got to the point where he could not go any farther, or even turn around. "Hey, guys," he radioed back.

"How's it going in there?" Zack responded.

"Not good. It looks like I reached a dead end. I'll start to back—" Logan stopped in mid-sentence. He caught a glimpse of something farther down in the corridor of the cave, but the passage was too narrow for him to crawl into.

"Logan? Are you okay?" Zack called over the radio.

"Yeah, sorry. Just give me a minute."

Logan pulled a small but powerful LED flashlight out of his pocket, shining it down the narrow passage. He could see the top of a sign sticking out of what appeared to be a hole in the floor of the cave. It was about twenty feet down the passageway, but the height where he was at now was less than two feet, and the passageway looked like it narrowed to about a foot.

"Do you guys have a deck of cards?" Logan asked over the radio.

"What the hell are you talking about? You hit your head?" Zack asked.

"No, but it looks like I'm going to be here for a while. I've got to tunnel through about twenty feet of ice. After that it looks like a hole in the mountain."

"This is starting to make me nervous, Logan. Be careful," Zack said. Savannah stood quietly beside him, her forehead wrinkled with worry.

With firm ground, and rock beneath him, he began to work on icy ceiling above him. Logan found it painstakingly slow as the cramped area made it hard for him to get any leverage to chip away the ice with any power. "God, this will take three days," Logan muttered as he swept the ice slivers behind him as he chipped away. His efforts almost seemed to be in vain.

An hour passed. His whole body cramped up from being squeezed into the tight space. He set down the axe, picking up a sliver of ice, sucking on it, and thinking how many thousands of years old it was. "At least I won't die of thirst here," he snickered, rotating his stiff shoulders to work out the kinks and cramps. Then everything changed fast.

Out in the main cave, Zack had been monitoring the radio and holding the rope attached to his friend. Suddenly, he felt a tremendous pull, and his shoulder and head smashed against the edge of the cave opening. Almost simultaneously, Savannah's scream echoed through the cave as she saw Zack hit the ice wall and blood spray from his nose. In seconds, he fell stunned to the floor of the cave.

"Oh, my God, Zack! Are you okay? What happened?" Savannah screamed.

Zack yelled in pain, not as much for his nose that turned the pristine ice into blood spattered modern art, but for his arm that had been wrenched down the passageway. The rope he had been slowly feeding Logan was wrapped around his arm. He felt the rope dig deeply into his flesh through his thick jacket, and his shoulder throbbed in pain.

"Help me, Savannah!" Zack spat blood. "Help me hold the rope! It's ripping my shoulder out of its socket." Cursing himself for not being more prepared, knowing something like this could happen.

Savannah crawled into the passageway to grab the rope, and began to heave on it, to take the pressure off Zack's arm. Her efforts seemed in vain. She braced herself with her legs against a crack in the ice of the blood-spattered wall, and pulled with all her strength, barely taking enough of the strain to give Zack the slack he needed. "I think I got it," she said.

Feeling some of the pressure release from his arm, Zack used his other arm to unwrap the rope. He saw Savannah struggling to hold on, so as soon as he was free, he helped her handle the load on the rope. They both strained to keep more of the rope from playing out. Zack tried to ignore the shooting pain in his right shoulder, which he figured was separated from his arm. There was about thirty feet of rope left, and Zack had no idea what Logan was dealing with at his end, so he couldn't afford to let him fall any farther.

"What happened?" Savannah cried, tears streaming down her face. Horrible scenarios whipped through her mind.

"I don't know! Can you reach your radio?"

Savannah took one of her hands off the rope and reached for her radio. "Logan? Logan? Logan, are you okay?" She hysterically yelled into the radio.

Just then, they flew backward onto the cave floor as the rope went slack.

CHAPTER 16

Logan spun around, gasping to catch his breath. The wind had been violently knocked out of him when he'd jerked to a stop after a six-foot plunge into the black abyss. He fought to draw that first life-giving breath. A few minutes seemed more like an eternity, but finally his breathing began to return to normal. He closed his eyes for a few seconds, allowing his spinning head to clear. Opening his eyes, he looked up toward the hole he was heading for, which was now about triple the size. He realized it was an opening to a dry cave and the thin ceiling had collapsed under his weight. He had dropped his main waterproof light as well as his LED flashlight, but fortunately, his headlamp remained tightly fastened around his forehead, held on by his helmet that was strapped firmly around his chin. He searched for his radio, which had also fallen to the cave floor below.

He had been so busy worrying about trying to breathe, he hadn't realized the pain shooting through his back and ribs. "Yeah, that's going to leave a mark." Logan snickered, causing himself more pain. He twisted his neck around. "Oh, shit," he said as he peered down about fifteen feet to the uneven rock floor of the cave.

Logan wrapped his wrist around the rope above him to give himself some slack and began to untie it from his waist. As soon as the rope dropped from his waist, he reached up and grabbed it, lowering himself down to the end of the rope so he only had about eight feet to drop. He let go and felt it rip through his hands as he prepared for his landing on the cave floor. To his surprise, he landed soft, although even the gentlest of landings irritated his extremely sore ribcage. *Well, Logan, you were trying to get to the opening*, he thought, *and now you have.*

He looked around for the radio, so he could let Zack and Savannah know he was okay. Although he had no idea how he was going to get out of there, but knew if he couldn't find another way out, his friends would send out a search party—eventually. After a few minutes, Logan spotted the radio, or rather what was left of it, which had broken on the rocks. He started to put it back together, but he realized after a few minutes that it was beyond repair. He hoped that his friends were okay, but he knew they would be worried and he knew Savannah would be in a panic. Unfortunately, his LED flashlight was also broken, and his fluorescent yellow waterproof light had mysteriously disappeared. "How do you lose a bright yellow light?" he said.

As Logan scanned the large chamber, he noticed a narrow passageway and headed toward it. All ambient light from the sun penetrating the glacier was long gone, so he relied on the small light on his head to illuminate the blackness. *I hope these are good batteries*, Logan thought. He realized that if his headlamp went out, he would be in utter darkness.

"Well, I'll be," he exclaimed as he approached the opening to the smaller passageway. It was another warning sign with the initials C. E. B. in the corner. Immediately he wondered, *If Colton Braxton had come down here, how did he get back up? Where would he have tied off a rope? It was all ice up there. Did he have help? Someone holding the rope? Was there another way out?* The questions swirled around in his head as he cautiously began his way down the narrow passageway.

Meanwhile, Zack and Savannah discussed what to do. They were fully aware that Logan did not want them to contact the authorities, but this could be a life or death situation. Zack enlisted the help of Savannah as well as the cave wall to pop his shoulder back into place. After a few agonizing tries, it seemed to pop back into place, although pain still pulsed through his shoulder down his arm, leaving it feeling weak and half paralyzed.

"I have to go down there and find out what happened," he said.

"And leave me alone here?" Savannah shrieked, her face ripe with fear.

"It's not safe for you to go down there. Plus, we need someone here just in case something else happens. I'll call you every five minutes," he said as he took the third radio out of his backpack. "If I don't check in and you can't reach me, then go for help, okay?"

Savannah nodded silently with worry on her face.

With a deep breath and a loud sigh, Zack was off down the icy passageway, following the limp rope that at one time had been tied around Logan.

After a few minutes, Logan found himself stooping over as the cave began to shrink. Fifty feet farther ahead, the passageway seemingly ended with only a miniscule opening that Logan seriously doubted he could fit through. Then he saw the sign: "Danger. Do Not Enter. Dead End … C. E. B." The sign was wedged in a crack just before the entrance to the extremely small opening.

Logan wasn't at all claustrophobic, but he knew if he did manage to squeeze in, it would be like being trapped in a coffin. There would be no way to turn around, and he didn't even want to entertain the idea of being stuck. *Colton said to follow the signs!* he thought. He got down on his belly, extending his arms in front of him and pulling in his shoulders to make himself as compact as possible.

"Damn, this is a lot worse than the Cu Chi Tunnels," Logan muttered. He snaked his way along the narrow tube, thinking of the time he spent touring the famous tunnels used by the Vietcong.

Well behind him in the passageway, Zack stopped. He was panting from the exertion, and he was trying not to panic in the small dark space. He pressed the transmit button on the radio. "I'm to the point where Logan had to dig through the collapsed ice," he said to Savannah.

"Be careful, Zack."

"Count on it."

Zack followed the rope down the narrow secondary passageway until he came to the gaping hole in the cave floor. "Holy crap," he exclaimed. "Savannah? Savannah?"

"What's wrong, Zack?"

"I think I found out what happened," he replied. He pulled up the limp rope from the opening, careful not to get too close, as the collapsing floor caused some of the ice to break away while other huge sections sat precariously in place, ready to fall at any time. "There is a huge dry cave below this ice cave, and when the floor collapsed, Logan must have fallen in. He either untied himself from the rope, or he wasn't tied off very well, because the rope is intact."

"Can you see him?"

"Not yet. The ice is unstable, and I don't know how much I trust this floor. I'm going to try to get a look."

To spread his weight out, Zack crawled gingerly toward the edge of the hole, grimacing in pain with every inch. "Okay, I'm at the edge."

"Be careful."

"You said that already."

"Just be careful."

"Yeah. Right."

Zack peered over the edge into the deep hole. He saw no sign of Logan, but he shouted his name, hoping he might hear a response. The sound vibrations from the echo in the large chamber sent several large chunks of ice plummeting down, one glancing off Zack's head as it fell. The hit snapped his neck forward, grinding his chin against the rocky edge of the hole. He wanted to cry out in pain, but held it in, knowing he might receive an encore performance.

"Savannah, I can't see him and he's not answering. His radio is smashed. It must have fallen into the hole. So he can't call us. The hole—"

"Shit," Savannah said, her voice thick with emotion.

"It looks like the entrance to another cave," Zack said quietly, not wanting to dislodge any more projectiles.

"Logan must be trying to find another way out. There's no way I can get down there, especially in the shape I'm in now. I'm coming back to you."

"Are you sure? You sure you can't get down there to help him?"

"Yeah, I'm sure. I'm sorry, Savannah. There's nothing I can do for him now."

Before leaving, he tossed the rope back into the hole, pulling it until it almost reached the floor of the cave. He figured if Logan couldn't find a way out, he would come back to the rope, so he would keep a hand on it, waiting for a tug at the other end. With that, Zack slowly backed up until it was safe to turn around and began to find his way back to Savannah.

Deep in the hidden cave, Logan heard a voice echoing through the cave, but didn't dare call back, for fear he would cause a collapse. He could see some loose rocks blocking his way. He painstakingly had to push the rocks ahead one at a time, since putting them behind him or going past them wasn't an option. "Oh, thank God!" Logan exclaimed a few moments later. The passage widened a few feet ahead, and the sight seemed to energize him as he slithered along the last few feet. The passageway appeared to open into another large chamber. He emerged from the small opening and stood up like a ninety-year-old arthritic man. "Oh, I need a hot tub now," he mumbled. He stretched and rotated his neck, working out the kinks from the last forty minutes on his belly.

The chamber wasn't as big as the one he had fallen into, but it was still large enough to move around. Soon, his dim light illuminated something shiny. He'd seen it out of the corner of his eye. He moved closer and saw an object on a rock ledge that almost looked like an altar. He could scarcely believe it. He gasped. He was looking at a small treasure chest with a half-rusted silver lock.

Logan stood in front of the treasure chest. *No, this is too damned easy,* he thought. He was about to pick up the chest, realizing what he had just been through was far from easy. He then began to look for booby traps. *Maybe I've just watched too many of those adventure movies.* After a comprehensive inspection of the surrounding area, he found no boulders about to come down and no poisonous darts ready to shoot out. He cautiously tipped back the chest from all angles, looking for any wires. Nothing. The lock didn't appear to be too secure, so Logan picked up a rock and struck it. On the second try, the hinge came loose, and the lock flew onto the cave floor.

Cautiously, Logan lifted the lid of the treasure chest. He smiled in satisfaction as he saw the next map, and then held it up in front of his light. A momentary surge of elation made him almost jump for joy, but then the reality of his situation damped his mood. *Now, how the hell do I get out of here?* Since it didn't weigh much, Logan took the small treasure chest, along with the map. With it tucked under his arm, he scoured the cave, looking for a way out, but it seemed to end with the large chamber. "God, I hope I don't have to go back the way I came." He shuttered at the thought.

"Idiot!" he yelled to himself, as he turned out his light. It had just come to him. *What do you do if you are disoriented in a shipwreck and don't know which way is out? Cover your dive light and look for where ambient light is coming from! It just might work!* Logan thought. Hope was building within him.

He shut off the light and blackness enveloped him as he peered into the darkness for the faintest sign of light.

At first, he thought his eyes were playing tricks on him, because from one corner of the chamber a slight sliver of light shone through. He clicked his headlamp back on and headed toward it. The source disappeared when he turned his light back on, but he headed toward the spot he had marked in his mind.

Once there, he again turned off his light to get the exact location. "You clever little bastard, Colton," Logan said. He found an entrance to the cave that had obviously been deliberately blocked with a collection of small rocks. Logan began clearing them away, only to be met by a thick collection of deadfall, which was covered with about a foot of snow. It was placed over the outside entrance, completely concealing it from view. He managed to clear aside just enough logs, snow, and debris to squeeze through the opening. Logan inhaled a deep breath of the fresh glacial air and looked down toward the glacier from the mountainside. Despite his body aching from the fall and exertion of the day, he felt happy, filled with a sense accomplishment.

He checked his watch, wondering how long he'd been stuck, and how long it had been since he'd lost radio contact with Zack and Savannah. *Shit, they must be worried sick about me,* he thought. It was 2:50 p.m. He had to get back to his friends right away. After a quick assessment of his location, he began to make his way back down to the entrance of the ice caves, although he had no idea if Zack and Savannah had already gone to find a search party. As Logan approached the cave from its top slope, Zack and Savannah hastily exited the cave as they were formulating their rescue plan. He stood only ten feet from them as they emerged from the mouth of the cave, oblivious to his presence. He could hear every word they said as they scurried back down the glacier.

Having a bit of a warped sense of humor, he snuck up behind them. "I would just leave the bastard down there to rot."

They stopped in their tracks and turned, a look of total shock on their faces, as if they had just seen a ghost.

"You asshole! You almost got yourself killed. And for what? A damn map?" Savannah screamed as she first began pounding on Logan's chest, which quickly turned to a tight embrace with tears of joy flowing down her face.

"It's okay, baby. It's okay." He turned to Zack. "Holy shit! Who the hell beat you up?" Despite Logan's light-hearted banter, the look on his face showed the concern and relief he truly felt towards his friends.

Zack's face had begun to change color from his two encounters with the ice and rock.

"That would be you," Zack replied in a stern voice, although the relief of seeing Logan told another story. "I guess it's my own fault. I should have braced myself instead of assuming a clumsy oaf like you could walk along without falling into a hole."

"You won't be any uglier than you were before, and let me remind you that we would both be a lot better off if we were wearing our harnesses, don't you think?"

"Yeah, yeah—Murphy's law. You know if we had our harnesses on, you probably wouldn't have fallen down that hole."

"What the hell is wrong with you guys? After all we've been through, you're still joking around like a couple of children," Savannah said. She scolded them but enjoyed their banter.

"I'm going to assume that mini treasure chest you're carrying contains the next map," Zack said.

"You bet it does, but all I want right now is a stiff drink and three hours in the hot tub."

Logan told them about his adventure in the ice cave as they returned to the hotel. The ratty-looking trio cleaned themselves up, followed by time in the hot tub, before they met up for a celebratory dinner. They were all so excited that their exhaustion did not interfere with the dinner, nor did it get in the way as they relived their adventures of the day by the roaring fireplace in Logan's suite. While Savannah and Logan huddled together like a couple of infatuated teenagers, Zack sat a few feet away, already banging away at his laptop, inputting the clue from the new map and scanning in the new piece of the map puzzle.

"Yes!" Zack screamed, causing Logan and Savannah to jump. "When you're good, you're good! And I'm really frickin' good!"

"What's up?" Logan asked.

"Remember that shoreline recognition program I told you I developed?"

"Yeah."

"It extrapolated the island where the treasure is! Of course, we'll still need the other maps to find the exact location of the treasure, but we now know where we will eventually end up." Zack was brimming with pride. "I guess now's a good time to talk about my cut of the booty."

"Okay, two cases of beer instead of one. Are you going to keep us in suspense?" Logan asked.

Zack smiled, leaned back in his chair, and cupped his hands behind his head. "If you must know, the treasure is hidden on—"

CHAPTER 17

Logan smiled. "Maybe someone up there likes me."
"No doubt. I think you owe Mr. Colton Braxton III a big thank you for hiding the treasure in your backyard," Zack replied. It wasn't where Logan lived, but one in which he had spent a lot of time and knew well.

"You know it, Zack. I love Thailand, and how ironic that it's on the island that I just spent a month on last year. You gotta love Koh Lanta."

"I think we better find a couple more clues before we book our tickets to Krabi," Zack said, referring to the closest airport to Koh Lanta.

Logan knew they had a lot more work to do before they could even think about finding the treasure, but possibilities still swirled in his mind. He had explored the jungles, caves, and beaches of the island. *Where would he hide it? Concentrate on the task at hand.* Logan's mind drifted back to the map, although not so far in the back of his mind the wheels continued to turn, searching for any possible hiding places that made sense.

Logan and Zack looked at each other, and then back at the clue. It read:

"This eastern dynasty begins its reign as a black cloud lay over half this seaborne power. Gather ye rosebuds while ye may, made of wood, and then of stone from hence you'll go." A long set of intricate walking instructions was followed up with the final words of the clue: "Up the stairs and to your right, you'll lay your head whilst picturing a moonlit night."

"It's a long one, Zack. Hope you got your thinking cap on and your computer revved up."

"No problem. It just gives us more to work with," Zack replied. He hoped he could back up his words.

Logan was also confident that they would figure it out, as the clue seemed to follow a pattern of finding places from events or people only related by dates, although some were quite arcane.

Savannah sat quietly, taking in everything the two men said. She hadn't talked to Victor in days and knew he would be furious. She decided that she wouldn't tell Victor about the final location, not yet anyway, but she would have to tell him about Logan finding the next map.

"Logan, I know you guys are going to be playing on your computers for the next few hours anyway, so do you mind if I go for a little walk?"

"It's quite late. Will you be okay?" Logan asked, worried about her going out alone at night.

"Remember I'm from New Orleans. I'll be fine."

Logan gave her a quick kiss and then pulled out his laptop. Zack was already busy and thoroughly engrossed, his fingers swiftly gliding over the keyboard, an intense look on his face. Before Savannah had left the room, Logan was already banging away at his keyboard, although not nearly as efficiently as Zack.

She quietly clicked the door shut, her head hung low as she slowly shuffled her way down the hallway, knowing she was again about to betray the man she was falling in love with. She had become all consumed with figuring out a way to escape the grasp of Victor Kane, although the only way she knew he would let her go was for her to kill him. She knew she never could; he was too strong. Tears began to well up in her eyes as she headed out into the brisk Arctic air of a clear Juneau night. She paid little attention to the crude comments of a pair of drunken roughnecks that stumbled out of a rundown bar, nearly knocking her over. Before she had realized it, she had walked over half a mile from the hotel to the waterfront, where the slight breeze was even more biting and damp. She sat down on a cold wooden bench and pulled out her phone.

"Victor it's—"

Before she could say another word, he was shouting at her for not calling him. Tears streamed down her cheeks. When she spoke to Victor, she didn't even feel like a woman. She felt worthless, like one of his pawns that he used any way he wanted. She told him what had transpired, and that Logan had found the next map, but she again stressed that he never let the maps out of his sight, so it would be impossible to copy them. This only ignited another barrage of profanity from him. He refused to believe she couldn't get the maps away from Logan long enough to copy them.

Savannah reassured him that she would call more often, especially if they made progress on the newly found map.

Victor hated not having complete control, but after his venting session, he realized that he needed Savannah and had to trust that she could do the job. But that didn't stop him from sending a few of his trusted contacts to keep an eye on them all from a distance. When Victor hung up the phone, Savannah was overcome with emotion. She dropped her phone, and with her elbows on her knees, her face fell into her hands. Her flowing tears became a raging river.

"How can I do this to Logan?" she blubbered through the torrent of sobs. Every time she had to speak to Victor, it was like a piece of her soul was torn out. How to escape the claws of Victor had become an obsession for her. She felt small, insignificant, and powerless against him. In contrast, when she was with Logan, she felt alive, sexy, important, wanted, and loved. These were feelings she had never had, but desperately craved. It had become a reoccurring theme with her, her own personal roller coaster. It was an emotional ride she didn't know how much longer she could stand. She felt she was on the verge of a complete breakdown, and she knew that Logan had to have questions about her behavior on occasion, but he never pushed her for answers.

"Oh my God," Savannah said aloud. She looked at her watch, realizing that she had been gone for almost three hours. She had been lost in her thoughts and tears of desire for the dreams she desperately wanted. *The guys will be worried*, she thought. She composed herself and began to make her way back to the hotel. When she arrived, she stood outside the door of their room. She closed her eyes and took a deep breath as she got ready for all the questions she'd have to answer as to why she had been gone for so long. Then she slowly opened the door and stepped inside.

Logan and Zack had not moved from their positions from three hours earlier. In fact, neither even looked up as she entered. They sounded excited, talking with each other as they banged away on their keyboards. She silently stood in the doorway listening to them, thinking that they sounded like kids who had just been to the candy store. She figured they must have been close to figuring out the latest clue.

"Hi, guys. How's it going?" She feigned enthusiasm, still torn apart inside.

"Hi, baby. Sorry I didn't hear you come in. Did you have a good walk?" He was completely oblivious to the amount of time that had passed.

"Yeah, it was okay. Sounds like you guys are making some progress."

"I actually think we've figured it out," Logan said. "We're just double and triple checking our findings. We got really lucky with this one! As soon as we got some dates to cross reference, they jumped out at me."

"What do you mean?"

"Well, not to brag, but I consider myself a bit of an expert on our next destination, as it is one of my favorite places in the world, a place that has intrigued me from the time I was a child."

"You're just torturing her now," Zack said. "I think she just wants to know where."

"Okay, okay! Jeez! Where's your sense of drama?" Logan laughed. "It's the incredibly romantic city of Venice."

"No way! Venice? In Italy? You have no idea how much I've always wanted to go there." She was elated at the thought of going to Venice, so much so that she had temporarily forgotten about her situation with Victor.

"Yeah, well, I know it's not quite as sophisticated as Juneau." Logan laughed.

Zack interrupted him, pulling him away from the conversation back to the keyboard to show him something he had found.

The moment of pause brought a slap in the face from reality, as her situation with Victor came storming back into the forefront of her mind. If you had told Savannah that she could only travel to one place in her life, she would not have hesitated for a second to tell you that one place would be Venice. Her mind was already dreaming of the romantic adventure she and Logan would experience there. She selfishly hoped that Zack couldn't make it. It was not that she didn't like him; she thought he was a great guy and enjoyed his company, but she dreamed of having Logan totally to herself. Her mind again turned to the situation at hand.

I can't tell Victor about Venice, she thought, knowing he would ruin her dream of romance. *Maybe I can lie to him, send him somewhere else.* She plotted in her mind, only to conclude that if he ever found out, he would put her in the ground without batting an eye. *Who knows what would happen to Logan then?*

Watching the two men work was intoxicating. The passion with which they approached their task seemed almost unreal to her. In her entire life, she couldn't remember meeting anyone who loved what they did so much. She could tell it wasn't about the money. This was who Logan really was. This was his passion, what fulfilled him. She loved his adventurous spirit and his lust for life. He didn't drift. He truly lived his life to the fullest. She wanted to be part of that dream, part of that life. Every day she was falling deeper in love with Logan. It was completely out of her control. Her head told her to slow down, but her heart had different ideas. Savannah squinted as she looked out the window, only to see the light of daybreak glowing on the horizon. She was hit by a wave of exhaustion, more mental than physical.

"Guys, I hope you don't mind, but I have to get some sleep before I fall down."

"Shit!" Logan exclaimed, not realizing that the entire night had flown by. He groaned as he got up to give Savannah a good night kiss, the stiffness of his muscles letting him know that he had been glued to his chair and hunched over his keyboard all night, and all that after taking quite a beating throughout the day.

"Good night, baby. I'll be in soon," Logan said. He gave her a quick kiss.

Savannah wrapped her arms around him, holding him tight as tears again welled up in her eyes. She didn't want Logan to see her crying again, so she just held him tight until she composed herself. She glanced back at him as she closed the door to the attached bedroom, catching his eye and shooting him a seductive smile and wink. He did the same, which set her heart racing. She undressed and climbed into the luxurious bed. The cold crisp sheets felt good on her naked body. She closed her eyes and fell asleep almost immediately, descending into dreams of Venice, the haunting serenade of a gondolier providing ambiance as they drifted down the Grand Canal, the moonlight shimmering across the water.

CHAPTER 18

Savannah stared out the taxi window at the train that flanked them across the Ponte della Libertà on the way to Venice. Automotive traffic came to a halt at the end of the bridge. From there on, it would be the true romantic Venice: free of cars, traffic jams, and honking horns. The city was built on an archipelago of 117 islands connected by 455 bridges spanning canals from the narrowest, those resembling a back alley of water, to the Grand Canal that snaked its way through the heart of the city.

Logan was more than happy to leave the hustle and bustle of traffic for the romantic cobblestone streets and canals. He had always thought of Venice as the most romantic city on Earth, and he went out of his way to spend time there whenever he could. He could easily see why Colton Braxton had chosen it as one of the hiding places for the maps; he would have chosen it himself. Logan had no need for a map because over the years he had spent many a day aimlessly wandering its streets. He would often find little hidden gems that weren't on the tourist highlight list. Normally, he would be arriving at the Venice train station to begin his adventure, and because they were dropped off close to it, he had no problem getting his bearings.

Only steps away, it was easy to forget that automobiles even existed. It was a different world, a place that oozed romance. He longed to share that with Savannah, but he knew business had to come before pleasure. From the clues on the map, Logan knew the starting point to find the next map was at the Rialto Bridge, so as fate would have it he and Savannah could enjoy a nice long romantic walk from the train station to the bridge, albeit a bit more rushed than what would normally be the case.

She was awestruck by Venice. It was the same look Logan knew he had the first time he found himself wandering alongside the city's many canals. Better yet, she had Logan all to herself, knowing Zack probably could have made it, but chose to give them some time together. Logan's feelings for Savannah were genuine, but he also felt sorry for her. She had an emptiness in her that was begging to be filled, and to see that sparkle in her eye as he did now was as valuable as any treasure. As much as he loved the sights of Venice, he found himself spending more time observing her and the expressions on her face.

As they walked arm in arm down the crowded streets, the sound of romantic Italian ballads emanated from the myriad of restaurants. Despite all the distractions, Logan tried to work backward in his mind and was almost certain that the map was hidden in a building along the very street where they now strolled.

"Oh my God, it's like a postcard," Savannah gasped. They began to ascend the stairs of Rialto Bridge, to a breathtaking view of the Grand Canal winding its way through the heart of Venice, its shores lined with the unique architecture, while the canal bustled with boat traffic ranging from canal buses to gondoliers serenading couples young and old with their haunting songs.

She stood silently taking in the sights, sounds, and smells of the fascinating city. As the sun glistened over the canal, the songs of the gondoliers, the music of the waterside restaurants, and the salty smell of the water all mixed with the animated banter of the locals, who, to Savannah, always seemed angry or at least overly excited.

Logan was eager to begin the search, but he couldn't bring himself to pull her away too quickly. Even though he had stood in that location many times before, he was always taken back by the splendor of Venice.

He stood behind Savannah with his arms wrapped around her as she stared out over the water. Twenty minutes had passed when he finally rubbed his hand on her back.

"Okay, baby. We'll be back here. Let's go find ourselves a map."

Without saying a word, she swung around, wrapped her arms around his neck and passionately kissed him. It was a thank you that didn't need words. He grabbed her by the hand as they began following the instructions that they hoped would lead them to the next map. Logan was waiting for some sort of surprise since this map seemed all too easy, although being so familiar with Venice certainly didn't hurt.

"I knew it," Logan exclaimed. "This is it!" He recalled the clue: Up the stairs and to the right, you'll lay your head whilst picturing a moonlit night." The place the clue indicated was almost right where he thought it would be from his backward workings on their way to the Rialto Bridge.

Logan pointed up to a window on the second floor, or what the Europeans liked to call the first floor. "I bet you a shiny nickel that is the very room we need to be in." They went inside.

"Bon journo," Logan said to the hotel front desk clerk.

"Good afternoon, sir. My name is Mario. How may I be of assistance?" He replied in English, recognizing that Italian was not Logan's native tongue.

"Yes, I'm hoping you can help us. A year back, we stayed in a room on the second floor, uh, the first floor on the right that overlooks the canal. We were hoping to have the same room again for old times' sake. We had such an incredible time here."

"Oh, I'm so sorry, sir, but that room is rented. We do have a second-floor room directly above it, with an even better view," Mario replied.

"Mario, we were so hoping to have that same room. It's so important to us. We will definitely make it worth your while."

"I honestly would love to, sir, but a young couple on their honeymoon just checked in yesterday for a week's stay."

"A week?" The annoyance was plain in his voice. "Is there any way you could upgrade them at our expense?"

"Again, sir, I am very sorry, but I couldn't do that."

"Fine then. We'll take the room on the second floor," Logan replied.

Even as Mario checked them in, he again apologized, as he could see the displeasure on Logan's face.

Logan silently walked up the stairs, carrying both bags, followed closely behind by Savannah.

As soon as the hotel room door closed, with a worried look on her face Savannah asked, "What are we going to do?"

"We can't wait a week, but I think I came up with quite a clever plan."

"C'mon genius. Let's have it."

"If you must know, there's a little café right beside the hotel. We can sit there and watch when they leave for dinner, as I can see they are in their room right now, and then we'll make them an offer they can't refuse."

"Now you're just sounding like the Godfather. Why not just knock on their door?"

"First of all, I didn't mean that kind of offer. They're newlyweds, so who knows what the hell they're up to, and that might just freak them out."

"Yeah, stalking them from a distance is much better." Savannah laughed.

"I didn't say it was perfect. Got a better idea?"

"No," Savannah said sheepishly. "What are you going to offer them?"

"A week at the Rialto Hotel."

"Is that the beautiful hotel right on the Grand Canal?"

"You bet that cute little ass of yours."

"That's where we should be staying," Savannah said, giving Logan a firm slap across his backside.

"Maybe if we find the next map." Logan winked. "First we need to get some good costume jewelry."

They went to a nearby jewelry store. The eyes of the jewelry salesman lit up when Logan said he wanted to purchase an engagement ring and two wedding bands. The big smile and friendly demeanor were quickly replaced with a scowl and contempt in his voice as Logan explained he just wanted fake costume jewelry. The jewelry store clerk took many liberties to jab Logan on his cheapness and didn't mind saying how that was no way to treat the woman he loved. Logan thought that if and when the time came with Savannah, he would definitely buy her a stunning ring, but one thing was certain: it wouldn't be from this store. Just outside, Logan put on his wedding band and handed the rings for Savannah to put on. He almost put them on for her but stopped himself. If he ever put a ring on her finger, it would be a real one.

"Boy, Logan, you really know how to treat a girl," Savannah said. She slipped on the fake rings, desperately wishing that they were real, and Logan really wanted to marry her.

"Hey, only the best for my babe." Logan laughed, which only got a dirty look from her.

"Oh, thank God. They're still up there," Logan said as he looked up into the hotel room window.

They walked over to the café and sat down at the table with the best view of the hotel door and window. "The rings may not be real, but let's enjoy a real glass of Italian wine," Logan said.

They ordered a bottle of one of Tuscany's finest reds, and with one eye on the hotel room window and the other on Savannah, Logan raised his glass. "To Venice."

"To Venice," she replied softly, hope filling her voice.

CHAPTER 19

Logan snapped to attention as the hotel room lights went out. Less than a minute later, a young couple walked out the front door of the hotel, draped over each other.

"That must be them," Logan said, quickly placing some money under a wine glass to cover their bill. The young couple was almost parallel with them now, so he grabbed Savannah's hand as they scurried out to meet the couple as they passed by.

"Excuse me," Logan said as he approached the man. "My name is Logan Nash, and this is my wife Savannah. May I speak with you for a minute?"

"Hi, I'm Wagner," the man replied in perfect English, although with a German accent. He looked suspiciously at what looked like the typical Barbie and Ken American couple.

"I'm so sorry to bother you," Logan said. "I understand you're on your honeymoon."

"Yes," Wagner replied, now beginning to look a bit worried.

"We, too, are on our honeymoon. In fact, last year I proposed to Savannah in the same hotel room you are now staying in, and it was our dream to spend our honeymoon in that same room. It would mean the world to us."

"I don't know," Wagner said, looking at his new wife for advice.

"I'll tell you what I'll do for you guys. You know the Rialto Hotel by the bridge?" Logan asked, hoping that they had seen it in their walking about.

"Yes, far out of our price range, though," Wagner replied.

"I'll pay for you two to spend a week there in a room overlooking the canal."

Wagner's wife grabbed his arm with excitement.

Logan laughed. "I think I know what your wife wants. By the way, I didn't catch your name," he said. He offered the pretty woman his hand and flashing his dazzling white smile.

"Ingrid. Pleased to meet you… Logan?"

"Yes, and this is my wife, Savannah." She gave Ingrid a courteous nod.

"Savannah. I love that name. It's very unique," Ingrid said.

"Thank you."

"Oh, can we, Wagner? Don't you remember when we were standing on the bridge we talked about how much we wished we could stay there?"

"How can I refuse you?" Wagner replied. He rolled his eyes and gave Ingrid a quick kiss.

"Okay, you have a deal," Wagner said to Logan.

"Thank you, Wagner," Logan replied. They exchanged a firm handshake.

The four of them then walked down to the Rialto Bridge, the sun dipping below the horizon. Soon it was replaced by the full moon that shimmered like magic across the Grand Canal, silhouetting the numerous gondolas that slowly made their way along the picturesque waterway.

They paused at the top of the bridge. Venice had never looked so romantic.

They made their way to the Rialto Hotel, where Logan paid for the week's accommodations in an incredible canal view room for Wagner and Ingrid. Wagner in turn asked if he could buy Logan and Savannah dinner.

"We'd love to, but it's my treat for doing us a favor," Logan replied.

"I would have to say that you did us a much bigger favor," Wagner said.

"At least we agree it was a win-win situation," Logan replied. They walked down to one of the many restaurants that lined the canal.

For the next couple of hours, they sat at a charming canal side restaurant, spending time swapping tales of travel and starting a life together as a married couple. The latter Logan and Savannah made up as if they were actually married, perfectly adlibbing and feeding off each other's comments. After an entertaining and relaxing dinner, they walked back to their hotel, finally getting a chance to check out the room, after Wagner and Ingrid packed up their luggage.

Mario still was on shift at the front desk, and he seemed annoyed that Logan had done an end run around him to get the room he wanted. In a not so sincere voice, he greeted them. "Mr. Nash, I'm glad you were able to obtain the room you desired. However, I cannot refund your money for the other room. I hope you understand."

"No problem," Logan replied with a big smile on his face. As he shook Mario's hand, he gave the clerk a fifty Euro note. Mario's attitude changed instantly.

They quickly ran up the stairs to their old room, grabbed their bags, and headed down the narrow stairs to their new room. As soon as the door opened, Logan smiled.

"A view of moonlight over the canal at the foot of the bed. Almost like the real view we saw tonight," he said. He headed for the painting but decided to look for the obvious first and carefully lifted it off the wall. Before he even had a chance to set it down, Savannah squealed and pointed. Taped to the back of the painting was a piece of paper. Logan peeled it off, careful not to rip it.

"Thank you, Colton, for making this an easy one."

"I've got to get this scanned and sent off to Zack, although I don't even know if I'll need his expert computer skills on this one."

Reading over Logan's shoulder, Savannah gave him a puzzled look. "You can't possibly know the answer already, do you?"

"Not the exact answer, but I know a few things that should help me figure this out in no time. I really think that Colton Braxton made this quest just for me."

To the regular person, the clue would make no sense whatsoever, as it didn't to Savannah, but Colton Braxton III, being the intrepid adventurer he was, had his thoughts running along the same tracks as Logan.

Savannah stood there waiting for Logan to explain what he knew. As if on cue, Logan began to read the clue aloud.

"Forty years past to the day another kind of flight began and this one not a play. On the year this lady first did sail, the world's most famous found the one that failed. Through the graveyard you must go to the place the leader once did stand to watch many die where life now thrives."

Logan paused to soak it all in, causing Savannah to grow impatient. "Well, are you going to let me in on your wealth of knowledge?"

"Sorry. I drifted off somewhere for a bit. I don't know the exact location, but I know the map will be on a shipwreck that was discovered by Jacque Cousteau in the same year that a famous ship began to sail—ships are often referred to as ladies. The ship was sunk forty years to the day after a play with a flying theme began. Given these parts of the clues already figured out, I'm sure that I can have it in no time. Just to test my knowledge, I'm going to send Zack the clue, but not tell him what I know. We'll see who finds out what wreck it is first." Logan laughed.

"Oh, you're such a boy sometimes." Savannah shook her head, causing him to laugh even harder.

The quaint hotel was full of charm, but it lacked an Internet connection or Wi-Fi. Logan scanned the map to a PDF file, loaded it unto his USB drive, and headed out to one of the many Internet cafes along the streets.

"I'll be back in a few minutes," Logan said. He ran out the door as excited as a schoolboy. He could feel he was so close to the end of the treasure hunt. It was even greater than the adrenaline rush he had when he had first begun treasure hunting many years before. A few doors down from the hotel, he found an Internet café and sent off an e-mail with the attached scan to Zack. He immediately sent his friend a text message telling him to check his e-mails ASAP, which was kind of silly since Zack was virtually attached to his computer and was always alerted when new e-mails came in. Logan had completely forgotten to tell Savannah that he was going to spend some time working on the clues, but he was sure that she would figure it out.

Less than an hour passed when Logan yelled out a loud, "Yes!" It startled most of the patrons in the Internet café, drawing several dirty looks. At this point, he didn't really give a rat's ass, as the fourth and final map was not only on a wreck he had heard of, but one he had dived to several times before. It was in his favorite diving spot in the entire world. It was almost too good to be true, but he had checked and doubled checked. It all fit. He headed back to the hotel, not sure how Savannah was going to react, but there she was just sitting there all wide eyed, waiting for him to tell her some news.

"You'll never believe where the last map is hidden! It's way too good to be true." Without even waiting for a response, he carried on. "The play was "Madame Butterfly," the lady was in fact the QE II, and, of course, the most famous was indeed Jacque Cousteau, who discovered the wreck of San Francisco Maru, a Japanese ship sunk in World War II by the Americans, the deepest of Truk's famous wreck dives. I guess I'll be heading to the bridge of the good ol' San Francisco Maru again," Logan explained, grinning ear to ear.

Savannah looked as puzzled as ever, still no further ahead. "I'm sorry, babe, but I don't know exactly what you're saying. Where is the next map?"

"Oh, I'm sorry. I guess in the diving world everyone knows about San Francisco Maru. It is one of the most famous wrecks of Truk Lagoon. Well, actually, it recently changed its name to Chuuk from Truk, although most divers still call it Truk," Logan explained.

"You're going to think I'm really stupid, but I don't know where Truk Lagoon is." She looked as if she had disappointed Logan.

He laughed. "No, not at all, most people have never heard of it, unless they're a diver or a World War II history buff. I'll show you on a map later, but it's in the South Pacific past Guam. It's the ultimate wreck diving destination. I spent a month there a couple of years back and I've been dying to go back."

"I'm so excited for you! I wish I could dive," Savannah said.

"I'm going to see if Zack wants to head to Truk. Unfortunately, he's far from a hardcore tech diver, but hopefully he'll be game. You can be there with the champagne when we get the last map. Okay?"

"I will be," Savannah replied. She gave Logan a big kiss for being so understanding.

Just then, the phone rang. It was Zack. "Logan, you'll never believe where you'll be heading next! Never!"

"It's Zack," Logan whispered to Savannah. "I think I'll have some fun."

"Ah, let me guess. The wreck of San Francisco Maru in Truk?"

"Oh, very funny. How long have you known?" Zack asked, feeling his surprise was ruined.

"Hey, buddy, how do you feel about a trip to the wreck diving capital of the world?"

"You know diving is not my forte. Thirty feet looking at the colorful fish is good with me, but diving to over two hundred feet inside a wreck? I don't think I could do that."

"Are you sure? I could really use the support."

"I think I would be much more of a liability than an asset."

While Logan was busy talking with Zack, Savannah motioned to him that she was going for a walk. Logan nodded and blew her a kiss.

"Okay, but be ready to receive the last map so we know exactly where on Koh Lanta we will be going to."

"You bet. Talk to you soon."

"I'll call you as soon as I know anything." As soon as Logan hung up the phone, he again picked up the map and smiled, formulating a plan in his mind for their trip to Truk.

Meanwhile, Savannah stood beside the canal, tears streaming down her face as she dialed her phone, mentally preparing to make the regular call she hated to make. She knew she couldn't do it anymore, no matter what the consequences were, yet there she was, calling Victor to betray her lover again.

Victor picked up the phone after the first ring. "Good girl. You finally called on time. So, do you have some news for me?"

"Yes, Logan found the location of the next map. It's on a shipwreck in Aruba. I'm sorry, but he never lets the maps out of his sight, so I can't copy it," Savannah said.

"Ah, one of our ex-colonies. Maybe I'll have to head down there myself."

"Why not just let Logan find the final map for you?" Savannah asked.

"If I didn't know better, I would think you didn't want to see me there." He was quick to anger, as always.

"No, Victor, you know I just don't want anyone to get hurt. I'll make sure that you get the map. Please, please don't hurt him. He's a good man."

"Just let me know when you hear anything," Victor barked. He slammed the phone down. Immediately after he hung up, he picked up the phone and began to dial.

Savannah slumped to the ground and began to cry. She felt like she just signed not only her death warrant, but Logan's as well. She knew what she had to do. She slowly shuffled back to the hotel, unable to slow the onslaught of tears. Along the way, several people asked if she was okay. She waved them away and carried on. She kept her head low on her way through the hotel lobby, and before long, she stood at the hotel room door. She couldn't bring herself to open it for a long moment, but then she got a grip on herself and went inside. Logan was still smiling from the good news, but when he saw Savannah, he knew she'd been crying again. He wondered what brought those strange attacks of emotions on. What was she hiding?

"What happened, Savannah?" Logan's heart began beating rapidly. He was worried that something had happened while she was out, but he also knew it could be another one of her breakdowns, which he found hard to handle.

Her voice cracked, and her eyes flooded with tears. "Logan, please sit down. I have something I have to tell you."

"What is it, baby? You can tell me anything."

Savannah began shaking her head, crying even harder now. "No, no, no! You're going to hate me. No, more than hate me. You'll despise me!"

"Please, Savannah. Let me into your life. I want to be a part of it."

"Logan," Savannah began, pausing to compose herself. "We didn't meet by accident in Bangkok. I was sent to seduce you by Victor Kane. I've been in touch with him all along." Through her tears that again began to flow, she went on to open up to Logan about the horrors of her past, from her traumatic childhood, to how she became entangled with Victor Kane.

CHAPTER 20

Logan immediately felt a chill run down his spine. He knew what was coming next, but hoped he was wrong. His heart pounded, and his head spun as if he stood at the edge of a cliff and might fall off.

"I love you, Logan. I'm begging for your forgiveness." Tears streamed down her face.

Logan sat speechless, stunned. *How could I not see what was happening? How could I be so completely duped by someone?*

"Logan? Logan?" Savannah called out to him, but he said nothing.

He simply sat staring at her in utter disbelief, trying to take it all in. He felt so betrayed, and the worst part was that he had fallen madly in love with her. In fact, until that moment, the split second after she'd told him, he had not even realized himself how deep his feelings were for her, which made her betrayal all the more painful.

"Logan, I know you probably hate me now, but I just thought you should know that when I called Victor tonight I told him that the final map was hidden in a shipwreck in Aruba. It started out all wrong, but I fell in love with you. There were so many times I wanted to tell you or just run away. I never wanted to be a part of you getting hurt, but Victor said he would kill me if I didn't do what he said. It doesn't matter for me now. When he finds out I lied to him he'll make sure I die a slow painful death. I just want you to have a chance to find the treasure without him breathing down your neck." She desperately hoped that he had a little forgiveness in his heart.

"Savannah, I don't know what to say, let alone what to do. I have never felt so betrayed in my life." Logan softly spoke, a deep hurt apparent in his voice.

"I know. I'm not saying I deserve a second chance. In fact, I know I fully deserve whatever Victor will do to me, but I want a second chance. I know my word means less than nothing to you right now, but you can trust me, Logan. I would do anything for you."

"No, you don't deserve to be handed over to that madman."

Logan had never been one for second chances. He had always lived by the old saying, "Once burnt, twice shy." A whole new set of questions joined in the tornado that whipped around in his head. *Can I ever trust her again? Should I give her a second chance? If I do, how would our relationship be? Could it ever be like it was? Even half of what it was? Could I just leave her to be ripped apart by Victor?*

The long silence worried Savannah. Finally, she said, "Logan, please let me know what you're thinking." She fought back her tears and looked at him intently.

"My mind says run, but my heart says to forgive you. It took a lot of courage to do what you did tonight, and now I understand a bit more about those other times."

"I think you should listen to your heart."

Logan saw things in Savannah that he had never seen in anyone before. He saw things in her that he was sure she didn't even see in herself. Despite her extremely hard life, with her abusive father, on the street, and then under Victor's thumb, there was an innocence about her. Despite everything that had happened to her, she had not given up on life. She was still so full of hope and promise, something that he would have thought would have been long beaten out of her. That inner strength made the decision for him.

"Savannah, I love you." Before he could continue, Savannah shed more tears and grabbed Logan around the neck and squeezed him tight.

Those were the words that she was longing to hear, and no matter what came after, they could never be taken back.

Logan held her tight for a while and then pulled her away, holding her at arm's length by the shoulders. "Savannah, I love you, and because of that I'm going to do something I wouldn't normally do. I will give you a second chance. I don't know if I will be able to trust you fully again, but I will try. I guess sometimes the heart has a mind of its own."

"I totally understand. I know I don't deserve your trust, but I'm going to show you with my actions that you can trust me. I can't blame you for being skeptical. I don't think I would trust me either if I were you."

"I guess I'm just scared we're going to lose what we have now, and that it will never be the same."

"I know, and that scares me too. If it doesn't work out, I will never blame you. Just giving me a second chance after the way I betrayed you is more than I could ever hope for."

"Do you mind if I go out for a walk alone? I really need to clear my head," Logan asked.

"I understand. I'll be waiting here for you when you get back." She smiled, although inside she feared he would change his mind as soon as he left the room.

"I might even stop and check into some flights to Truk if you still want to go."

Without saying a word, she nodded, wiping away her tears. The fact that he still wanted her to be a part of his quest was something she didn't expect.

Logan walked out the door in a haze, feeling like he was recovering from a six-day bender. He had always been blessed with an innate sixth sense, which seemed to have been shut down by the events of the night. He didn't notice the indiscreet man that began following him as soon as he left the hotel. Logan walked for a long while, weaving up and down the narrow side streets of Venice. It was lucky for his pursuer that he was utterly lost in his own mind, since the surveillance effort was as comical as a B-grade movie. On any other night, he would have noticed the man following him straight away.

After some time, Logan slowly walked into an Internet café and sat down. His poor excuse for a shadow sat at a row of computers behind him, so he could watch exactly what Logan was doing. After a bit of searching, Logan found a website that offered the best prices and easiest time schedule and booked tickets. Despite it being a slightly longer flight, flying out of London worked out to be cheapest by far, so Logan had them flying via Venice. London. Bangkok, Guam, Chuuk, Guam, back to Bangkok, then down to Krabi. Knowing the location of the treasure was definitely a bonus, or so he thought. As Logan printed out his itinerary, the man hastily went to leave the café, causing a shout from the attendant when he forgot to pay. He quickly paid and hurried out the door. Through all the ruckus, Logan still didn't realize that he had been followed.

Outside the café, the man couldn't wait until he was ten steps away to call Victor, knowing he would be rewarded handsomely. "Mr. Kane? It's Paul. You were right. She was lying to you." Paul spoke like a kid tattling on his sibling.

"That bitch! I knew I couldn't trust that damn bitch!" Victor screamed. "Where the hell are they heading?"

"Chuuk. I don't know where that is, but I'll find out for you, sir." Paul said, stuttering out of fear as he realized the level of Victor's anger.

"I know where Chuuk is, you fricken' moron." Victor seethed at the utter incompetence of some his hired thugs, asking himself how so many people could be so stupid.

"I'm sorry, sir. So sorry, of course—"

Victor interrupted him, tired of hearing his babbling. "Shut up and listen. Do you have anyone else in Venice you can trust?"

"Yes, sir, a friend of mine, who's also named Paul. He is reliable and trustworthy. He would be honored to work for you, Mr. Kane." Paul's voice was trembling. He had seen Victor Kane's cruelty firsthand.

Oh, just fricken' splendid, Victor thought. Two idiots named Paul. He felt he almost needed to go there himself, but in Europe, he was closely watched in all his activities.

"Are you listening?" Victor barked.

"Y… yes, sir," Paul stuttered.

"I want you to get Savannah and take her to a good hiding place until I give you further instructions. Do you understand?"

"Yes, Mr. Kane. No problem at all."

"Yes, Paul, there may be a problem. I don't think Logan Nash is going to let you waltz up and take her away. Do you?"

"No, sir. We will kill him then," Paul replied, hoping to please Victor.

"Idiot. Are you the stupidest frickin' ape on the planet? I don't have all the pieces to the puzzle, and if you kill him, I'll never find the treasure. Do you understand?" Victor was now far past irate. He hated incompetence, and his anger often flustered people and made them appear even more incompetent than they really were.

"I need them both alive. For now. Can you handle the job? If you can't, I'll find someone else who can."

"Yes, Mr. Kane. You can count on me," Paul replied.

Victor rolled his eyes, having serious doubts about the man he had chosen for such an important task. "Okay, I'm counting on you to get this done. Hopefully tonight. I don't need to tell you what happens if you fail. Do I?"

"No, Mr. Kane, you don't." Paul knew that if he failed in a task of this magnitude, it would most certainly mean his life.

Paul was a typical Italian tough guy. He stood about five-foot nine and was built like a no-neck bulldog that had had its nose broken on more than one occasion. Not only did his friend Paul have the same name, but they were also cut out of the same cloth. More than once people had commented that they looked like brothers, although neither would ever admit to there being any resemblance. Paul ended the call to Victor and dialed Paul's number, anxious to reach his friend, whom everyone called Pauly. He'd been called that ever since they'd begun hanging around together as teenagers.

"Pauly? It's Paul. Yeah, yeah, yeah, I'm fine. I've got a big job for us. It will open a lot of doors for us."

"What's the job and who will we be working for?" Pauly asked.

"I don't want to give specifics on the phone, but I'll say two words. Victor Kane."

"Victor Kane?" Pauly sounded nervous. "Then I guess we better not screw this one up. I'll meet you at the usual place. Let's say twenty minutes."

"Twenty minutes. And bring the boat."

"The boat?"

"I'll tell you when you get here." Paul ended the conversation, trying to come up with a feasible plan before Pauly arrived.

Paul looked back through the Internet café window. Logan was back on the computer again. Paul squinted to make out what was on the screen, and it seemed that Logan was reading e-mails. Paul stared at his watch, hoping it would make Pauly appear faster. He thought if they could grab Savannah at the hotel before Logan got back it would make life a lot easier.

Paul began getting nervous as Logan finished his Internet session and went to pay. "Shit, what do I do now?" Paul whispered to himself. It seemed fate was on Paul's side. Logan turned the opposite way and walked toward the Rialto Bridge. Paul breathed a sigh of relief. *At least that buys me a bit more time*, Paul thought.

Suddenly, he realized he was so preoccupied with watching Logan that he had forgotten to go to their regular meeting place. "Oh, crap! Maybe Victor is right. Maybe I am an idiot," he mumbled. He scurried along the narrow streets.

Pauly was waiting at their usual meeting spot with his boat. "I thought you said it was an emergency," he said, holding up his wrist and pointing at his gaudy watch.

"Don't ask," Paul said, hopping in the boat and giving Pauly directions to the hotel.

Paul hoped that Logan hadn't made it back yet. He hadn't been too long, so he thought she would still be alone if they hurried. Paul gave Pauly the details about the job.

"What about the front desk clerk?" Pauly asked. "He may do something when we haul a woman out of there kicking and screaming."

"We'll just have to take him out before we go upstairs," Paul said.

The men parked the boat right outside the hotel and walked into the hotel foyer where Mario was working. "May I be of assistance, gentlemen?" Mario asked.

Without saying a word, Pauly delivered the first blow. Paul joined in. The men savagely beat Mario unconsciousness with repeated blows to the head. Mario slumped to the floor in a heap, and Pauly gave him two solid kicks to the ribs for good measure. Blood flowed from Mario's deep wounds as he lay motionless on the floor.

"We got to hurry before someone comes into the lobby," Paul said. They hurried up the stairs.

Paul knocked on the door, his knuckles still dripping with Mario's blood. He was still trying to come up with a believable line when the door swung open.

"I'm glad you're ba—" Savannah had only opened the door because she thought Logan had forgotten his key after all that had happened, but when she saw the burly men with blood on their hands, fear flooded over her. She tried to slam the door. They pushed violently on the door, snapping it back and sending her flying across the room. Savannah kept her wits. Her many years on the street had made her a lot tougher and meaner than she looked.

Pauly rushed in, and he reached down to grab the pretty blond. With all her might, Savannah lashed out, kicking at Pauly and landing a fierce blow right to his mouth. Blood and teeth flew across the room. Pauly screamed. She kicked him again on the inside of his knee, sending him crumbling to the floor. Savannah braced herself to stand up when suddenly all went black.

CHAPTER 21

Logan's heart began to race as he saw a trail of blood leading into the hotel from the edge of the canal. He ran into the lobby and saw Mario bleeding badly behind the desk, but he knew he was still alive because he could hear him moaning. Logan saw that the blood trail was not from Mario. It led to the stairway in spatters of gore, and he knew it would lead straight to his door. Sprinting up the stairs, Logan called an ambulance on his cell phone. When he got to his room, he froze in the doorway. The room looked like a murder had been committed there. There was blood on the floor, on the wall, and all over the furniture. There was even blood spatter on the ceiling. Map or no map, it was time to get the police involved. Logan reached for his cell and even before he could punch in a single number, his phone rang.

"Logan!" Savannah screamed into the phone, terror in her voice.

"Savannah? Savannah? Savannah?" Logan frantically screamed.

"You want her to live?" Victor asked, as he clicked off the recording of Savannah's voice.

Logan would never forget Victor's sinister voice, the voice of the man who had left him for dead years earlier in the Caribbean. "You hurt her, you fucking maggot, and I'll slit your throat ear to ear." Victor didn't scare or intimidate Logan one bit. He was afraid for Savannah, but Victor Kane was nothing but a cockroach that needed to be squashed.

Victor snarled. "How dare you threaten me? I should just kill her for the hell of it."

"You lay one hand on her and I'll destroy all the maps, and no one will ever find the treasure. I would gladly do that just to chap your ass, and don't worry about looking for me because I'll find you."

Victor laughed. "Logan Nash. That's why I respect you as an adversary. You're not so spineless as ninety-nine percent of the people in this world. I can't even stay mad at you."

Logan stood silent, his blood boiling. Victor may have thought the situation was humorous, but he would gladly follow through on his threats without batting an eye.

"Who am I to stand between true love? Obviously, she must love you to betray me like she did. So, here's how it's going to work. First of all, you will tell the police that it was a robbery. You will not mention anything about Savannah being kidnapped. Secondly, you will give me all the original maps, and then you can be reunited with your little girlfriend."

"You must be smoking crack. The minute you get those maps, you'll kill her and then come for me. How stupid do you think I am? Those maps are my only leverage."

"I had a feeling that you wouldn't go for that one. What I think we—"

"No, let me tell you how it will go down. First, I don't give a shit about you. You can have the treasure. All I want is Savannah and to be left alone to live our lives. I'm going to compile as much proof as I can against you, and I'll have that locked away only to be opened if something happens to either Savannah or myself." Logan knew that Victor wouldn't stop until he and Savannah were dead, but he had to make Victor think otherwise.

"And what about the treasure?" Victor asked.

"We'll cross that bridge later. I will make sure that there is a safe escape for us both. Also, if you had any plans for your thugs to get the maps from me, well, that won't be happening. They are already safely locked away." The maps were actually sitting three feet away from him in his backpack.

"Fine, we'll play it your way for now, but double cross me and I'll spend every resource I have hunting you down."

Logan skipped the formalities and just hung up. He immediately called Zack.

"Hey, Logan! How's romantic Venice treating you love birds?"

"Drop whatever you're doing and get on the next plane to Venice," Logan said.

Zack knew that there was a serious problem. "What's going on?"

"They ha—" Logan stopped talking as two policemen rushed into the room. "Zack, I'll call you back." He ended the call but kept the phone to his ear, as if he was still on the line. "Yes, dear. I'll be fine. No, I don't blame you for wanting to get out of town after what happened."

"Sir, are you okay?" the policeman asked in a strong Italian accent.

"Yes, I'm fine. How is Mario? The front desk clerk." Logan asked, genuinely concerned.

"Sir, it was you that called the ambulance? Yes?"

"Yes," Logan replied. He was frustrated that he had to spend even a minute with this situation, instead of finding Savannah.

"Why not the police?"

"Sorry, I just thought that the ambulance was a lot more important."

"So, whose blood is this?" one of the policemen asked.

"One of the burglars. When they were trying to rob the place, my fiancé, who happens to have some self-defence training, got a few good shots in and frightened the men away." Logan made up the story on the fly.

"Where is she now?"

"She was very shaken up, and she said she needed to get out of town."

"So soon? Did not this just happen minutes ago?" The police fired back, now leery of anything Logan said.

"Yes, she said she didn't want to spend another minute here, so a friend that had just come to Venice to meet us is driving her to Switzerland. I'll meet them in a day or two. I know you're going to say you need her to give a description of the men, but she assures me that she could not identify either man." Logan kept talking, hoping that they bought his extremely far-fetched story.

"You know, sir, your story is hard to believe. We really need to speak with her to make sure she is okay. You understand? Oh, and one more thing. We would appreciate it if you didn't leave town until we can verify your story," one officer said. "And don't touch anything else in the room. We don't want you contaminating the crime scene."

Oh my God, Logan thought. *They think I did something to Savannah!*

Logan complied with the officers, left the room and went downstairs. Mario had already been taken away and there was a new man behind the desk. The police had obviously said something to the new clerk regarding Logan. The clerk had a bad attitude, as if he felt he was harboring a criminal responsible for the disappearance of a woman and the brutal beating of his co-worker. Logan tried to be polite to the new clerk. "I'm sorry to hear what happened to Mario. I hope—"

The new front desk clerk turned and walked away.

Logan went back up to the room he and Savannah had initially rented, before they'd managed to finagle their way into the room where they'd found the map. Fortunately, he had kept the key since he was paying for the room. He could hear the police rummaging around directly below him. He shook his head and called Zack back.

"Logan, what the hell's going on?"

"You mean other than Victor Kane kidnapping Savannah and almost beating the front desk clerk to death? Oh, and as an added bonus, the police think I'm responsible for all of it. I'm just lucky they didn't haul me away," Logan said.

"Holy shit! What do you need me to do?"

"Get here as quick as you can. We need to find Savannah, and I absolutely need you here because I know the police will be watching me until they can verify the bullshit story I gave them. God, usually I come up with something better."

"What did you say?"

"It doesn't matter. I'll fill you in when you get here."

"I already checked, and I can be on a flight to London in less than two hours, and from there it will be easy to connect to one of the Venice airports," Zack replied.

"Great. See you soon." Logan ended the call, glad he could always rely on Zack. He wasn't even sure where he would begin to look for Savannah. If he had to, he knew he could always buy time for her by finding the last map, but he hated to leave Venice without her. If she was even still in Venice. Suddenly, his cell phone rang. He was expecting it to be Zack calling back, but he didn't recognize the number. "Hello?"

"So how did it go with the police?" Victor asked.

"Not good, now they think I had something to do with Savannah's disappearance because they wanted to talk to her about the beaten hotel clerk. You can thank your stupid goons for the mess we're in."

"Don't worry, I will," Victor said.

"The only way I'll be able to leave Venice and look for the next map is for Savannah to call the police and talk to them."

"Out of the question. They're not going to be happy with a phone call. They are going to want her to come in."

"Look, Kane, you know as well as I do how much of a smooth talker Savannah is. You don't think she can smooth talk a couple of macho Italian cops?"

"You aren't wrong. She could sell air conditioning at the South Pole. I will contact my people and have her call the local police. I will be listening in on the call, and if she says one thing she shouldn't, it's game over for her. By the way, do you have a contact number for the detective in charge? It will add a lot of credibility if she actually knows who she is to be talking to."

"I agree," Logan said. He dug out the card the detective gave him, not believing he had just agreed with Victor Kane. "Have your goons call me so I can tell her that she should go along with the plan. I really need her to do this. No offense, Kane, but she might not believe you."

"You'll hear from her in a few minutes." Victor hung up the phone, annoyed that had he let Logan have so much control over the situation.

As Kane had promised, a few minutes later the phone rang. "Savannah?"

"No," a gruff Italian voice responded. "Make sure you watch what you say to her. We'll be listening."

Logan was happy that it was a goon and not Victor listening in on the call. He thought that Victor might listen in, but he had to take the chance that he trusted his own henchmen to do the job. After all, he couldn't be everywhere. The henchmen didn't seem like the sharpest tools in the shed, so he figured he could put his plan in action without Victor's dimwitted thugs catching on. He also figured that Savannah would get the meaning behind the words he would emphasize, seeing them as a sort of code. It may have been a long shot, but it was the only thing he could think of.

There was silence for a moment or two, and then he heard Savannah's voice. "Logan, I'm so scared."

"Savannah, it's very, very important that you listen to me."

"Okay, I'm listening."

"They are going to give you a number of a policeman who's heading up the case of the hotel incident. The cops think I beat up Mario and kidnapped you, and now they are watching me. I can't even leave town. I need you to be more convincing than you ever have been. Tell the cops that you walked in on a robbery attempt, but you're fine. I know you can take it from there. I love you, Savannah, and no matter where you are, know that I am thinking about you. It will be okay. Do you understand everything you are to do?

"Yes, Logan, I understand. I will be extremely convincing, I won't be surprised if they apologize for hassling you. Listen, Logan, like I told you in the letters I wrote to you."

Oh my God, I think she got that I want her to send me a message. Logan surmised, listening intently.

"MY feelings for you ARE as real TODAY as ever. OUR bad experiences in VENICE will never UNDO what we have. I love you." Savanah said, not no subtly stressing certain words, which still seemed to fly right over the heads of Victor's goons.

"Yeah, yeah, yeah. Very touching," Paul yelled. He ripped the phone out of Savannah's hand and hung up on Logan.

"Letters, not words," Logan mumbled. He thought about the words she had emphasized, and that he had written down. "My Are Today Our

Venice Undo. Matovu! Shit!" Logan wondered if he had written down the wrong words. He wondered if he was losing his mind, but he'd been careful. He thought he had been so careful. Would she have used the last letter of each word? Probably not, she would have made it simple as possible.

Logan called Zack.

"Hello?"

"Oh, thank God I got you before you were in the air," Logan said. "Can you get on the Internet where you are?"

"Does a bear crap in the woods?" Zack replied.

"Sorry, I forgot the level of nerd I was talking to. What does Matovu mean to you?"

"Could you spell that for me?"

"M – A – T – O – V -U."

Logan could hear Zack's fingers already gliding over the keyboard.

"Hmm. I guess you learn something new every day."

"That was fast even for you. So, what does it mean?"

"Actually Logan, it's two words: Ma Tovu. It's a prayer that's said when you enter a synagogue. I don't understand why this would be important. What gives?"

"Savannah is a genius! Oh my God, I have no idea how she would know that, but I think I know where she's being held."

"In a synagogue?"

"Yes! There is a Jewish ghetto, actually two Jewish ghettos, in Venice. She has to be in one of the synagogues in those areas."

"I know you can handle yourself, but please don't do anything before I get there, especially with the police still watching you."

"Okay, then tell that pilot to step on it."

"Speaking of that, my plane is starting to board." Zack hung up, fumbling along with his computer equipment as he hurried toward the gate.

Logan had walked around the old Jewish section many times, but he didn't know exactly how many synagogues there were. He pulled out a tourist map that had been placed in the room, but it wasn't much help, so he thought he would head over to an Internet café. On his way, his phone rang again. With everything that was happening, it made him feel a bit apprehensive every time the phone rang.

"Mr. Nash, it's Detective Milano."

Logan noticed the man's voice was much friendlier than it had been the last time they spoke. "Yes, detective? What can I do for you?"

"Sorry to call you so late, but we just spoke to your fiancé and she cleared everything up. Maybe I shouldn't tell you this, but I think she will call and apologize to you soon. She realizes now that it wasn't your fault that you weren't there to protect her, and that you can't be at her side twenty-four hours a day. Of course, I too owe you an apology. I jumped to conclusions before we knew all the facts. We have identified one of the men, thanks to your fiancé. One of them left several good fingerprints in the blood. She also left us quite a substantial DNA sample to work with." The detective laughed. "Seems she got one of the burglars really good."

"Yes, she's a tough chick. You see how you should be worried about me getting hurt, not the other way around." Logan joked with the detective just to put on a good show, but all he really wanted was to get out there and find Savannah.

A few minutes later, down in the Internet cafe, Logan had the locations of every synagogue in Venice. He looked at his watch. "Shit." He knew that he had promised Zack he would wait, but he couldn't. Every second was valuable, and now that the police weren't on his back anymore, he was free to go wherever he wanted. He was certain that Victor would have some of his goons watching his every move, but he was confident that he could lose them with minimal effort.

Logan ran back up to his hotel room and threw open his suitcase. He always liked to be prepared, so he took a lock blade he had with him and strapped it to his lower leg. He then pulled out a can that looked like a can of body spray. Every time he looked at it he laughed, just waiting for the minute that some unsuspecting baggage checker thought he'd freshen himself up. Instead of smelling sweet, he'd be enjoying the disabling power of extra-strength pepper spray disguised as body spray.

Logan wore a pair of nondescript jeans, put on a lightweight windbreaker, and then a heavier bright red jacket. He stuffed a ball cap in the jacket pocket. He would make sure that Victor's men got a good look at him, and then, after he ditched them, he would also ditch the bright red jacket and put on the cap. It wasn't the most high-tech of disguises, but it would be something they weren't looking for. Logan looked at his watch again, knowing Zack was still in the air, his flight winging its way ever eastward toward Venice. He took out his cell phone and punched in Zack's number. His friend would get the message as soon as he landed. Logan said, "Sorry, Zack, I just can't wait any longer about checking out the synagogues. Thanks for everything. You've been a good friend. Hope to see you soon. Will leave a voicemail on your cell if I find anything. Bye."

Logan could hardly believe that only a few hours earlier he was on top of the world, ready to head off to his favorite diving destination with the woman he loved to find untold riches. It all seemed like that was weeks ago. He was tired, dog-tired. It was almost two o'clock in the morning. *It's late. Maybe it's too late*, he thought.

Logan took a deep breath and headed out into the crisp night.

CHAPTER 22

The night air hung like a thick wet blanket. The cool breeze filled Logan's nostrils with the strong smell of sea air, and the tangy scent took his mind back to the Pacific Northwest and a typical late summer's night there. Those were happier times for him. Times he wanted to get back.

Within five minutes, he spotted what he thought had to be two of Victor's cronies. He would walk for a while longer to see if the parade got any longer. After fifteen minutes, Logan was sure that only two men were tailing him. *Time for a bit of exercise*, he thought. He picked up the pace and started weaving up and down the narrow streets. It was almost comical watching the two bulky men not only trying to keep up, but also trying to look inconspicuous in the process.

If the street was too narrow, they had to let Logan get a fair distance away from them, so as not to appear like they were chasing him. As soon as he turned a corner and was out of their sight, he sprinted as fast as he could and then slowed down to a walk. The men seemed perplexed about why they were losing so much ground. When he turned the corner down a long narrow street, he saw the two men about a block behind him. They were all but abandoning their stealth strategy. Logan broke into a full sprint, and he didn't stop until he turned the corner at the end of the long street. The two bulky men also began their version of a sprint, trying to close in on him and expecting to do so at any moment.

When they rounded the corner all they found was an empty street. There was nothing but the echo of the wind through the ancient buildings. They began checking doors and gates as they went down the street, never even entertaining the thought that Logan could make it down the long street that fast. By the time they had made it to the end of the street, he was a mile away, heading toward the Jewish ghetto.

They weren't expecting company, but Logan had to assume that Victor would have been careful and posted guards inconspicuously a block or two from the synagogue. Logan approached the first synagogue as stealthily as a cat burglar. No guard, no lights on, no sign of life. From a hidden vantage point, he lobbed a small rock just hard enough to make a loud noise, but not hard enough to break the glass. He melted back into his hiding place and waited.

Nothing, Logan thought. *One down, four to go.*

The next synagogue was being used as a museum. After a few minutes of recon, Logan could see one guard that looked more ancient than the building itself. Definitely not one of Victor's men, but still, they could have her hidden somewhere in the bowels of the building. To make sure, Logan dug around a trashcan until he found an empty wine bottle. He took the bottle with him and pretended to stumble toward the synagogue, incoherently mumbling as he approached. In a feeble voice, the guard said something Logan couldn't understand, then moved silently away, unable to speak and not wanting any confrontation.

"Two down, three to go," Logan said, energized by his covert operation, despite his lack of sleep.

He moved on, walking swiftly for about two blocks until he arrived at the next synagogue. He quickly threw himself against a building. "Shit! More guards?" He watched a man standing in the darkest shadows of the quiet street. The man was smoking a cigarette and not paying much attention to anything around him. Three cigarettes later and Logan was convinced that the man was probably one of Victor Kane's thugs. *No one stands out on a cold night and chain smokes three cigarettes like that,* he thought. *Unless you must.* Logan backtracked, coming around toward the synagogue from another direction. He saw two other sentries. After another hour of careful recon, Logan was convinced that there were only three of them.

Suddenly, the two men that were supposed to be watching Logan came up and began to speak to one of the guards. The guard was obviously in a position of authority over them, as he began to rip into them, saying that they should never have left Logan unguarded under any circumstances. Logan knew just enough Italian to understand the basics of the conversation. The two men who had been chasing him said it was okay to leave him unguarded because they'd seen him get ready for bed and turn out the lights. It was apparent to Logan that they were afraid to inform their superiors that they had lost him because they feared what Victor might do to them. They told the guard that they were returning to their posts.

The eastern sky began to shed its charcoal cloak as the sun inched its way above the horizon. With the break of day, Logan could feel the energy draining from his body. He had been running at top speed for most of the day and night. He was so close to rescuing Savannah, but he knew he likely faced a half-dozen men. No doubt all of them would be armed to the teeth. Logan knew he would need more than a pocketknife and some pepper spray.

He decided to head back to the hotel, grab a couple hours of sleep, if he could, and hopefully come up with a plan by the time Zack arrived later in the morning. On the walk back to the hotel, he passed one of Victor's men from the previous night, not letting on at all that he recognized him. Out of the corner of his eye, he could see the man's head whip around so fast Logan was amazed he didn't get whiplash.

At the hotel, he lay in bed unable to sleep. His body was exhausted, but his mind still raced. The woman he loved was out there, alone and scared. As he tossed and turned, various scenarios ran through his mind. Most importantly, he needed to get Savannah out of there safely.

"Logan? Logan!" a voice shouted through the door, jarring him out of his deep sleep. Even in his groggy state, he recognized Zack's voice. He held his watch in front of his bleary eyes.

"Shit!" he shouted, seeing that he had overslept by two hours. The last thing he remembered was thinking he might as well get up since his alarm would go off in thirty minutes. He hadn't even remembered falling asleep, and for a brief second he forgot where he was, but unfortunately, the grim situation was more than the slap in the face he needed to be wide awake. Logan opened the door for Zack.

"Jesus, I've been pounding on that door for five minutes! I thought maybe they got you too," Zack said.

"I found out where they're keeping her," Logan said. "After I spoke to you, I did a bit of recon."

"I thought you were going to wait for me. I know I'm not exactly a ninja, but at least I could scream like a girl for help if something happened."

"Sorry, Zack, I just couldn't sit around and wait."

"So, what did you find out?"

"It looks like there are three sentries posted in the perimeter around the synagogue, and I can only imagine there are going to be at least that many on the inside, if not more."

"And am I to assume they are all armed?"

"Without a doubt, my friend."

"So how are we, two unarmed civilians, not even on home turf, going to take on a half dozen or more armed men?"

"The element of surprise."

"Yeah, right."

"No, really. We can do this," Logan said. "Trust me."

"Uh huh."

"I don't know if you noticed the two goons outside the hotel, but I'm sure they noticed you."

"Sorry, Logan, you know I'm not nearly as good at this cloak and dagger stuff as you, but hey, give me a keyboard and I'll do wonders for you."

"Here's the plan. We are going to book you a ticket to Chuuk, and we'll change mine, making it appear we are leaving in a few hours. You make sure those two Neanderthals see what we are doing and let the others know. Hopefully, the idiots will let their guard down long enough for us to get into the synagogue and rescue her. The element of surprise is a powerful thing."

They went to the Internet café and booked the tickets. Logan had to laugh because the goons following them were so obvious. To complete the charade, Logan and Zack carried their bags out of the hotel and grabbed a water taxi. As they sped off down the canal, Logan glanced back and saw the goons scrambling to find a boat to follow them.

"Hopefully they'll be on the phone to Victor and his henchmen, letting them know we're on our way to the airport," Logan said. He was pleased that the first part of his plan seemed to work so well.

Logan had the boat driver weave around the canals headed toward the edge of the Jewish ghetto. "Stop right here," Logan yelled. They paid the boat driver handsomely and went into a small hotel and checked in under assumed names. Being a bit more of a rundown place, the desk clerk didn't ask for identification or a credit card.

"Okay, Zack, you ready for this?"

"Ready as I'll ever be," Zack replied.

"I think if we take the sentry around the back side, we can get to the synagogue without being seen. Besides, he looks like the easiest guard to take out."

"That's not like you, Logan. I thought you always liked a challenge." Zack managed a joke, despite the seriousness of the situation.

They approached within fifty feet of the sentry. "Okay, he doesn't know what you look like, so I want you to wander aimlessly down the street like some tourist, and when you get in front of him, start asking some stupid questions. Then I'll come up from behind and take him out."

Zack hated violence, but he enjoyed the adventure. He realized this situation required decisive action. There was no other choice.

Logan watched intently as Zack casually walked toward Victor's henchman. He would never forgive himself if anything ever happened to

Zack, but he knew that even if he didn't feel comfortable with the situation, he would still be there a hundred percent. Zack began playing the part of the annoying American tourist. The sentry was getting noticeably upset, trying hard to get rid of him.

The timing was perfect, as the out of the way street was now abandoned, except for Zack and the sentry. Logan crept down the street with the stealth of a jungle cat, and with a sharp blow to the back of the neck, the man dropped in a heap.

"Quickly, before someone comes. Roll back the tarp on that boat and we'll toss him in there," They tossed the thug into the boat, gagging and hog tying him. Then they covered him with the tarp.

They arrived at the back door just as one of Victor's men stepped outside. His eyes widened as he saw Logan standing five feet in front of him. He reached for his gun, but Logan was too quick with a debilitating kick to the groin, swiftly followed by grabbing the man by his hair and driving his face into his knee, culminating in a sickening crack of bone and cartilage as blood sprayed across the steps. Logan peered inside. "Okay, let's drag him inside," he said. They dragged the blood-soaked, unconscious body inside the door, and then relieved the guard of the nine-millimeter pistol.

Logan held up his hand for Zack to stop for a moment. Logan didn't like it. Everything was deathly quiet. *Do they know we're here? Is there a trap waiting for us?* He motioned to Zack to proceed. They crept around as silently as they could, temporarily freezing every time they made even the slightest sound, as to them it sounded like a snare drum banging. They could hear no voices. Logan began to fear the worst, that they had already killed Savannah.

Suddenly, from a dimly lit hallway appeared a door. Light shone through the crack at the bottom of the door. Logan's heart began to pound so loudly that he was afraid Victor's henchmen would hear the thumping in his chest. He crept right up to the door, firmly gripping the pistol he had taken off the guard. He waited for a minute, but still no sound. He motioned to Zack that they would enter on the count of three. Silently mouthing the words, Logan began the countdown. *One, two, three!* Logan viciously kicked the door in and aimed the gun around the room, ready to shoot the first thing that moved.

The room was completely empty, except for one small table on which sat a portable cassette player—a stereo that would have been popular ten or fifteen years ago. Logan handed Zack the gun. "Shoot anything that comes through that door," he said.

Logan walked over to the table and pressed the play button.

CHAPTER 23

The tape in the stereo began to play and Logan stiffened, recognizing Victor's Kane's voice.

"Logan Nash, I expected more from you. Do you think I would let you talk to Savannah without listening in? I'm assuming if you're listening to this, you have probably disposed of a few of my men. That's just as well. They were so stupid that none of them even realized that you and Savannah were sending messages. You should realize by now that you can't beat me. Just get to Truk and find that last map. Don't forget. I'm watching you all the time."

"Damn it! I should have known better than to think he wouldn't be listening in. Damn it! Damn it all to hell!" Logan shouted. He picked up the stereo and flung it as hard as he could against the wall, shattering the machine into a hundred pieces.

"Let's get going to Truk," Logan said to Zack, trying to calm himself.

Zack just nodded, thinking it was probably best to leave Logan with his thoughts for a few moments.

They headed out the back door, retracing their steps in hopes of avoiding any encounters with Victor's other men. They headed back to the hotel, checking out only hours after checking in, and began the trip to the airport. Logan didn't want to waste any time, so he called the airlines en route, getting them on connecting flights as soon as possible.

"Zack, when was the last time you strapped on a tank?" He knew it had been a while since his friend tumbled off a boat into the deep blue.

"I think Nixon was president," Zack said, pretending not to notice the pain Logan was masking with his humor. "Honestly, Logan, I will keep guard on the boat or do any logistical support you need, but I'm not sure if I'm up for a two hundred-foot dive. In fact, I don't think I've ever been up for one of those."

"Don't worry, I would never do anything to endanger you—much." Logan laughed, knowing that no matter what they did, they often ended up in some kind of scrape.

"Yeah, I know. Never!" Zack replied in a dry sarcastic tone. He knew that Logan would never purposely endanger him, but it seemed that ninety percent of what they did contained some danger. Strange as it was, Zack felt Logan led a charmed life, and if he were with him, somehow they would come out of it fine and with a great story to tell.

Logan loved travel, but this certainly fell into a category of its own. The joy of the treasure hunt had been replaced with the worry and burden of rescuing Savannah. Logan thought. *Even if we rescue Savannah, it's now doubtful that I will ever get my hands on the treasure.*

Micronesia was one of the world's top diving destinations, but it was certainly not one of the most accessible. The day became a surreal blur of airports, immigration, bad movies, and endless plans in his mind, mixed with the occasional catnap when Logan became too physically or mentally exhausted. On the other hand, Zack was sound asleep for hours at a time or banging away on his laptop.

More than a day had passed when the pilot came over the intercom and announced that they would be landing in Weno in twenty minutes, which was Chuuk's capital city and made up almost a third of the island's population. It was more like a moderately sized town, but the closest thing Chuuk had to a city. It was music to Logan's ears, although as the time got closer his apprehension built, not knowing what Victor Kane had in store for him next, not to mention the state that Savannah must have been in already. The tropical heat swept over them as they walked down the steps down to the runway. It was a welcome feeling after the icebox of a plane. He never understood why the airlines often felt it was necessary to have the air-conditioning set to sub-zero temperatures.

The last time Logan had gone diving in the region, he had gotten to know one of the dive masters quite well. He didn't want to use a dive shop for this particular dive. It was too sensitive, too fraught with danger. Instead, he just wanted to rent a boat and hire his friend Andres as the captain. He was thoroughly impressed with Andres's knowledge of the area, and the captain was friendly and reliable. Logan had made a habit of making sure to keep the contact information of people he had met over the years, and to stay in touch with them every so often. The practice had made him some good friends, and many times they had proven invaluable because of local information and connections that they could provide. All of which would have been almost impossible to otherwise procure.

Logan scrolled through his cell phone's contact list, while soaking in the midday sun that beat down on him. It had been quite a while since Logan had been in contact with Andes. He had sent him an e-mail the other day but had not received a response. Logan hoped that Andres remembered him and that he could get a bit of time off from the dive shop. Logan punched in the number.

"Good afternoon, Wreck Tek Divers. Andres speaking."

"Andres, this is Logan Nash. It's good to hear that friendly voice of yours. I—"

"Yes, Mr. Logan, I got your e-mail. I was very happy to hear that you are coming back to Truk," Andres said. He still referred to the country by its old name. "Are you at the airport now?"

"Yes, my friend. I am at the airport, as well as a friend of mine that came along for this trip. When I see you, I have a business proposition I'd like to discuss."

"I have a lunch break coming up, and the morning dive group is already back, so I can close up for a few minutes. I'll come pick you up at the airport." Andres was always willing to help.

"As long as it's no problem."

"Not at all. I'll see you shortly." Andres hurried to close the shop down, fired up his old pickup, and drove to the airport.

Zack and Logan stood outside as Andres pulled up. Logan smiled as he remembered thinking how badly Andres needed a new truck, and here they were a few years later and the man still had the same one, though it was in worse shape than ever. Andres jumped out to greet Logan, leaving the engine in idle. His wide smile seemed extra bright against his dark skin, partly due to his heritage and the many hours he spent on the water.

"Mr. Logan, it is so nice to see you again." Andres said as he pumped Logan's arm up and down, and then reached out his hand to Zack. "Hello, my name is Andres."

"Hi, Andres. I'm Zack Cook. A pleasure to meet you." He received the same exuberant handshake as Logan.

"Yes, very nice to meet you, Mr. Sack," Andres replied, flashing his big smile.

"Sorry, that's Zack, not Sack." Logan had a hearty laugh at his expense.

"Don't worry, Andres, he's been called much worse, and that was by people that really liked him," Logan said. Andres looked worried that he had offended Zack.

Andres nodded, again feeling comfortable. He was in his early forties but was wiry and fit and had the sense of humor of a teenager. Maybe that was why he and Logan had gotten along so well. Logan knew that Andres didn't make a great deal of money, and he was hoping that he could come up with a win-win situation for them both.

"Andres, remember I said I had a business proposition for you?"

"Yes, Mr. Logan," Andres replied.

"I would like to hire you as our private boat captain. I will hire the boat and pay for any expenses relating to diving equipment. All I want is your expertise."

"Mr. Logan, we have plenty of diving spots available, and we can try to get the dives you desire," Andres replied. Clearly, he didn't understand.

"This isn't exactly a pleasure diving trip. I can't go into it in detail, but we would like a private guide and driver, and I know that no one knows these waters better than you. I will pay you five hundred dollars a day for your services. What do you say?"

Andres's eyes widened, and his jaw dropped. "You could have any guide for much, much less than that. I couldn't possibly ask that much money for my services."

"Then you will do it?"

"Yes, my boss is flexible, so I don't think it will be a problem. I would love to make that much money, but I wouldn't feel right," Andres replied.

"I'm not just paying you for your services, but also for your discretion. I'm asking you to keep anything we do totally to yourself, and I'm also paying you extra because what we're up to might be a bit dangerous."

"Okay, Mr. Logan, but I must insist that you and Mr. Zack stay at my home. Our children can stay over with friends and you can have their rooms."

"I would hate to impose," Logan said.

"It's no problem at all. We would feel insulted if you didn't stay with us."

"Then we will accept," Logan replied. He shook Andres's hand, knowing it would be nice to stay somewhere not so public, but also worrying that his presence might endanger the family.

Andres grabbed Zack's suitcase and Logan's diving gear and began to struggle toward his truck. Logan quickly relieved him of his dive bag, knowing that it alone weighed over a hundred pounds.

"Please, Andres, you don't need to get a hernia before we head out diving," Logan joked. He easily carried both his dive bag and his luggage.

Andres looked slightly embarrassed, noting the ease with which Logan tossed the heavy dive bag in the back of the truck, his muscular tanned arms glistening in the sunlight. Zack noticed the look on Andres's face, laughed, and put his arm around his new friend. "Don't let the big guy intimidate you, Andres. He's always showing off. You should see him if there's a lady around. It's shameful."

"Hey, I wasn't showing off! I was just being helpful," Logan said.

Zack nimbly hopped in the back of the truck with the luggage. "I think it might be a bit crowded up there with three of us, so I'll ride back here in second class."

"Okay. I'll make sure Andres gives you an interesting ride." Logan laughed as he climbed into the passenger side and slammed the door.

The old truck sputtered and groaned. Zack frantically waved his arms, trying to clear the cloud of blue smoke that lingered in his face. With a few violent bone-jarring jerks that sent Zack tumbling to the floor of the truck bed, they were off. He shook his head as he could hear Logan roaring with laughter in the front seat.

Through all the frivolity, Logan had been keeping a close eye out for anyone that may have been watching them. He was certain that Victor would have sent his men ahead of time and might possibly have even came to the island himself. Logan desperately wanted to rescue Savannah, but he didn't even have any idea where to begin to look. He would play the treasure swap game, knowing that the second Victor got a hold of the treasure, he would not stop until they were all dead. He also knew that the treasure was the only leverage he had to get Savannah back.

Was she still in Venice? Would Victor bring her here? Was she still alive? Logan's mind raced with questions as they drove out of the city to Andres's home just past the edge of town. *No, I have to believe she is still alive.* He scolded himself for letting negative thoughts enter his head.

"What? Sorry, Andres, my mind was somewhere else," Logan said. He realized that Andres had been speaking all along. Logan hadn't heard a single word.

Turning off the main road, the trunk bumped along a rutted path. *Hmm, no wonder the truck is in such deplorable condition*, Logan thought. He glanced in the side mirror to see Zack hanging on for dear life. With a deafening screech of metal on metal, the truck jerked to a stop, again going into its death cough as Andres turned off the engine. Andres jumped out of the truck, ran to the back, and helped Zack out of the rusted truck bed. "I am so sorry, my friend! Are you okay?"

"Yeah, nothing that an hour with a masseuse wouldn't cure," Zack joked, his sense of humor still intact.

Andres reached in the back and grabbed the two pieces of luggage, deciding to leave the extremely heavy dive bag for Logan. Before they got to the door, a trio appeared on the front porch to greet them. A beautiful dark-haired woman in her early thirties stood there with a curious look on her face, no doubt wondering who the strangers were that Andres had dragged home. Logan was aware of her beauty, her unique looks, and he thought she might possibly have Micronesian and Asian lineage. Flanking her on both sides were a boy and a girl of similar ages.

"Logan, Zack, this is my beautiful wife, Tasi, my daughter Kaikala, and my son Brad," Andres said. Just by the look on Logan's face, he could see he wondered why one name was so different, so American. "Don't ask," Andres mumbled under his breath. Logan nodded. Both Logan and Zack shook hands with Tasi and nodded to the children, while Logan tussled the hair of the boy, who he guessed to be ten or eleven years old.

"You have a beautiful family, Andres," Logan said, causing Tasi to blush.

Andres thanked Logan and excused himself, pulling Tasi aside to tell her of his plan to have Logan and Zack stay with them. Logan's charms must have been working their magic since, to Andres's surprise, Tasi had no objections at all. No doubt, the kids would not be crazy about giving up their rooms, but in this matter, they had no voting rights.

After getting settled in and freshened up, Logan and Zack sat on the front porch. Tasi brought a couple of cold beers out to them that went down extremely smooth in the heat of the afternoon. While they relaxed for a few minutes, Andres began arranging for tomorrow's dive. He was well connected and respected around town, and in no time he lined up a boat and all the necessary diving equipment, except for helium, which Logan would have preferred to use on this dive, as there was a chance he would be diving beyond two hundred feet.

Logan knew if he had to dive to the deepest part of the wreck, he would be pushing the limits of oxygen toxicity, but he had dived on the wreck of San Francisco Maru on air before and he'd been okay. Besides, according to the clues he and Zack had gathered, the next map was on the bridge, so he shouldn't have any serious problems. However, he would have nitrox for faster decompression. Logan went over the dive plan with Zack like it would be any other dive.

It wasn't the dive that Logan worried about, it was whatever surprise Victor Kane had waiting for him.

CHAPTER 24

The sun rising into a cloudless sky shimmered across the water as Andres skipped the moderately sized uncovered skiff over the small waves. The speed of the boat brought a welcome breeze as the temperature crept north of ninety before Logan's watch read 9:00 a.m.

Logan scanned the horizon for anything unusual. He should have been glad that he hadn't seen or heard anything from Victor or his henchmen, but he felt like he was being watched through a two-way mirror. It was as though he was straining to see who was on the other side and couldn't. Logan knew it was a case of when, not if, Victor Kane would try something nefarious.

Andres shut down the boat's engine as they drifted toward the mooring buoy that marked the location of San Francisco Maru. Logan remembered the last time he had gone diving on the wreck Andres found the site without a buoy or a GPS, but having a mooring buoy in place prevented damage to the wreck and surrounding coral from the anchors of all the dive boats. Andres scurried to the front of the boat and tied off to the buoy with ease, having done it hundreds of times before. The heat seemed to intensify the moment they came to a stop.

"God, it's hot," Zack said. He wiped his dripping forehead with the back of his hand.

"Nah, it's a perfect day for a dive. The seas are fairly calm, and the sun is shining," Logan said with a smile. He was much more comfortable with the heat.

On any other day, this would have been a perfect day, but the circumstances made it a dive of necessity rather than pleasure. Logan closed his eyes. The air was still. He could feel the sun baking his skin, and he could hear the waves softly lapping against the side of the boat. He inhaled a deep breath of the humid sea air and slowly exhaled.

"Damn it!" Zack yelled, breaking Logan's trance. Zack was struggling to put his wetsuit on over his sticky body. "I hate these damn suits."

"Here." Logan laughed, reaching into his dive bag and tossing Zack a bottle of talcum powder. "Try this on for size."

"Do we really need these suits? The water is eighty-four degrees."

"You may not, but with the decompression stops, I may be under the water quite a while, and even in water this warm, heat will drain away from the body over time. Besides, whenever I do wreck penetrations, I always wear a suit," Logan explained.

Logan did an equipment check of his friend's gear. Zack didn't bother to reciprocate the process, knowing that if Logan didn't spot something wrong, he certainly wouldn't. Recreational divers were always taught to practice the buddy system, whereas technical divers were taught to be much more self-reliant. Logan had done solo diving in harsh conditions on many occasions.

As he did on every dive, Logan sat on the edge of the boat and took a deep breath, keeping his eye on his pressure gauge. Normally, he would now have placed one hand over his mask and regulator, while the other would be placed over his weight belt, but as he was diving with double steel eighties, a weight belt wasn't necessary, although he stuffed a two-pound weight in each of his front two BCD pockets. Logan didn't have any worries about the dive itself, just the possibility of unexpected visitors, so Zack would hover at about one hundred feet, watching for anyone either coming from above or approaching the wreck from the side. The visibility was even better than normal, so Zack would have a perfect view of what was happening around him.

Logan made sure that Andres had armed himself. The captain didn't feel very comfortable about it, but he'd brought along an old shotgun and a shiny new spear gun. To Logan, the spear gun looked a whole lot more reliable than the rusty antique shotgun.

"Okay, Zack, you ready?" Logan asked, regulator in hand at the ready.

"As ready as I'll ever be," Zack replied. He wished he had done a few more dives and spent a bit less time on the computer.

"Let's rock and roll." Logan winked at Zack, placed his regulator in his mouth, and fell backward into the crystal-clear waters of Truk Lagoon, followed closely by Zack, who not quite as gracefully also fell backward into the water. Logan slid into the blue abyss with the ease of a fish, while Zack struggled at the surface to rid his BCD of excess air, finally beginning his descent. By the time Zack had begun his descent, Logan was already a small shadow more than a hundred feet below him.

Logan was intoxicated by the silence of the underwater world. The only sounds were the hollow hiss of his regulator as he inhaled and the rush of bubbles floating toward the surface as he exhaled, but the pause between the two when there was no sound Logan referred to as the symphony of silence. No matter how many thousands of different shapes and colors of fish raced around, going about their daily routine of survival, it all happened in surreal silence. It was like traveling to a different planet, with every possible shape of alien you could imagine. He had always taken time to appreciate every creature, from the smallest crustaceans to the majestic whale sharks.

He was taken back to the first time he dove on the wreck as the huge ship came into focus. It was one of his favorite wrecks in Truk Lagoon. There were many with brighter coral and more marine life, but the wreck of San Francisco Maru held a special place in his heart. The wrecks of Truk were so much more than your run-of-the-mill ones. They were underwater museums, left as they were on the day they slipped violently below the waves in 1944 during a successful American attack, a sort of payback for the devastation the Japanese had dealt out at Pearl Harbor. The ship lay proudly on the bottom, her guns now reclaimed by the coral, her tanks and trucks once ready to be offloaded to join the battle were still proud as well, but too tired to fight anymore, slowly losing the battle with the relentless sea. The holds were filled with personal items, all with a story to tell, every artifact a piece of history. The lagoon was a place of solemn remembrance.

Logan slipped his small dive light from its sheath on his BCD as he entered the bridge of the wreck. He slowly and meticulously made his way through the bridge, careful not to stir up any silt. He knew the map would be placed somewhere it wouldn't be accidentally found. After searching the bridge twice, Logan began thinking that maybe someone had indeed accidentally found it. He thought of what that meant: no treasure, which meant no leverage with Victor Kane to get Savannah back. No, Colton Braxton wouldn't have been that careless. *Think, Logan! Think like he would!* His pep talk encouraged him, making him feel positive that he and Colton Braxton thought along the same lines.

Suddenly, Logan stopped and swung his dive light to a spot against the forward bulkhead. At first glance, what he saw appeared to be a rusting metal plate bolted onto the bulkhead, but instead of bolts around the edges of the plate, they formed an X. *Could X mark the spot? Would Colton have been that brazen?*

He grabbed the plate and it moved. It was not at all bolted to the bulkhead but had the appearance of being part of the wall. It was another case, just like the one in Angkor. Logan assumed it would be waterproofed and opened it. To his surprise, inside the case was a note, which read: "Follow the signs down at the keel and there a surprise, oh, so surreal."

I don't think Colton would have made it as a poet, Logan thought.

Logan glanced at his dive computer. He had plenty of air, but time and oxygen toxicity had become his enemy, especially now that he was headed to the deepest part of the wreck. *Follow the signs? Hopefully, whatever clues he had left are still there now.*

Logan began to make his way slowly along the outside of the wreck, skimming just above the sea bottom. *Oh, Colton,* Logan thought, as he came across a few rocks that to the normal person would have appeared to just be strewn along the ocean floor. But they were clearly arranged in the shape of an arrow pointing to a spot at the bottom of the wreck. He swam over to the exact place the arrow was pointing, but nothing was there. *Am I imagining things, seeing signs that really aren't there?*

Logan dug in the sand around the area where the arrow pointed. He was about to abandon his search when close to two feet down, his hand hit something hard. He redoubled his efforts, moving as much sand as he could. *No, no, no, it can't be!* Logan screamed in his mind, not believing what he saw. He quickly moved some more sand. *My God! It is!* Logan reached his hand into the end of a large cannon that had once sat on a Spanish galleon and pulled out a clear tube. Inside he could see the fourth and final map. In a strange twist of fate, the San Francisco Maru had landed directly on top of another wreck. Maybe this is a bonus piece of treasure that Colton wanted someone to find.

He'd been so engrossed that he almost lost track of how long he'd been down. He looked at his dive computer and noted that he had already exceeded the safe limits for oxygen toxicity. Everyone reacted differently to its effects, but he knew he needed to get into shallower water very fast because once oxygen toxicity hit, it would almost certainly be fatal. A few of his tech diver friends had died that way, usually from diving too deep on nitrox mixtures that were not labeled correctly. It was a horrible way to go. They'd gone into convulsions as their central nervous systems shut down, causing them to drown. Logan quickly shoved as much sand as he could back into the muzzle of the cannon to conceal it and began to ascend. He would also need a few decompression stops along the way, but right now, his priority was to get to a shallower depth. When it came to his deco stops, Logan was always extra cautious, spending a couple minutes longer than what was required.

Zack was met by a stream of bubbles that rose from Logan's exhaled breaths. Zack had crept down a bit closer to the wreck, obviously enthralled by the awesome spectacle that lay beneath him. Logan motioned for Zack to join him at a hundred feet, where they made a quick stop, although it was not totally necessary. Zack was happy to keep Logan company through all his stops on the way to the surface, except for Logan's last deco stop at ten feet. Zack struggled to stay neutrally buoyant, eventually gave up, and went up to the boat, thinking Logan would be fine. A few minutes later, Logan broke the surface and climbed up the ladder onto the boat, almost tipping over the small skiff since he was so laden down with his tech dive gear.

"Any problems while we were down, Andres?" Logan asked. He began stripping off his dive gear.

"No, Mr. Logan, everything quiet up here. Did you find what you were looking for?" Andres asked.

"Oh, yes, I certainly did," Logan replied. He smiled to himself, knowing he found much more than what he was looking for. The wreck of the galleon was something he would keep to himself until he could both research it and log a few more dives, inspecting it firsthand. Logan didn't know what to make of the fact that Victor or his band of goons hadn't made an appearance yet. He was sure Victor would make a play for the maps, but he must have believed it when Logan had told him he didn't have the maps with him. *After all, bringing the maps along with me is probably not the smartest thing I've ever done*, Logan thought. He knew it was dangerous having all the maps together, but he was constantly on the move, so he didn't have much of a choice. Plus, there could be something hidden in the map that he couldn't get from a copy or scan, which was why he liked to have them handy.

A light breeze had come up, adding a slight chop to the azure sea. The sun beat down relentlessly on the uncovered skiff as it slapped its way toward the distant shoreline. Both Logan and Zack were too engrossed in studying the map to notice the heat. From the outline in the other maps, Zack had already ascertained that the island the treasure would be found on was Koh Lanta in Thailand.

Logan was familiar with the island, and now that they had all four maps, they could read the numbered clues to find the approximate location of the treasure. They still wouldn't know the exact location until they were there in person. As they studied the map, Logan tried to recall the other clues by number, but there were twenty that had to be followed in order and he would have to wait until they got back to Andres's home. Andres pulled the boat alongside a beaten-up old dock just outside the town of Weno. Each of the men grabbed as much gear as they could carry and tossed it into the back of the weary pickup. Miraculously, the truck fired up on the first try, and with a cloud of blue smoke, they were on their way.

A battle of emotions raged within Logan. He was elated at finding the final map; it would give him the leverage he needed over Victor, but he also felt a little guilty because the adventure was fun. He should have been worrying more about Savannah. Even as the old truck coughed and lurched, Logan and Zack were already on their way into the house to study the maps. Zack went into his room to grab his laptop while Logan went into his room, closed the door, and from behind a family photo hanging on the wall, he removed an envelope taped to the back.

Zack entered the room with his top-of-the-line laptop already fired up. "I think we'll have to give Andres a huge thank you gift. I wasn't sure he would have Internet access, let alone a wireless router."

"Yeah, and running water too," Logan joked.

"No, I'm just saying the house looks pretty humble from the outside, but it has most amenities."

It wasn't long after studying the clues alongside a detailed map of Koh Lanta that Logan shouted, "I knew it had to be!"

"What?" Zack asked.

"Near the center of the island there is an extensive cave system called Tham Khao Maikaeo. I have done some spelunking there before. The cave system is huge and very challenging in places. There is no way we can get an exact location of the treasure until we are actually in the caves. There are just so many places it could be hidden, like in the many branches just a few feet apart. There are also deep crevasses and extremely narrow passageways. I think Colton picked a perfect place to hide his treasure."

"Let me get us booked on the next flight out of here," Zack replied. He was showing more excitement about the adventure than he previously had. "Shit, can you get packed up in about three minutes?"

"If I have to. Why?" Logan asked.

"There's a flight out of here in less than two hours, which I booked us on. Otherwise we have to wait until tomorrow."

"No problem! Consider it done."

In minutes, both men were packed and carrying their luggage into the living room. Andres looked surprised at seeing the men packed up just minutes after getting back from their diving.

"Mr. Logan?"

"I'm sorry, Andres, but we really need to catch a 3:50 p.m. flight. It's an emergency."

"Mr. Logan, I was hoping that you would stay for a day or two. Besides, of all people, you know you cannot fly right after diving. You are supposed to wait at least twenty-four hours." Andres seeming shocked that Logan would be willing to break a cardinal rule of diving.

"I know, I know, Andres, especially after a deco dive, but it's a chance I'll have to take," Logan said. He was trying to convince himself that he would be okay. However, he realized deep down that he truly would be flirting with the bends if he got on an airplane. He could not afford to get decompression sickness, but he also knew what an extra day could mean for Savannah.

"Andres, what is the highest nitrox mix you have?"

"I have an 80/20 deco tank."

"I know it's not a foolproof answer, but I'll suck back on that thing the whole way to the airport. It will at least get a few more of those bubbles out of the ol' system." Logan sheepishly smiled at Andres, who shot Logan a disappointed look as he grabbed the tank. Zack again bounced along in the back while Logan took deep steady breaths on the oxygen-heavy mix, trying to rid his body of as many nitrogen bubbles as he could before they got to the airport. Logan stepped out of the truck and grabbed his luggage from the back, while Zack again climbed out looking disheveled from the rough ride.

"Andres, thank you for everything. I wish I had a chance to say bye to Tasi and the kids." Logan gave him a firm handshake.

"You're welcome, my friend. I wish you could have stayed longer. Thank you for your generosity. I know they would have wanted to say goodbye to you as well. I have no idea where Tasi and the kids went. Maybe into town?" Andres thanked Logan, genuinely wishing that they had more time to stay.

Andres waved as the men headed into the airport. While checking in, they could hear and smell the environmental disaster that was Andres's truck as the man fired up the engine in a cloud of smoke and chugged down the road.

"I hope he spends some of that money on a new truck." Logan laughed, shaking his head at the thought of the old truck. He had given Andres five hundred dollars for the one day of work, but he'd also left an envelope on the bed with a thousand dollars in it. He knew Andres wouldn't have taken it otherwise.

Andres's eyes got wide as he arrived back at his house. Three men walked out the front door and jumped into a new four-wheel drive, completely ignoring him. He quickly ran into the house to see what the men had wanted. On the couch, Tasi sat weeping and hugging the two children tightly. On the coffee table in front of them was strewn a wad of hundred-dollar bills.

"What happened? Did those men hurt you or the kids?" Andres asked.

"I'm so sorry, Andres. I'm so, so sorry. I had no choice. He said he would kill us," Tasi said. She was choking back the tears and trying to comfort the traumatized children.

"I don't understand what you're talking about. What happened?" Andres asked, near frantic now.

Tasi stopped sobbing, and with tear-filled eyes she began to speak. "As soon as you left to go diving this morning, those men came in and searched all around Logan and his friend's room and suitcases. The one man was very angry when he couldn't find something. I tried to stop them, but one of the men pulled out a gun. They put a bunch of hidden cameras in Logan and Zack's rooms, and then took us at gunpoint to a hotel room. When you took your friends to the airport, the men seemed to be happy. They brought us back here and threw this money on the table. He said if we called the police, he would come back and kill us all." She immediately broke down again as soon as she finished.

"Logan said there were some men after the same thing he was. I think they must have gotten the information they needed from the cameras. I think Logan is in danger. I need to warn him," Andres said. He hurried toward the old truck to drive back to the airport.

"No!" Tasi cried. "Please don't leave us! It's too late, anyway. You'll never make it."

Andres rushed to the phone and called the airport. "Damn it!" he screamed. "Can you stop the plane? I have an emergency message. Damn, damn, damn!" He swore, slamming the phone down. "The plane is already on the runway." He picked up the phone to leave Logan a voicemail, telling him everything that had happened, desperately hoping he would get the message before it was too late.

Sitting in the large leather chair that adorned his private jet, Victor Kane drew deeply from a huge Cohiba cigar and smiled. "Okay, let's go find us the treasure. And Mr. Nash, I have a nice surprise for you too."

CHAPTER 25

"Thank you for your cooperation, Mr. Nash," Victor Kane said. He was pleased about the ingenuity he had used to acquire a copy of all the maps. Logan and Zack had sat down studying them as Victor retrieved detailed pictures from every possible angle via the hidden cameras, and then he was able to produce copies.

"I knew you were lying to me! I knew you had the maps with you." Victor carried on talking out loud to himself and feeling extremely proud of his clever plan. He was sitting in the comfort of his converted Gulfstream V, the longest range private jet available. It was the choice private jet of many royal families around the world. It looked more like a luxurious office than an aircraft, and Victor knew that with a range of over 7400 miles, the pilot would not need to refuel.

As the sleek jet ripped through the cloudless sky, Victor studied the maps alongside a detailed map of Koh Lanta. Having already known the final destination, he had previously arranged for a half dozen of his most trusted men to meet him upon his arrival. He would be landing in Krabi, and his men were procuring a helicopter to hop over to the island. He sneered at the thought of catching the ferry across like a commoner.

Victor could see on the map the area of the island where the treasure was located, noting the cave system. He would be arriving on Koh Lanta much earlier than Logan and Zack, which would give him the upper hand, or so he thought. With a smug look of satisfaction, he was confident that he would possess the treasure long before Logan Nash was anywhere near Koh Lanta. He figured he had a solid eleven to twelve-hour lead.

While Victor was smirking in his private jet, the island hopper from Truk screeched in a puff of smoke as it touched down in Guam. As the aircraft taxied toward the gate, Logan reached into his pocket and turned on his cell phone. A few seconds later, a loud beep alerted him that he had a voicemail message.

"Who's the message from?" Zack asked as Logan punched in his code.

"Don't recognize the number." He furrowed his eyebrows.

"What? What's wrong?" Zack asked, deeply concerned as he saw Logan's face turn as white as a sheet.

"Shit, shit, shit!" Logan swore. "Victor Kane kidnapped Andres's family and planted a series of hidden cameras in his house. Now he has a copy of all the maps. He has no reason to keep Savannah alive after he finds the treasure. I don't know how, but we must find that treasure before he does. I can only imagine that he's halfway there already. I can't see him flying commercially."

"At least we have a bit of a jump on him because we know he was there after we were already at the airport," Zack replied.

"Remember that fancy jet that I commented on?" Logan asked Zack.

"Yeah."

"I bet you anything that it belonged to him." Logan fumed. He was angry with Victor, but he was also angry with himself for being so careless to allow him to gain possession of the maps, not to mention putting Andres's family and Savannah in danger. Logan had already previously checked, and there were no direct flights to Krabi commercially. He didn't think it would matter, but now he knew he and Zack couldn't afford to lose any time.

"Zack, what do you think the chances are of hiring a private jet on ten minutes notice?" Logan asked, only half serious. He knew it would not only be almost impossible, but very expensive.

"I might be able to arrange something," Zack said.

"What?" Logan asked. "What do you mean?"

"I just finished a major website project for a Japanese businessman who is based here in Guam. I know he always takes his private jet to Seattle, and, not to brag, but he loved my work and said if there was anything he could do for me—"

"Call him! Call him now!"

"Okay, I'll see if he's even on the island."

"God, I hope so. It could save us ten or twelve hours. That time could make the difference between Savannah living or dying."

"I know," Zack replied. He began scanning through his phone book. In less than a minute, he was punching numbers into his phone.

"Yes, could I speak to Mr. Akita please?" Zack asked the receptionist. "Damn it."

"What? He's not in?"

"Please, this is very important. Would you tell Mr. Akita it is Zack Cook on the phone and that it is a dire emergency?"

"What's going on?"

"He's in a meeting," Zack said, "but she's going to see if he will take my call."

"Yes, hello, Mr. Akita. Thank you for taking the time to talk to me. I have an extreme favor to ask of you, and I will understand if you can't do it, but it is truly a matter of life and death. I need to borrow your jet."

Logan could hear the man's voice over Zack's phone, but not what he was saying.

"Yes, Mr. Akita. Your jet! That's right," Zack said. He started answering Mr. Akita's many questions. "Thank you, thank you so much, Mr. Akita! You have no idea what this means. I don't know how, but I'll make it up to you."

"So, I'm assuming we have a plane now?" Logan asked.

"Oh, much better than that. Mr. Akita's pilot is here at the airport, and he is personally arranging to have us expedited out of here ASAP. We are supposed to head through customs right now, and the pilot, Mr. Kato, will be waiting on the other side," Zack said. He was proud that he was able to make such an important contribution.

"You are amazing!" Logan said, grabbing Zack by the arm and almost dragging him in his sprint toward the customs line.

They went through customs and met Mr. Kato, who, with a quick bow, escorted them directly to the plane. A few minutes later, the plane roared down the runway.

"You must have one powerful and influential friend there!" Logan exclaimed, more than amazed at how quickly they had gotten in and out of Guam.

"Yeah, he is rather well off. And he also told me that his sales had doubled in the last month since I finished his website, so he was more than willing to help."

"I knew you were good, but I didn't think you were that good." Logan laughed, feeling a sense of relief and hope.

Logan reached for a satellite phone attached to the front bulkhead. "I hope Mr. Akita doesn't mind me making a long-distance call."

"Go for it," Zack said.

Logan punched in the numbers. After several rings, a sexy voice picked up, answering in Thai. "I would recognize that beautiful voice anywhere," Logan said to Suchin, a girl who ran a travel agency in Krabi.

"Logan? Is that you?" Suchin asked, surprised to hear his voice.

"Yes, it is. I would love to catch up with you later, but I have a big favor to ask you."

"What is it?"

"I need you to arrange transportation from the airport and a private fast boat over to Koh Lanta. It's very important and time is of the essence."

"What's this all about?"

"It's very complicated. I promise I'll explain everything to you later over a seaside lobster and wine dinner." He skated past answering her question.

"Okay, you always know how to sweet talk a girl. I can have Daw pick you up at the airport, and my friend Kiet has a very fast boat that can take you over to Koh Lanta. I will also arrange a room at that little hotel by the sea you liked so much last time you were here."

"Could you make that two rooms? I have a friend with me that will need one as well. I'll look you up as soon as I'm done dealing with my situation on Koh Lanta. I'll make sure your people are paid well too," Logan said, more for the sake of Daw and Kiet than Suchin. If they knew they would be paid well, it always seemed to speed everything up.

Meanwhile, Victor grinned as he stepped out into the stifling humidity of the Thai night. He looked at his watch and saw that it was just 10:20 p.m. He nodded with approval, having picked up four hours since leaving Truk.

"Mr. Kane? Mr. Kane?" A stubby man came running up to the plane, bending over to catch his breath before continuing. "I found out that information you wanted."

"Are you going to tell me?" Victor snapped at the pudgy man, impatient that he had to wait.

"Sorry, sir. They will miss the first flight down here, so the earliest flight that gets here from Bangkok is at 11:40 a.m. They probably won't be on Koh Lanta till around 1:00 p.m."

"Excellent. Do you have accommodation arranged?"

"Yes, Mr. Kane, the best on the island. A private mansion that is currently up for sale."

"I assume that everything I requested is in place on the island already?"

"Yes, everything."

"Good, let's get over there and make the final arrangements. I want to hit the ground before the sun rises," Victor barked. He knew that it would be a lot more difficult to find anything in the jungle and caves in the dark. He felt comfortable in the fact that even if they began their search at 6:00 a.m., they would have a six- to seven-hour head start on Logan.

Time seemed to inch forward, but finally the shoreline of Thailand was approaching. Logan's heart raced as he went over a thousand scenarios in his mind, knowing that an encounter with Victor Kane was inevitable.

CHAPTER 26

Logan couldn't sleep. His senses were alive with anticipation as his mind raced with thoughts of what might happen in the morning. He listened to the sea through the bamboo walls of the humble beachfront cabana where he was staying. He had always loved the sound of surf. He had lived with it all his life, and it soothed him. Tonight, was different though. There was no gentle lapping or rolling of waves onto a powdery white-sand beach. The Andaman Sea seemed angry, its harsh waves pounding the shoreline in a fitful rage. Logan slid open the glass patio doors and stepped into the sultry moonlit night. The moonlight bathed the sea in white, casting enough illumination for him to see clearly the foamy white crests of the breakers as they thundered onto the otherwise quiet beach. He gazed up at the starlit sky and smiled, although he felt uneasy. *Here I stand halfway around the world staring up at the same sky I always do,* Logan thought. He was overcome by a strong feeling of déjà vu, as he often found himself standing on his own deck staring up at the starlit nights both in Hawaii and back home in the Pacific Northwest. Logan realized how much more he loved the hot sticky nights of Southeast Asia over the cold biting nights of the Pacific Northwest, and even more than the comfortable warm nights of the Hawaiian Islands. *Maybe too much time in the tropics has made me soft,* he thought. He leaned his powerful forearms against the patio railing, standing there only in his boxers, his skin glistening with sweat.

Suddenly, the sound of the crashing Andaman Sea was broken by the wail of the early morning prayers from the mosque in the distance. Logan glanced at his watch and saw that it was 5:15 a.m. "Ah, right on cue," he whispered, appreciating the distinct difference of the Muslim/Buddhist mixture of the south to the predominantly Buddhist majority of the rest of Thailand. Logan hadn't managed to get any sleep, and part of him wished that they had headed off into the night as soon as they arrived, but he knew they had no idea exactly what to expect, especially from Victor Kane. Logan slipped into a pair of khaki cargo pants, ran over to Zack's cabana, and knocked on the door. "Up and at 'em sleepy head. We hit the road in fifteen."

A few seconds later, Zack snapped out of his slumber. "Jeez, do you have to be so damn happy in the middle of the night?" he said, still mostly asleep.

"Sure do. Come on. We got to get going soon," Logan said. He went back to his cabana, put on a black T-shirt, and double-checked his backpack for all the supplies they might need. He slipped the maps, along with a detailed map of the area, into his front pocket, and then strapped a large survival knife to his leg. He reached into his suitcase, pulled out a rolled-up towel, and unrolled it, revealing an old Llama M-82 nine-millimeter pistol that he had bought from Kiet on the way over from the mainland. Logan had made him promise not to tell Suchin. The old handgun showed signs of wear and the wooden grip was chipped and worn, but other than that, it looked like it was in good shape. Logan slid out the clip. Fifteen shots and no extra rounds. He hoped he didn't have to use the weapon, but he was comfortable and proficient with most firearms, so if it came down to a firefight, he was prepared. He tucked the pistol into the belt of his pants, the steel cool against the small of his back.

A few minutes later, Zack knocked at Logan's door, tossing him a protein bar as soon as it opened. "I'm going to assume we're not stopping for banana pancakes?"

"No, I'm afraid not," Logan said. His voice had turned serious as he mentally prepared himself for the day. "I would love to have you with me today, but I totally understand if you don't want to go."

"Hey, buddy, this is what friendship is. Getting your ass shot off for an adrenaline junkie of a friend," Zack joked. Inside, though, he felt he was going to vomit as his stomach did cartwheels.

"Thanks, Zack, it means a lot to me. Okay, let's do it." They jumped into the beaten-up Jeep that had been arranged for them. "At least it's sort of the same as mine," Logan mumbled as he cranked up the engine. The Jeep was the same make as his, but the similarities stopped there.

Logan had ascertained approximately where they would end up. However, to make sure they got the exact location, they would follow the clues from the starting point, which entailed driving to the east central side of Koh Lanta. When they got there, Logan found a clearing in the jungle a few hundred yards away and backed the Jeep in. Despite the complete lack of sleep, his senses were sharp. It was as if all his years of training and adventures were culminating in this ultimate trial. Not for a moment had he lost sight of the fact that Savannah's life was at stake and far more important than the treasure. He reached behind him and pulled the pistol from his belt. He yanked back on the slide to chamber a round and checked to make sure the safety was on.

"Where the hell did you get that?" Zack blurted out, shocked that Logan had somehow acquired a firearm.

"From Kiet on the way over."

"Where the hell was I?"

"I think you were busy hanging on for dear life as we sped through the night weaving in and out of the boat traffic."

"Yeah, yeah, but you have to admit that was a scary ride."

"Let's go Double O." Logan threw his backpack on, sticking the gun back in his belt.

Once they reached the starting point, they began to follow the instructions meticulously. Before long, they found themselves in the thick jungle headed up the jungle-clad slope to the caves that honeycombed the area. Logan had spent a lot of time in the caves known as

Tham Khao Maikaeo. There was an extensive labyrinth of caves and caverns with many entrances, so it was important not to take anything for granted.

"Shit," Logan whispered. He grabbed Zack by the collar and dragged him into the jungle behind a large rock.

"Wha—" Zack began to speak, only to have Logan's hand cover his mouth.

"I hear voices coming up the trail. I hear Victor Kane's voice!" Logan whispered.

As the voices drew closer, Logan heard someone crying, recognizing who it was almost immediately. Savannah! His heart was beating out of his chest, grateful that she was alive. His anger at Victor Kane was now almost uncontainable. All he wanted to do was just jump out and shoot every one of them, but he knew that only worked in the movies. If he tried it, they all might be killed in the ensuing firefight. As he crouched behind the rock, he slipped the pistol from his belt, ready to use it if he had to. Logan and Zack were well-camouflaged behind the rock and the dense foliage. Logan could feel the tears welling up in his eyes as he saw Savannah walk by, beaten and bloody, chained up like an animal, her spirit broken. Logan's blood boiled, and he could hear himself breathing heavily.

"Not yet," Zack whispered to Logan, being the voice of reason. He could see Logan rising from his crouch, pistol firmly in hand.

Without a word, Logan nodded as the men with Savannah drew abreast of his position. From all the noise they were making it was obvious that Victor was not expecting Logan yet. "The element of surprise will be our advantage," he whispered.

As the men passed by with Savannah, Logan carefully watched, assessing the force arrayed against him and Zack. The two men flanking Victor were obviously a couple of Victor's goons, as they spoke to Victor in Dutch, and when they had something for everyone to hear in English, their thick Dutch accents were obvious. A pack of heavily armed thugs took up the rear, and Logan noted with disappointment and annoyance that guards were being dispatched along the way, both on the path and in the surrounding jungle. *Those guys are going to try to ambush us,* Logan thought. *They're ready and waiting for us to come waltzing up that path.*

"I counted fifteen including Victor," Logan whispered to Zack.

"Great. Is that all? Piece of cake."

Logan just shook his head. "We're going to have to either take out the guards or try to sneak around them." He paused. "We are going to have to take them out. We need to stay on the path, so we can follow the instructions."

"You know I hate violence, Logan. I'm a lover not a fighter."

Logan chuckled softly, realizing that Zack was extremely nervous and was using humor to cover it up. He didn't like violence either, but it seemed on several occasions trouble found him on its own. He was more than capable of taking care of himself in almost any situation.

Victor had posted a guard about fifty feet up the path. "Stay here until I take that guy out."

Zack nodded and stayed where he was.

Logan picked up a softball-size rock and began to creep through the jungle parallel to the path. When he got about ten feet from the slight, but hardened-looking guard, the jungle began to thin, making it impossible for Logan to get closer without being seen. He rummaged around on the ground, picked up a small rock, and tossed it into the jungle on the other side of the path. The sudden crack made the guard whip around to look for the source of the sound, pointing his AK-47 assault rifle into the jungle. The jungle was always alive with noises from the many insects and other creatures, so the guard lowered his weapon, reaching into his pocket and pulling out a pack of cigarettes. With his back still to Logan, he put a cigarette in his mouth, reached in his pocket again, and pulled out a Zippo lighter. Covering the flame with his left hand, he raised the lighter to his mouth.

Logan chose that moment to strike.

The unlit cigarette cartwheeled to the jungle floor as the man dropped to his knees, slumping face first into the thick undergrowth of the jungle. Logan stood behind the collapsed body, breathing heavily, blood dripping from the rock that he still firmly gripped. He tossed the rock into the jungle, reached down, grabbed the man under the arms, and dragged him behind some thick foliage.

Logan hurried back to Zack. "Okay, let's keep pacing things out until our next dance party."

"What happened to the—" Zack hesitated. "Oh, never mind I don't want to know."

As they climbed higher up the mountainside, the jungle off the path became almost impenetrable. The normal jungle sounds gave way to the overpowering buzzing of the cicadas that all but drowned out everything else. To many unfamiliar with the song of the large fly-like insect, they thought they were hearing a large piece of machinery at a deafening level of up to a hundred and seven decibels rather than an insect. Logan grinned. The cicadas would definitely work to his advantage, allowing him to make some noise undetected. Upon seeing the next guard, Logan used Zack as a noise-making diversion as again another rock found its way to the skull of a guard. After hiding the unconscious body in the underbrush, Logan and Zack slowly made their way through the jungle, skirting along the edge of the path so they could hide fast if necessary. A few minutes later, Logan gestured to Zack to step quietly into the jungle.

"I was hoping this is where we would come out," Logan said, keeping his voice low. "We arrived here from a different path, but this is the cave entrance I used the two times I explored on my last trip," Logan said. He was excited by the fact that he had spent considerable time exploring the Tham Khao Maikaeo cave system. In the distance, he could see Victor and four other men standing at the entrance to the cave. He could see Savannah lying on the ground. She was obviously crying. One of Victor's no-neck goons kicked in her the ribs. "Piece of shit," Logan said through his clenched teeth. The rage inside him grew.

The thick tangled jungle had given way to rubber trees, every one of them with cuts winding their way around the tree culminating in a slow white drip of liquid rubber that would soon solidify in the bucket below. Logan surmised that many of the guards must have been dispatched into the jungle. There was only one other guard that stood between them and the five men standing at the entrance of the cave. Logan saw one other guard farther down the clearing on the other side of the cave entrance. Logan's senses were sharp. He strained to listen to every word Victor spoke, tuning out the plethora of intense jungle sounds ranging from monkeys and birds to the uncountable insects, including the cicadas.

Victor was studying the instructions as he peered into the cave entrance. He looked at his watch and smiled, turning toward the two Dutch henchmen. "I'll be long gone by the time Logan and that friend of his arrive. Maarten, I want you to stay here with the rest of the men to make sure that they never walk out of this jungle. Rolf and I will go find the treasure and take it back to the house, where we'll wait for word about the unfortunate death of Mr. Logan Nash."

After a few minutes, Victor's face seemed to change. He would often have mood changes, most often for the worst, and this was no exception. With a scowl on his face, he turned to Savannah. "You traitorous bitch! After everything I've done for you, how dare you betray me!" He paused long enough to kick her viciously in the thigh, causing Savannah to yelp in pain, and then continued to shout profanities at her.

Zack was feeling very anxious, as he could see the situation could escalate quickly, especially as he saw Logan raise his gun, his face as stone cold as Victor's.

"Stand this worthless bitch up," Victor barked to Rolf and Maarten, who quickly jumped into action. Victor moved right up to Savannah's face, standing with his face only inches from hers.

Logan strained to hear what Victor was saying, but Victor was speaking to her so quietly that Logan had no chance to hear what he said.

Victor spoke softly, but he was obviously furious at being betrayed. "I'm going to leave you at the entrance to this cave as a present for your little boyfriend. Don't worry. He won't have long to mourn you until he, too, will join you in hell."

Logan could see the tears running down her dirty face. Suddenly, all color ran out of Logan's face as he saw a glint from a large knife Victor held in his hand. He watched as Savannah mouthed a single word. "No."

Logan's heart raced out of control and his breath heaved. *No, no—he wouldn't! He's only scaring her*, he yelled in the silence of his mind.

With a vicious scowl on his face, Victor raised the knife to Savannah's neck.

CHAPTER 27

Time moved in slow motion as Logan watched in horror. Victor coldly slashed Savannah across the throat. Even as Victor had begun his slashing motion, Logan had dashed into the clearing. Before he had taken two steps, the guard closest to Logan dropped to the ground, a gaping hole opening in his chest. Logan then raised the gun and fired toward Victor, grazing his shoulder as Victor and Rolf scrambled into the cave. Sprinting toward the cave, Logan continued to fire at Victor's men through a volley of bullets coming his way. In the longest few seconds of his life, he suddenly stopped twenty feet from the cave entrance. The gunfire had ceased as the last body slumped unto the ground. Logan looked around. Blood-soaked bodies littered the jungle floor.

"Logan, watch out!" Zack yelled, as one of Victor's men snuck out of the jungle with his rifle aimed at Logan.

The man immediately turned and fired in Zack's direction at the exact moment Logan spun around and fired at Victor's henchman. Zack cried out in pain as the man dropped his rifle, clutching his neck with both hands. Blood sprayed from the arterial wound caused by Logan's bullet ripping through his neck. Logan ran back toward Zack, keenly aware of the fact that Victor and Rolf could appear from the cave at any moment. "Zack? Zack?"

"I'll live," Zack groaned, holding his thigh. "Get those bastards before they get us!"

Logan tore off his shirt and wrapped it around Zack's leg to slow the bleeding. "That should hold." Logan retrieved the assault rifle from the dead guard and gave it to Zack. "I'll be back, Zack, but if Victor Kane walks out the entrance of that cave blow him away. The AK is ready to fire. Just pull the trigger."

Logan ran back toward the cave entrance, stopping to retrieve an assault rifle for himself as he neared the cave. There was no movement at the cave's entrance. Logan stood over Savannah's body, fighting back tears. Victor's henchman, Maarten, had fallen partially on top of Savannah. Logan swung his leg, kicking Maarten clear of her, giving him an extra kick for good measure.

Keeping one eye on the cave, Logan knelt beside Savannah. Despite his best efforts, he couldn't hold back his tears. He ran his fingers gently over her eyes to close them, and then brushed the blood-soaked hair out of her face. "I love you, Savannah. I will never forget you." He bent over and gave her a gentle kiss on the forehead. *I hope you find the peace in the next life that you never found in this one*, he thought. He recalled all the horrors that she had revealed to him about her torturous life, and then tried to put them out of his mind.

Now Logan just wanted justice for her—not court justice, real justice. He tucked his pistol back into his belt, checked the clip in the AK-47 assault rifle, and quietly snuck to the cave entrance. He quickly flashed his head around the corner. *At least I didn't get it shot off*, Logan thought, seeing no sign of either man.

He slipped inside the cave. He patted his pocket to make sure he still had his flashlight. He wouldn't turn it on until he lost all ambient light. He felt like a sitting duck. Rocks and offshoots were everywhere, which meant Victor and his henchman could be hiding anywhere. It was especially precarious at the start of the cave, where he was at a lower level with a narrow uphill climb to the main passageway. Logan stood silent, hoping to hear a sound that gave away where Victor and Rolf were. He closed his eyes, listening for even the faintest sound, but he could only hear the beating of his own heart. *Not a good thing*, Logan thought. *They must have an ambush waiting somewhere.*

Logan quietly moved behind a large rock that sat in the middle of the uphill passageway and again listened for sounds. Nothing. With his rifle at the ready, he crawled up the passageway until he reached the crest. He paused beneath the crest and then ran in behind a rock outcropping. As he slid in beside the safety of the protruding rock, he heard feet shuffling against the gravel that covered some of the less traveled passageways. *Next offshoot on the right. Has to be.*

Logan stood silent, waiting for them to make the first move. Time seemed to stop. Minutes seemed like hours, but finally in the extremely dim light Logan could see a shadow peek out from behind the rock entrance of the passageway. Suddenly, the bright beam from a powerful halogen light startled him. He fired the automatic weapon as he dove from his place of cover in a tuck-and-roll maneuver. The volley of gunfire had been successful, as the glass of the light shattered, leaving them again in near darkness. Logan heard the clang of steel as Rolf's gun hit the cave floor. Logan fired blindly again before Rolf had a chance to retrieve it.

As Logan's eyes adjusted after the blinding flash of light, he could see Rolf heading down the main passageway toward a deep chasm that Logan had navigated several times. The chasm had three thin bamboo poles that ran along a vertical wall that towered over the black abyss on its right side, making it a delicate process to cross safely. Logan waited until Rolf was a step from the bamboo bridge, and then fired two shots along the cave wall, causing Rolf to veer right. Rolf's left foot landed on the outside bamboo pole as his right foot hit nothing but air, causing his momentum to carry him into the deep chasm as he groped in vain for the bamboo bridge. He let out a terrified scream that ended in a sickening crunch of flesh and bone against the rocks far below. Logan only felt satisfaction.

"You never cease to amaze me, Mr. Nash." Victor's voice echoed in the distance. "You're like a cockroach. You just won't die. It looks like it's just you and me."

Logan knew that past the chasm he had to be very careful, as the cave system honeycombed into many offshoots, some coming back on themselves, which would allow Victor to get behind him. *How in hell am I going to get across this bridge without getting shot?* he wondered. There were a few other offshoots behind him, but he had no idea if they were dead ends or if they would take him in a completely different direction. If he crossed the bridge, he would be a sitting duck, and if he waited, Victor would certainly find the exit sooner or later on the other side, although it was not only cleverly hidden, but quite a tight fit. Logan weighed his options as his mind raced a mile a minute.

"I can wait here all day," Logan yelled, firing a single shot down the passageway. The round sang as it ricocheted off the cave walls. *That should keep him on that side for a while,* Logan thought as he decided which offshoot he should try.

"You're a dead man!" Victor screamed, firing a volley of shots that hissed around the cave, causing Logan to dive for cover, hoping a ricochet didn't hit him.

I must have come close, Logan snickered.

Victor swore under his breath as he held his hand against what was left of his left earlobe, feeling the warm blood on his hands.

Logan was presented with the option of three offshoots he could take. *Three has always been my lucky number,* he thought, starting his way down the third passageway. The offshoot began to narrow as he walked, but Logan was happy to see that it curved to the right, which would take him over the chasm. Before long, he was walking hunched over, as the ceiling had dropped to under five feet in height. Suddenly, the cave floor went black.

"Shit," Logan said in a quiet voice. He had almost stepped into the black abyss. He shone his small flashlight into the dark cavern. "Holy crap," he muttered. His light didn't even penetrate to the bottom of the chasm. Logan surmised that it must be a huge cathedral chamber below the upper cave. He pointed his light across the floorless passageway and shook his head. On the other side, the ceiling was around seven feet, but there was an eight- or nine-foot gap over the abyss. Under normal circumstances, Logan would hop across that distance without a second thought, but with the ceiling so low, there was no way he could get any sort of run whatsoever, let alone being able to jump without knocking himself unconscious on the rock ceiling.

With a deep breath and a loud sigh, Logan mumbled aloud "Well, here goes nothing." He tossed his flashlight across the chasm, where it landed facing the opposite direction, but at least it gave him a minimal amount of light. He sat on the edge of the abyss, his legs dangling over the side. He raised his legs until they were near the ledge, braced his powerful arms on either side of the wall, and after rocking back and forth a few times he uncoiled himself like a leopard pouncing on its prey, diving across the darkness with his hands outstretched, praying they would find the ledge on the other side.

He flew over the abyss, his forearms landing on the opposite side as he frantically began grabbing to get a firm grip on anything as gravity began to pull his body toward the seemingly bottomless pit. As his arms slid toward the ledge, he grabbed a small stalagmite; it was only two inches high. With his left hand braced on the cave wall, he pulled himself up from the grip of the abyss.

Logan lay there and caught his breath for a few seconds. *Okay, let's go,"* he thought. He picked up his flashlight and began to make his way down the slightly larger passageway. It seemed to parallel the main passageway, and Logan surmised that he had traveled at least as far as Victor's current firing position. *Shit, maybe the passageways never reconnect*, he thought. Then he spotted an offshoot to the right about four yards ahead. He quickly turned the flashlight and held the beam against his body, so if it was a connecting tunnel Victor wouldn't see his light. Logan froze in place as his motion disturbed the bats overhead, sending them squealing down the passageway. He waited a minute, but didn't see any sign of Victor, so he carried on. As he neared the end of the tunnel, Logan saw a faint light where only blackness should be. His heart began to pound as adrenaline surged through his veins. Victor was right around the corner.

Logan doused his light and edged up to the entrance back to the main shaft. He had now come out behind Victor, which would hopefully catch him by surprise. Logan carefully peered around the corner. Victor was covering the end of his light, allowing him just enough to see.

This is the best shot I'll ever get, Logan thought as he raised the AK-47 assault rifle and pulled the trigger. Click! *Misfire! Shit, shit! I thought these pieces of crap were supposed to be reliable.* Logan thought. Victor immediately turned and began firing in the direction of the sound. Logan darted behind the rock wall, reached for his pistol, and returned a single shot. At the same time, he worked on the jammed rifle. Within seconds, Logan cleared the jammed round and let loose a hail of bullets blindly in Victor's direction, hoping to get lucky. Victor returned fire. As the echoes subsided, Logan could hear Victor heading back out toward the main entrance. He knew he had a much better chance at getting Victor within the confines of the cave, although he knew Victor wouldn't go far, as he didn't appear to have found the treasure.

Logan now felt he had a great advantage as he entered the main passageway since he had made several excursions through there in the past. He wanted to make sure he got to him before he crossed over the bamboo bridge because after that, the terrain would favor Victor. In the utter blackness, Logan knew he was safe to move as long as he didn't make a sound. The part of the cave he was now in was almost free of small rocks and gravel. He squatted down against the wall as a sudden rush of bats filled the air, shrieking as they flew. *So, you're in the Bat Cave,* Logan thought, remembering a huge cathedral room that was home to thousands of bats.

Logan quickly made his way to the back entrance of the huge room, holding his rifle at the ready as he turned on his flashlight and shone it into the room. With a quick adjustment to the right, he saw Victor scrambling away as he squeezed the trigger. The hail of gunfire sent the bats into a frenzy as Logan tucked behind the rocks and covered his face and head. Several bats struck him in their frenzied flight. Logan's ears were ringing from the gunfire, and the screeching of the bats that filled the cave. Logan could hear Victor grunting over the noise. *Yes, I think I hit that son of a bitch*, he thought.

Logan moved along the wall as fast as he could with minimal noise. He could hear Victor heading down the main passageway toward the chasm. When Logan got to the other end of the Bat Cave, he shone his flashlight on the ground. "Damn," he said, seeing only a token amount of blood on the cave floor. *I must have just clipped the lucky bastard.*

Logan leapt into the center of the main passageway and again fired a volley of bullets.

"Ah!" Victor grunted in pain as a ricochet caught him in the shoulder, causing him to drop his gun.

With the grunt and the sound of metal hitting the floor of the cave, a sense of hope filled Logan, but only for a second, as he heard Victor running for the exit of the cave. He began to run after him, but caution slowed his progress as he realized that Victor would more than likely have several weapons.

By the time Logan had reached the chasm, he could hear Victor in the distance, so he crossed the bamboo poles without fear of being shot at. After a short level stretch, the cave took a downhill turn toward the cave's exit. Logan turned off his light, as there was more than ample ambient light. He scrambled in behind the large rock that stood guard ten feet inside the cave's entrance. He was certain that Victor had an ambush set up outside. He had thought about going through the cave to another exit, but he realized it would take him close to an hour. Anything could happen in that time.

Logan squinted out from behind the rock toward the bright noon sun. He couldn't see Victor straight ahead, and he had to decide which side he would have gone to avoid his ambush. Questions ran through Logan's mind. *Where was he hiding? In the jungle? Behind a rock? Right outside the entrance to the cave? Shit, why hadn't Zack fired when Victor came out?*

A sense of urgency came over him. He would never forgive himself if anything happened to Zack. "Time for the unexpected," Logan said. He took a deep breath and began to count to himself. *One. Two. Three!*

He sprinted straight out the cave entrance toward a small patch of bushes about twenty feet away. After five long strides, he began to dive toward the bush. At that same moment, Victor peeked his head above the bush, where he had been hiding and waiting for Logan to come out. Victor's mouth dropped open in shock as he saw Logan flying toward him. Logan was just as surprised. Before either man could even think of getting a shot off, they collided. The surprised looks on their faces changed to absolute hatred. The collusion knocked the guns from both men's hands as they struggled to kill each other. Victor tried to strangle Logan, and Logan let fly a barrage of right-handed punches to the side of Victor's head. As powerful as Logan was, he was amazed at Victor's raw strength, despite his injuries. It was that thought that gave Logan the idea to dig his thumb into Victor's shoulder wound.

With a grunt of pain, Victor released his grip on Logan's neck. Logan fell to the ground, gasping for breath. Still dizzy, Logan stumbled away to buy a few seconds to catch his breath. A sharp agonizing pain struck him as Victor came beside him, kicking him in the ribs hard enough to lift him off the ground. He fell hard.

"I'm going to enjoy killing you slowly," Victor seethed.

Logan felt on the edge of a blackout, but a surge of energy roared through him when he realized he had fallen on a rusty rubber tree knife that had been lost or discarded by one of the workers. He inconspicuously slid his hand to its handle, not letting on that he had any strength left.

While Victor raged and screamed insults at him, Logan gained his composure. He played opossum while Victor got ready to deliver another kick to Logan's broken ribs. As Victor's foot came rocketing downward, Logan rolled over, avoiding the kick and gaining an opening. He slashed the back of Victor's leg to the bone with the rusted, curved blade as he rolled one more time, grunting in pain. He got to his feet at the same moment Victor went down in a heap. Victor clenched his teeth and grabbed his leg. Logan unleashed a flurry of vicious kicks to Victor's ribs and groin. Unable to stand, Victor tried to crawl away on all fours. Logan relentlessly continued inflicting pain on Victor, his mind replaying all the evil things he had done, inspiring him to kick him even harder.

"You win! You win!" Victor gurgled through his blood-soaked mouth. "It's all yours."

"Are you on fucking crack? You're not giving me anything you piece of shit. You lose! You're going to get what you deserve, you bastard!" Logan raged toward Victor, all his evil deeds racing around his head.

It finally dawned on Victor that Logan had no intention of turning him in to the authorities but was planning to leave him on the jungle floor. "Mercy! Mercy! I swear on my life that if you let me live I will never bother you again. I'm Victor Kane. I don't deserve to die in the jungle like an animal."

"You piece of shit! Don't ever compare yourself to an animal. I would never hurt an animal!" Logan screamed at him as he delivered another flurry of kicks, knowing he had no choice. If he let Victor live, he would be signing his own death warrant. After all Victor had done, he didn't deserve to live. "No, you're right, Victor. You deserve the same chance as you gave me in St. Thomas."

Logan noticed that a few feet away from where Victor lay was a square pit with a drop of about twenty feet to the surface of the water inside. Logan reached down and grabbed Victor by the hair and dragged him to the edge of the pit.

"Please! Please! Have mercy!" Victor begged in a muffled voice through his pain and smashed up face, in a last-ditch attempt to save his own life. He finally realized that all his money and power were now meaningless.

"I'm all out," Logan coldly replied, driving Victor over the side of the pit with a solid strike from his right leg.

Victor careened downward, hitting the water with a slap and temporarily slipping below the surface before he popped up a few seconds later, struggling to stay afloat in the muddy water, his body void of strength. After less than five minutes of struggling, Victor drifted into his muddy grave. As Logan watched the ripples on the water settle, a sense of relief came over him. He realized it was finally over after all these years. Victor Kane would never inflict his evil on him or anyone again. Logan spat into the muddy water below. "Rot in Hell."

Certain that Victor was dead, Logan hurried over to Zack. "Hey, buddy, are you hangin' in there?" He was still conscious, but weak and groggy from the loss of blood. "We're going to tighten this up a bit and get you to a hospital. Are you okay to stand?"

"Logan, get back in there and get that treasure. This place will be crawling with the authorities in no time. This is going to be your only chance. Don't worry. I'll be around to be a pain in your ass for a long time yet," Zack said, his voice just above a whisper.

"God, I don't know how you can still have a sense of humor." Logan shook his head. He had surmised that the remainder of Victor's men that were not so loyal must have fled when the bullets started flying and their comrades were falling all around them.

"I can't leave Savannah's body here. She never had a break in life, so the least I can do is give her a good burial."

"No, Logan. You gave her so much in the last couple of weeks. Because of you she lived more than she ever would have dreamed."

Logan nodded, fighting the tears back, trying to remain focused despite his heart being torn to pieces. He quickly fixed Zack's makeshift dressing and hurried back into the cave to follow the instructions, tracking the clues to the point where Victor had gotten. "So close, Victor," Logan laughed, knowing how furious he must have been when he and Zack crashed their party.

The second to last clue had Logan crawling on his belly through an extremely small passageway. It opened into a small room that looked like a dead end. It was too small to stand up and would probably not have fit a coffee table. "Look where no one would look," Logan said, reading the last clue. He shone his light. "Is there a fake wall hidden in here?" Logan looked around and saw nothing but rock. He slowly scanned the room a couple more times when he realized where he wasn't looking.

The room was so small anyone coming to the end of the tunnel would just peer into it and see it was a dead end. Logan twisted around, sending shooting pain through his body thanks to his broken ribs. At first, there didn't appear to be anything but a rock wall. *No! There's a small break farther up!* He contorted his body a bit more, pain again shooting through him. After a minute, the pain subsided as he regrouped and shone his light toward what appeared to be a break in the rock.

He smiled. Above the opening there was a rock ledge that was invisible unless you contorted yourself into a space that was an obvious dead end. It was a perfect hiding place. Logan propped his light against a rock, which illuminated the small space. The rock ledge was deeper than Logan expected as he strained his sore body to reach and grasp the edges of what felt like a wooden case. His heart beat faster with anticipation as he drew the case into the light, revealing the proverbial pot of gold at the end of the rainbow.

Even as he pulled the case from the ledge, he realized he had found the true treasure. This quest had rekindled his insatiable lust for life and adventure. As he squatted and stared at it, he realized that it had never been about the treasure itself, it had always been about the quest and his lust for the ultimate adventure. That passion had driven him for most of his life.

Still the same, I wouldn't turn down a chest of gold doubloons, he thought. Finding doubloons was a possibility since the chest weighed approximately eighty pounds, although there were no clues left to say what it actually contained. He expected nothing less from Colton Braxton III. The treasure chest was sturdy mahogany with a black metal bracing around it. A heavy antique padlock sealed it, which looked like Colton had taken from the set of a pirate movie. "Maybe he did." Logan laughed.

He tried to keep his hopes from running wild, not wanting to set his expectations too high. Suddenly, he became nervous. He had spent every cent he had, plus money he didn't have, to fund what turned out to be an extremely expensive quest. It wasn't all about the money, but it would certainly be nice to find treasure to cover the expenditures. He reached for the rock that he had used to prop up the flashlight. He struck the lock once, and then again and again, pain shooting through his body with every jarring blow. "Damn, Colton, couldn't you have used a weaker lock?" he said, gritting his teeth and hitting the lock again.

Sweat dripped from his forehead as he pounded away at the lock, finally cracking it open. "Jeez, it's about damn time." He slumped against the cave wall. Kneeling in front of the chest, he slowly raised the lid.

CHAPTER 28

Logan's body sagged as he flipped back the lid of the treasure chest. It appeared to be filled with nothing but books. He began removing them and piling them beside the chest until he had taken them all out. He saw a simple white envelope. It wasn't all about the treasure, but still, Logan felt cheated. No matter how much he had tried to tell himself not to get his hopes up, he had believed deeply that the treasure would be one of great riches.

He picked up the envelope. "Let's see if this envelope contains a big fat cashier's check."

He slid his finger under the sealed envelope and pulled out a two-page letter, peering inside the envelope to make sure there wasn't anything left inside. "Empty." Logan shook his head as he began to read the letter.

"If you have followed the four maps that brought you here, you are already rich with adventures that you will remember for the rest of your life. Enclosed are my journals of my travels. I was never known in life, but my wish is to be known in death, to be remembered for who I really was. My biography should at least pay for your trip, and who knows? There may even be enough people that want to read about me that you could make a good buck."

Logan carried on reading the letter. It just went into a bit more detail of how he wanted to be remembered. Logan tossed the letter into the empty chest, slumped back against the cave wall, and started to laugh as he picked up one of Colton's journals.

"Oh, Colton, why am I not surprised?" Logan shook his head and began to read.

"Oh my God," Logan said. He had picked up a journal of Colton's travels to the Amazon. Logan read a quote that changed the way he saw himself. "Chance meeting with a young man after my own heart, with a sense of adventure that even exceeds my own. I have met presidents and kings, and none have impressed me more than that young man, Logan Nash."

"It was you" Logan said, thinking back to the photo he saw of Colton when he found out about the map, but then had convinced himself it probably wasn't him.

Logan continued to read, and he was amazed at how close Colton's journal read like his own. To be thought of so highly by someone like Colton Braxton III was something that Logan never expected. Suddenly, any feelings of being cheated were gone. He truly had found a treasure more valuable than gold. Life seemed to have come full circle for Logan. Victor Kane had stolen his identity as an adventurer and treasure hunter when he had left him for dead under the waters of St. Thomas. This quest had brought him back to where he was. Passion once again burned deep inside him.

His only regret was Savannah's death. This was a bittersweet time. He had fallen hard for her, and she had been taken away from him. As he sat there, he wondered if there was anything he could have done differently, any way he could have saved her. He knew that Victor never had any intention of letting her live after she betrayed him, but it didn't make it any easier. He knew time healed all wounds, but he also knew his heart would be very guarded for some time. He picked up another journal and read a few pages. It inspired him and further fanned the flames for adventure.

"It should be fun hauling this chest of books through the cave," Logan said. He moved the chest nearer to the passageway opening before reloading it.

Logan's heart jumped. He rocked the chest back and forth again and again. "No, no, Logan! Don't you dare get your hopes up again!" He felt something shift in the chest. *It must be a false bottom*, he thought. He tried prying it open with his fingers, but to no avail. He resorted to cracking the wooden bottom open with a rock. He snapped off pieces of wood until he could see an envelope lying in the extremely thin false bottom that was only about a quarter inch deep.

Logan opened the unsealed envelope, which contained a letter from a law firm and a safety deposit box key. "I should have known you wouldn't make it easy."

He tucked the envelope in his pants pocket and packed up the chest. He began his trek back through the cave to where Zack was patiently waiting outside.

"Welcome back. You were gone so long I thought you were just going to leave me here," he joked, despite being in obvious pain.

"Never, who would I get to fix my computers for free?"

"Looks like you're a rich man," Zack said. He saw how Logan labored carrying the chest.

"Books," Logan replied.

"Books?"

"Yeah, Colton put his journals in the case so whomever found it could write his memoirs. Oh, and one other thing. A safety deposit box key."

"Hmm. Probably old socks."

"I'm not going to get my hopes up because Colton was obviously quite unpredictable, but I'm sure he'll take care of a fellow adventurer."

"It had to sound like a war zone here. Where are the authorities?"

"I'm going to take a stab in the dark and guess that Victor Kane paid them to ignore everything."

"Well, let's get the hell out of Dodge."

"I agree," Logan said. He soon devised a makeshift sled to drag Savannah and the treasure chest out of the jungle. "Zack, are you going to be able to make it out on your own strength?"

"Yeah, just get me a crutch of some kind and I'll make it."

Logan quickly constructed a crutch and they began to make their way through the sweltering jungle.

"At least it's downhill," Zack said.

The hike down the hill was in silence. Logan's time with Savannah was short but intense, and she was on his mind. He tried not to picture the gash running along her throat, her matted hair, and her tattered clothes. With each step, his ribs screamed in pain, but he plodded on, pulling the heavy sled through the rough terrain. Like a broken record, the highlights of his time with Savannah looped through his mind over and over again, and the tears began to roll down his face as Logan thought of what might have been.

As they approached the Jeep, Logan composed himself, but the pain was still obvious in his face.

"You going to be okay, Logan?"

"Yeah, thanks. You know me; I always land on my feet," Logan replied, giving a forced smile that Zack immediately saw right through.

"You don't always have to be so damn tough," Zack said, knowing that Logan always seemed to take everything in stride, but he could see that this was different. He hadn't seen Logan open up to anyone like he did with Savannah, but he knew he would have to mourn in his own way.

Logan nodded as he strained to load Savannah's body into the Jeep, followed by the chest. He then helped Zack into the passenger seat. "I'll call Keit and see if he can discreetly get us off the island, and hopefully Suchin can arrange to have Savannah's body flown back to Hawaii. I know a place she would love to live an eternity."

Less than two days later, Logan and Zack touched down in Honolulu. Suchin had used her connections to get them medical attention and to arrange all the paperwork Logan would need to get Savannah's body back to Hawaii. He didn't ask if the paperwork was legit or not, mostly because he didn't care.

"There are a few things I need to take care of here before I go home."

"I need to get back to the mainland unless you need me here," Zack said.

"Thanks. I'll be okay. When I find out what's in the safety deposit box, I'll let you know. You've earned half of what's in there."

Zack laughed. "You know I didn't. You did almost everything, but thanks for the compliment anyway. Seriously, Logan, you know my business is okay, and I'm not hurting for money. You gave me a bigger adventure than I could have ever dreamed of. That's all the thanks I want."

"Funny, that's what I was planning on giving you—a firm handshake and a thanks for your help, buddy." Logan laughed.

He gave Zack a brotherly hug, followed by a knowing nod. No words needed to be said.

Zack knew that Logan deeply appreciated everything that he had done and that their friendship was stronger than ever. As Zack limped toward the departure level, Logan thought how incredibly lucky he was to have such a friend.

A few hours later, Logan found himself in the passenger seat of the hearse, staring silently out the windshield as the large black automobile glided toward the crematorium. His mind again reran all the highlights of his time with Savannah, and the next several hours seemed to move in a blur.

Not even remembering how he got there, Logan again stood at the airport waiting for his good friend Kabos, a large ceramic vase nestled in his arms. Kabos approached Logan, picked up his bags, and nodded to him with his lips tightly pressed together, tears welling up in his eyes. "I am so sorry, my friend, I, I—"

"Thank you, Kabos. It's okay. I just want you to fly me home on the exact same flight path you took us on last time we were here," Logan replied, tears running down his cheeks.

Logan sat in the co-pilot's seat in the helicopter, the same seat that Savannah had sat in as she was stunned by the incredible beauty of the islands. The small corner window was open as they began their flight. Little by little, Logan spread her ashes over the lush Hawaiian landscape and indigo blue seas separating the islands. She was inspired by the beauty of the islands, and now she was part of it. Logan knew she would have wanted it that way.

In the bottom of the vase remained a few tablespoons of ashes. Logan planted a small banyan tree in his backyard overlooking the ocean, and mixed the ashes in the soil, watering it with the tears that streamed down his cheeks in his final goodbye. She would live in the tree long past Logan's years, a reminder of a love lost. "I will always love you, Savannah."

EPILOGUE

Logan smiled as he stood on the steps of New England Bank in Boston. He zipped his rugged brown leather jacket up to his chin as a gust of the biting Atlantic fall wind buffeted his face. He couldn't believe that he had waited for almost three months to open the safety deposit box. He now felt back to his old self again. His heart had begun to heal, and he managed to write the first of Colton's memoirs in what would be a series of three books. He had just yesterday sent the manuscript off to his publisher for editing. He had read Colton's journals and with every page was further inspired to follow his dreams of adventure and discovery.

"I knew you wouldn't let a fellow adventurer down." Logan smiled as he took out a sheet of paper detailing his new net worth. *Fifty million dollars!* Logan screamed in his head. There had been one stipulation: that the person who found the treasure had to donate fifty percent of the money to a registered charity or to charities of their choice. Colton Braxton III himself had left most of his fortune to charities that were close to his heart. Logan had many causes he had always wished he could help, and now he could. Many people came to mind—people he had helped, but desperately wanted to do more for, which now would become a reality. Of course, he knew the taxman would take his ungodly share. Then there was Zack. He would offer him a huge portion of his share, although he knew Zack would try to refuse any reward, or at least only take a token gift.

Logan now could afford to follow his passion. His lust for adventure surged through his veins more than ever. There was a big world waiting to be discovered.

He knew it wouldn't change who he was one bit, but the money would allow him to pursue his quests without the worry of funding his adventures, which always seemed to be outrageously expensive. The Braxton treasure represented freedom to pursue his passions. Logan closed his eyes and drew in a deep breath of the crisp New England air. He felt totally free. With a twinkle in his eye, he strode down the steps with breathless anticipation of what amazing adventures the future would hold.

COMING SOON:

Watch for more upcoming Logan Nash adventures at:

logannash.com